Michael Shew began writing fiction after retiring as the head teacher of a London comprehensive school, following a forty-year career in education. This novel, whilst standing alone, is the sequel to *Lessons in Lying* (2019, Austin Macauley Publishers), published after he took a creative writing course at the University of Oxford. He still works part time at Sheffield Hallam University and shares his life between London and Derbyshire.

BACKLASH

MICHAEL SHEW

The Book Guild Ltd

First published in Great Britain in 2022 by
The Book Guild Ltd
Unit E2 Airfield Business Park,
Harrison Road, Market Harborough,
Leicestershire. LE16 7UL
Tel: 0116 2792299
www.bookguild.co.uk
Email: info@bookguild.co.uk
Twitter: @bookguild

Typeset in 11pt Minion Pro

Printed and bound by CPI Group (UK) Ltd, Croydon, CR0 4YY

ISBN 978 1915122 360

British Library Cataloguing in Publication Data.
A catalogue record for this book is available from the British Library.

To all the women and young girls, known and unknown, whose lives have been blighted, destroyed or ended by male violence.

PROLOGUE

Head teacher left with life-threatening injuries after domestic incident

The emergency services were called to a detached house in an exclusive close near Bollington yesterday after neighbours reported hearing a woman screaming for help. Police were on the scene in minutes and have sealed off the house as a crime scene. One of the occupants, believed to be local head teacher Robert Mason, was taken to hospital with critical injuries. His wife, Emily Fowler, a lawyer with the Manchester-based firm of Pearson, Shallice and Grant, was admitted with minor injuries and later discharged.

Christine Black, a friend and neighbour, spoke to our reporter at the scene. "This is really shocking. We've known the family well since they moved in next door five years ago – we went to their dinner party only recently – and they've always seemed a normal, happy couple. I was in the kitchen yesterday afternoon when I heard shouting, then an awful scream, followed by police arriving almost immediately. It was as if they'd been tipped off. A few minutes later two ambulances arrived. Robert was stretchered out to one, which race away with the siren going, then a policewoman led Emily to the second. They've got an eleven-year-old daughter, Lily."

A police statement confirms that Robert Mason remains in a critical condition. Emily Fowler is making a good recovery and is helping the police with their inquiries. Officers are not currently looking for anyone else in connection with the incident.

– *Manchester Evening News*, September 2010

He was in the middle of a lake, pushing an airbed that supported a woman's body. The cold was excruciating – he'd lost all feeling in his arms and legs – and the airbed was deflating. Finally, he pulled out the bung and the body started to sink, but as he turned to swim back to shore, the corpse bobbed to the surface in front of him. She smiled, taunting him. As he tried to push her under again she wrapped her arms around him, pulling him down. He struggled free, swam to the surface and screamed for help.

"Shut the fuck up, won't you? I haven't slept a fucking wink since you were moved in here."

He jerked awake, terrified and disorientated. He looked around, slowly focusing on the cell walls, the metal bed frame and the mattress of the bunk above him. Of course, he'd had a nightmare, and he was still in the prison where he'd been remanded for the past ten months. But in a different cell, clearly. How much worse could it get?

"And don't start again, or I'll come down there and shut you up. Got that?"

"I've got that." He'd learned over the past month that you didn't give excuses or long explanations in prison; you just apologised and kept your head down. He had twenty years minus parole to look forward to; a minimum of fifteen years, but more if it was decided that he remained a danger to women. *And you can bet that my wife will do everything she can to keep me locked up as long as possible*, he thought.

"You're the guy that murdered that teacher, then tried to strangle his wife, aren't you?"

"I didn't try to—"

"Oh, for fuck's sake, save me that bollocks. Everyone's innocent in here. I was going to say good on you. I don't know about the first woman you did, but from what I read about your missus, she testified against you and helped the police stitch you up. She fucking deserved it. Most blokes in here agree. It's like women have got the upper hand now and men's rights count for nothing."

Robert didn't sleep much for the rest of that night. His conversation with his cellmate, if that was what you'd call it, had given him something to think about. All the reports he'd read in the papers were sympathetic to Emily's side of the story. Following the verdict, one newspaper had splashed 'Head teacher guilty – a danger to women, says judge' across the front page. If his empathetic cellmate was tapping into something – a big 'if' – then maybe Robert should try to get his own account out there. He had plenty of time to think about how.

1

THE VERDICT: AUGUST 2011

"Members of the jury, have you reached a verdict on both counts?"

Emily Fowler looked across from the public gallery to the dock, where her husband stood staring impassively at the foreman. Ever since the bastard had decided to plead not guilty to both charges – murder and attempted murder – she'd known that her private life would be raked over in public.

Once Robert had recovered from the serious injuries he'd sustained during their struggle a year ago when he'd tried to strangle her, the police had quickly put together – with Emily's help – the evidence they'd needed to charge him with the murder of his former colleague Sue Goodall. With charges of murder and attempted murder against him, bail was out of the question and he'd spent over nine months on remand before the trial.

The last four weeks of the trial had been the toughest of Emily's life. Her glossy chestnut-brown hair was now dull and streaked with grey at the temples. Fresh lines at the corners of her eyes drew attention to the puffiness underneath. She remained an attractive woman, but friends and colleagues had noticed the change to her once-striking appearance. Normally that would have depressed her, but she'd had more serious issues to worry about. As a solicitor, she'd seen first-hand what defence barristers could put prosecution witnesses through during a murder trial. Witnesses like herself, and her daughter Lily.

Emily knew she'd cope with the trial and hopefully come out at the end with her self-respect and reputation intact. But it would be a huge challenge for Lily. The prosecution had fought bitterly to prevent the defence from questioning Lily about her father's behaviour in the days leading up to his attempt on her mother's life, but their objections had been overruled. The judge's only concession had been to allow Lily to give her evidence by video link. Concession! They were forcing a twelve-year-old to give evidence about the father she adored. Emily wouldn't ever forgive her husband for inflicting that on Lily, who'd found it just as traumatic as she'd feared.

The foreman's hands were shaking slightly as he finally responded. "We have, Your Honour."

"How do you find the defendant on the charge of the first-degree murder of Sue Goodall?"

In the few seconds it took for the foreman to respond, Emily felt her heart thudding in her chest.

"Guilty."

Shouts and whoops of "Yes!" erupted from those around her in the gallery, as Emily took her first breath in half a minute.

Robert remained impassive as the judge asked the foreman if the jury had reached a verdict on the second charge of attempted murder. *Emily's* attempted murder.

"We have, Your Honour."

Emily fell into a trance, hearing nothing but a hiss of white noise, until she became aware of the people around her erupting again. The same shouts of "Yes!", the same fists punching the air. He'd been found guilty of attempting to kill her.

After Robert was led out of the court by two prison officers, the clerk gave the instruction for all to rise and the judge walked out. Everyone else took this as their signal to leave, but Emily just slumped back on the bench and looked up at the ornate ceiling. It was weird; at this moment, when she should have felt elated, there was a recurrence of the niggling doubt that had troubled her throughout the trial.

In the witness box, she'd put up robust and convincing responses during her cross-examination by the defence barrister.

"Ms Fowler, are you really asking the jury to believe that your only aim when you repeatedly slashed at your husband with that razor-sharp blade was to cut his tie?"

"Yes. I was totally focused on cutting the ligature that was choking the life out of me."

"But you knew that killing the person holding it would do the job just as well, and release you from a marriage you were desperate to get out of."

"Believe it or not, solving our marital difficulties wasn't my top priority at that moment."

(Muffled laughter from the gallery.)

Remembering that exchange, Emily's face showed the faintest glimmer of a smile. *But can I ever be sure that I wasn't trying to kill him? And if not, what does that make me?* she thought.

She picked up her bag and made her way down the stairs. The thought that this was the last time she'd be making this journey lifted her mood. As she walked down the curving marble staircase towards the exit, she saw a crowd gathered in the street outside. Julie, her solicitor, had warned her that there would be a large press presence; the trial had generated unforeseen levels of publicity. Emily spotted Julie immediately among the throng in the lobby – above average height, highlighted light brown hair and a huge smile on her face – and walked up to her.

"It's over, Emily. You and Lily can finally start to rebuild your lives. You've been so strong and resolute; a wonderful role model for women everywhere, standing up to male violence. There's just this last, manic part to get through. Remember, let me do all the talking, and resist any urge to respond to questions. As long as I'm talking, we can hold the line, but if you utter one word, the journalists will take that as their cue to ask anything they want. They're very good at getting people to say things they didn't intend to – it's their job, after all."

Emily gave an ironic smile. "We both know I'm rubbish at taking instructions, but I promise I'll keep my mouth shut on this occasion. Is the car waiting?"

"Yes, I've checked. Eric's our driver today. Ready?"

"*Once more unto the breach.* All I want after this is anonymity, closure and several large glasses of wine."

The pavement was packed with photographers, journalists and Emily's unofficial (and unrequested) supporters' group, holding the same placards they'd waved throughout the trial.

Stop Male Violence Now!
The Patriarchy Won't Go Quietly.

As they shoved through the gap created by police officers, cameras in her face, Emily felt relieved that she'd agreed to let Julie do the talking. Many of the journalists were smiling, but she'd learned that that meant nothing. She also noticed a small group of scowling middle-aged men standing apart from the crowd, watching. Most were dressed casually in the manner of men who didn't worry much about their appearance – baseball caps, nylon waterproof jackets, jeans and trainers. But one was smarter. Navy overcoat, shirt and tie, leather shoes.

She heard Julie's voice and realised she'd begun their prepared statement.

"Good morning. I'll be reading a statement on Emily Fowler's behalf, and she won't be taking any questions. As you can imagine, Emily and her daughter have been under an incredible strain over the past year and she requests that they're now left in peace to rebuild their lives."

Emily knew the statement by heart, having prepared it with Julie two nights ago over a bottle of Merlot, and she let the words wash over her. As she glanced at the faces in the crowd, she thought about the afternoon in her house a year ago when she'd nearly died. When her husband had tried to kill her. The memory of Robert's tie tightening around her neck with such force still produced an involuntary quiver.

The moment Julie finished speaking, the press started firing questions at Emily, just as Julie had predicted. Emily looked straight ahead as Julie and Eric each took hold of one arm and led her to the waiting car.

"Do you think justice has been done today, Emily?"

"Do you intend to stay in your home?"

"Is there anything you'd like to say to your husband?"

Emily turned to confront the journalist who'd asked that last question, but Julie gave her arm a sharp tug, pushed her into the back of the car, got in after her and slammed the door shut.

"Christ, I thought you were going to tear that journalist's head off," she said, turning to Emily. "Thank God I got you into the car before you said anything."

Emily burst out laughing, an uncontrolled release of emotion. *I can't remember the last time I did that*, she thought. *I used to love having fun, but life has been such a serious business over the past year.* As Eric eased the car through the crowd, faces smiling at her through the windows, she took several deep breaths. "You're right. God knows what I'd have come out with." Leaning forward, she spoke to Eric. "We're going to pick up my daughter now. Are you OK with the route?"

"All sorted, madam."

She turned to Julie, who'd put her arm around her. "I was amazed at the size of the crowd; I had no idea that our case had generated so much interest. Where've they all come from?"

Julie looked at her quizzically. "Come on, Emily, you must know your case has become a cause célèbre. When it comes to titillating the British public, what *hasn't* this story got? A body in a lake, adultery, respectable head teacher accused of murder and attempted murder? And, of course, you've become a heroine for many women; a strong woman successfully fighting back against male violence. I'm with them all the way. You're amazing, Emily, and I'm a little in awe of you. Professionally, I've had to be careful about revealing my feelings."

Emily felt humbled. Julie had lobbied to be her trial solicitor, which many colleagues had seen as a career risk. Although Emily hadn't been on trial, if she hadn't performed well under cross-examination, Julie's reputation could have been damaged. But it was clear that Julie thrived on risk. In private, they'd become good friends, and that friendship had provided support Emily hadn't received from some people she'd thought would be there for her during the past nine months. Occasionally, she'd wondered if Julie had wanted more than friendship. Sitting beside her in the back of the taxi, she felt the adrenaline rush that had sustained her since leaving the court being replaced by something more ambiguous. "That's a lovely thing to say, Julie, though it's scary being a standard-bearer for a campaign against male violence. If things don't settle down, I'm going to need your help to extricate myself from the role."

"I'll be there for you, Emily, I promise."

"Guilty."

As Robert stared at the foreman of the jury, strong hands gripped him firmly on each arm and began to lead him out of the court. He looked up at the gallery and saw his wife leaning back in her seat, staring at the ceiling. Since their fight in the kitchen a year ago, his loathing for her had increased tenfold. He was only trying to give her a shock, for Christ's sake; make her see how she'd betrayed him by going to the police. But she'd gone mad and tried to kill him, slashing open a main artery. The doctors had told him that he'd lost so much blood his heart was on the point of shutting down. *Yet she hasn't been accused of any crime – nothing! – and is now free to get on with her life with Lily, while I'm going down on two counts. British justice? More like trial by feminist outrage.*

In the past few months an unrealistic hope that the jury would see his side had kept his thoughts positive, but as he was forcibly escorted down the four flights to the cells, a sickening fear took over. Incarceration. He was about to be locked up for twenty-two hours a day in a high-security prison cell. For the remaining two hours, he'd be mixing with hardened career criminals and psychopaths – any one of whom could decide on a whim to take offence at his presence.

As he was half-pushed through the cell door, he felt his insides liquefying and just made it to the steel toilet as the door slammed shut. He heard the court officers laughing as he released his bowels. When the worst was over, he wiped himself as best he could with what passed for toilet paper, gingerly moved over to the bed and lay down. If Emily had backed up his story about their fight – it was just a domestic that had got out of hand, he wasn't going to strangle her to *death*, for God's sake – he wouldn't have been accused of attempting to murder her. The jury would then have probably gone for manslaughter instead of murder for Sue Goodall's death, in which case he'd be looking at around six years maximum with parole, instead of fifteen.

That's the difference that her desire for revenge has made. Looking at the obscene graffiti scratched into the grey gloss-painted wall next to the bed, he promised himself that he would do everything he could to make his wife's life hell.

Lily heard her phone ping and opened the message. Mum.

It's over now, Lily. Dad was found guilty, as we expected. I know his trial has been very tough on you, but you've been amazing through it all. We should be with you in half an hour. Looking forward to spending lots of time together again. Mum xxx

Reading the text, Lily felt only sadness. Her dad had been found guilty of killing one woman and then trying to kill her mum. Part of her couldn't believe it; couldn't accept that he could have done such terrible things. When she'd been collected from school and taken to the hospital to see her mum on that day a year ago, the horrible, ugly marks around her mum's neck had frightened her. Her mum had explained that she and Lily's dad had had a terrible fight. Dad had tried to strangle Mum, and she would have died if she hadn't fought back by trying to cut herself free. Lily could accept that they'd had a fight, but not that he'd tried to kill her. She felt her mum must be exaggerating; lying, even. But why would she do that? Her mum wasn't a liar.

Once her dad was out of danger, she'd been allowed to visit him once in hospital. Although Mum had been very upset when Lily told her she wanted to see him, she didn't try to stop her. Lily had hoped that seeing her dad would help her to see things more clearly, but she'd only got more confused. When she'd walked into his room she was surprised to see two police officers beside his bed; then she'd noticed her dad's wrist handcuffed to the bed rail. He'd looked asleep, but as she approached the bed he turned towards her and smiled a little.

One of the officers got up and asked to look in her backpack. "It's just a precaution, love; we need to do this with every visitor."

Lily felt angry, but knew she shouldn't argue, so took off her backpack and held it out. As the officer sorted through her pencil case, markers, Fruit Pastilles and phone, she stayed calm, looking into her father's pained face as he tried his best to maintain a smile. As soon as the policewoman returned her bag, she walked over to the bed, bent over and kissed her dad's cheek.

"Dad, they're saying that you tried to strangle Mum, tried to kill her, but it's not true, is it? You and Mum love each other. Please tell me it's a terrible mistake."

In spite of his weakened state, Dad had raised himself a little from the bed, grasped her hand and said, "Of course it's not true, Lily; you mustn't believe it. It's true that we had a terrible argument and we both lost our tempers. I was so angry with your mum that I pushed her backwards really hard, but then she came back at me with a knife. I'm sure she wasn't trying to kill me, though; she was just lashing out."

Sitting in Tamsin's bedroom now, looking at her mum's message, Lily remembered how she'd struggled to take in her dad's words. Her happy, secure world, built on the foundations of her parents' love for her and for each other, had disintegrated. The counsellor that social services had arranged for her to see each week had been understanding, and Lily looked forward to their time together. It helped to speak to someone who was there to listen and not judge whether she was saying the right thing. She'd given her useful advice on what to do if she felt overwhelmed by a world that had become an incomprehensible, uncertain place.

But how could Lily and her mum ever be as close again as they'd been before that horrible fight? Those feelings had been so special, and while Lily tried not to show that she didn't feel the same way anymore, she could see that her mum was very sad that she'd lost their close bond. Mum had been so stressed out by the trial most of the time, it was difficult to make things better between them. Her parents' stupid fight had turned everything she'd relied on upside down, and Lily blamed both of them.

She heard a knock as the door opened slightly, followed by Tamsin saying, "Sorry to disturb you, Lily. Have you heard from your mum yet?"

"Come in, Tams, I've just heard. Dad was found guilty on both charges."

"Both charges?"

"Yeah, don't you remember, they said he killed that other poor woman whose body was found in the lake, as well as trying to kill my mum? I'm sorry, Tams, it upsets me so much just to say it. Now he'll spend years in prison!"

Tamsin gave Lily a tissue and put her arm around her as tears began to run down her friend's face.

"Mum said they've just left the court and should be here in about half an hour. I know she'll be pleased, but I can't be. What am I going to say to her?"

Inspector Deepak Singh muted the television, looked at the name of the incoming call and pressed 'Accept'. He'd been expecting Tony Hawkins from the *Chronicle* to ring him with the verdict, remembering what the journalist had said the last time they'd spoken: "You should be there to collect the glory when that bastard goes down, seeing as you put him away and saved that solicitor's life."

"Hi, Tony. Thanks for ringing."

"You've done me enough favours over the years; it's the least I can do."

"I've heard the verdict went as expected."

"Too right it did. Guilty on both counts. The court erupted after each verdict; the judge wasn't impressed at all. Mason looked sick; I think he actually believed he had a chance, right up to the end. Talk about denial. Now, when can we do that interview so that the great British public know who the real hero of this story is?"

"You know that's going to be difficult with my hearing hanging over me, but I appreciate the thought, I really do. How did his wife take it?"

"She looked exhausted but relieved, to tell the truth. Just sat for several minutes in the gallery composing herself, then walked slowly out. I'd better go; I've got a deadline! Take care, Deepak."

"Thanks, Tony."

Deepak slumped back on the sofa. The case he'd been instrumental in solving had ended with the right outcome and he should be on a high. But all he could think about was how the events of a year ago might have ended very differently. If he'd arrived at the house a minute later, Mason would have died and Emily could have been charged with manslaughter.

As he'd smashed down the front door and barged in, the scene in the kitchen had resembled a Tarantino movie. Emily Fowler was slumped on the floor, leaning back against a cupboard with an angry, deep red mark around her neck, a terrified stare on her striking green, now bloodshot, eyes. Robert Mason, her husband, was lying less than a metre away, staring in terror at the blood spurting from his upper arm covering a fast-growing area of the floor. Deepak's eyes met Emily's just long enough for him to see that she was shocked, injured, but not in immediate danger, so he'd picked up the tie lying on the floor and tied it tightly around Mason's upper arm.

Mason had gripped his hand with his uninjured arm. "Save me, please," he'd said, a look of hopeless fear in his eyes.

Singh had looked around the kitchen, seen what he needed, grabbed a dirty tea towel and pressed it against the wound. It was a bad one. The brachial artery had been sliced open for at least ten centimetres; a laceration that was almost surgical in its precision. *Christ, Emily, remind me not to get on your bad side*, he thought.

Seconds later he'd heard the ambulance siren outside. He'd kept pressing as hard as he could until a paramedic rushed into the kitchen and pushed him aside. "Good job, mate, I'll take it from here."

Once he knew that Emily's injuries were relatively minor and that Mason was going to survive, he'd returned to his new two-bedroomed flat in Castlefield ('breathtaking views, beautifully fitted, replete with executive detail'), – had two bottles of Peroni, a takeaway curry, and reflected on solving one murder and preventing another.

The murder of Sue Goodall, 'the Woman in the Reservoir', had frustrated him and his team for weeks. When the evidence finally aligned to establish a strong case for arresting Mason, Deepak had quickly realised that Mason might suspect that his wife had colluded with the police and attack her. Which was exactly what happened. Ironically, Emily had successfully dealt with her husband's attempt to murder her before Deepak turned up – it was Mason's life he'd saved.

Yet now, at the end of the trial, Deepak's success left a bitter taste. Shortly after he'd given his evidence in court, the chief constable had told him that he was opening an internal inquiry into why early opportunities to link Robert Mason conclusively to Sue Goodall's murder had been missed. Initially Deepak had felt he was being treated unjustly, but as the chief constable had gone through the list of errors, he'd had to admit that there'd been missed opportunities. For now, he was on routine duties until the inquiry was over.

There was only one thing he wanted to do now, and that was to send Emily a message and wish her well. He'd got to know and like her in the weeks leading up to Mason's arrest. Like her a *lot*. He opened another bottle and began the text.

2

THE FOLLOWING DAY

That morning's papers lay strewn haphazardly over the kitchen table. Half an hour earlier, Emily had been woken from a deep sleep by persistent calls from Julie on her mobile.

"Have you seen the papers? You're all over them, even on the front page of a couple. You should get them; they'll cheer you up."

She'd made herself a coffee, pulled on the jogging top and leggings that should have been washed three days ago, then bought every title in the nearby mini-market, ignoring the smirking young man behind the counter.

Julie was right... to a degree. There were various pictures of them leaving the court. Emily looked tired and unsmiling, and though one showed Julie looking at her admiringly, the content of the stories surrounding the pictures gave her an uneasy feeling. She was painted in an almost adoring light: the brave and feisty professional woman who'd fought back against her vicious husband. Robert was universally vilified:

Evil killer brought to justice after his lawyer wife fights back.
Why was this monster not caught sooner?
Headmaster murders former colleague, tries to strangle his wife.

Emily knew that Lily and her friends and classmates would be reading the very same headlines and stories and promptly texting each other with increasingly exaggerated versions; not that the story needed any exaggeration.

Pouring herself another coffee, she went up to Lily's room. Before she got there she could hear her daughter shouting tearfully to someone on the phone. "My dad wasn't trying to kill my mum! They were having a horrible fight, but loads of parents do that. And I don't believe he killed that other teacher deliberately – he couldn't; he's a good man."

Emily felt nauseous. Throughout the period of the trial, Lily hadn't wanted to talk to her about Robert, and Emily hadn't pushed it for fear that she might increase the gulf between them. She'd carried on with this approach yesterday evening after picking Lily up from her friend's house, hugging her daughter and saying little. But she needed to confront Lily's denial sooner rather than later.

She heard Lily end the call, and with uncharacteristic impetuosity pushed the bedroom door open. Her daughter was sitting on the bed, propped up with pillows, tearful and red-faced. She looked up, and Emily saw from the look on her face that the conversation that she wanted – needed – to have with Lily would end badly. But she had to challenge this narrative now, before it became an undisputed truth in her daughter's head.

"I'm so sorry that you'll be hearing and reading horrible things about your dad in the next few days, sweetheart. Please believe me when I tell you that the story will be forgotten by the papers in a few days. However, I couldn't help hearing you on the phone just now, and it's really important that you understand what your dad did, and why he's gone to prison."

"Mum, it's no good trying to turn me against Dad. I love him and he loves me. I don't know what that other woman did to make him so angry, but she must be partly to blame for what happened. But I do know that he can't have been trying to kill you; he really loved you and he wouldn't do that. Why don't you admit that you overreacted? You could have just kicked him hard and brought him to his senses. Instead, you tried to kill him…"

Lily's final words shocked and hurt Emily more than her daughter could possibly know. She paused, taking several deep breaths, then said, "There were only two people in that room when your father came up behind me and pulled his tie around my neck with such force that I knew, in that instant, that he'd lost control and was trying to kill me. So please don't say thoughtless and hurtful things about me like that. He's a strong man, your father, and in a trial of strength I stood no chance. I had to cut that tie if I wanted to live, and I used the only thing I could reach. I didn't want to kill him, or even injure him. I just didn't want to die, Lily, and I knew I would if I didn't stop him. So please never say that I tried to kill your dad, ever again. It hurts me so much to believe that even a part of you thinks that."

"Can you just leave me alone now, Mum?"

Emily was on the point of saying that they couldn't leave their conversation like that, but then thought better of it. She just said, "OK," closed the door and went downstairs. Looking around at her surroundings, her mood lowered even further. The lounge and kitchen-diner looked just the same as a year ago; they were perfectly pleasant in a John Lewis way, but constantly reminded her of her life with the man who'd tried to kill her. She'd contemplated re-decorating the whole of the ground floor after their fight, but knew that any changes to the house would upset Lily; they'd even had a row when Lily realised that Emily had removed all traces of Robert from their bedroom, but Emily hadn't budged. "I'm sorry, Lily, but I'm not prepared to be confronted by happy family photos of your father when I wake up every morning, or see his clothes in the wardrobe."

Lily began crying with frustration as soon as Emily closed her door. *I shouldn't have to choose between Mum and Dad's stories. It's so unfair.* She'd spent the past year convinced that her father would somehow escape a prison sentence. Surely the court would take account of the fact that he had a twelve-year-old daughter? Mum had worried about her giving evidence in court, but Lily had wanted to tell them what a good man her dad really was. But she'd had to sit outside the courtroom, in a room with a video link. She'd wanted to look at her dad, smile and show everyone that she supported him, but she couldn't. And it was her mum's lawyer who had asked the judge to keep her out! The questions they'd asked her hadn't given her any chance to really speak up for her dad, to convince them what a good man he was.

"Did you ever see your dad hit your mum?"

"How many times did he hit you?"

"How often did he lose his temper?"

Lily lay back on her bed, tears running down her face. She hadn't ever felt like this before: alone, angry, despairing. Yes, that was the word – she was in despair, and she couldn't see a way out of it. Up to now, there'd always been her mum, or her dad, or both of them to turn to when she'd felt unhappy. But now, when she was unhappier than ever, there was no one. She had nothing to say to her mum; no longer really liked her. All through the trial, she'd known how Lily felt about her dad, but hadn't made any allowances for those feelings, so determined was she to see her husband go to prison. And now he had, she made no attempt to hide how relieved she was. Couldn't she see what that felt like for Lily?

The image of her dad locked up in a prison cell for years brought further tears, but she fought them back. *I've got to do something to make his life better, not lie here crying and showing Mum how weak*

I am. I can start by going to see him, whatever Mum says. She'll probably try and stop me, but I don't believe she can. As his daughter, I have the right to see him. I've often heard Mum use human rights to win rows with Dad.

The thought of her mum and dad arguing brought up unwanted memories. Her parents had started to argue more frequently in the six months or so leading up to their fight and Dad's arrest. Their family holiday in France the previous summer had been awful. When they weren't having rows they were drinking too much, making feeble attempts to hide how drunk they were in front of her. But that didn't prove that he'd tried to kill her; all parents did stuff like that. Lily would tell her mum her decision tomorrow, whatever the consequences.

3

HATRED GROWS

"Goodnight, Colin, see you tomorrow. Last to leave again – they should be paying you overtime."

Without looking round, Colin Stroud waved his arm in the general direction of the schoolkeeper's office and called out, "That'll be the day, Bennie. Have a good evening; see you tomorrow," then hurried out of the swing doors leading to the staff car park.

The chill of the mid-October evening made him wish he'd worn a jacket. The floodlights came on as he walked into the car park, illuminating the obvious fact that he wasn't the last one to leave. The head teacher's car was still there, along with a Mazda MX-5 two-seater belonging to the head of maths, Shirley Hazlitt. He could clearly see Shirley in the driver's seat, and next to her the figure of Roy Milton, an assistant head teacher, and her lover since she'd joined the school two terms ago. Their affair was a badly kept secret among the staff, although it appeared that Roy's wife Joan was either happy with the arrangement, didn't want to know or was clueless beyond comprehension.

The indicators on Colin's old Audi blinked twice as he unlocked the doors and got in. Thinking about his head of department had started to work him up again. He'd been virtually promised that job by the previous head, as he damn well should have been, having provided the intellectual drive in the maths department since he'd joined twelve years ago. But of course, it wasn't to be. *The unstated requirement for getting a senior position in the school over the past few years has been the possession of a vagina*, he thought resentfully. A requirement that Roy would soon be confirming that Shirley met in full, judging by the speed at which the Mazda departed. *I'm better qualified, more experienced and a better teacher than Shirley Hazlitt*, Colin thought. She had a third-class degree, for God's sake! But he'd realised from the moment they'd met during the pre-interview briefing that the job was hers, as she'd spieled on about pupil-centred approaches and the amazing potential of interactive whiteboards.

Don't get mad, get even – wasn't that the phrase? Colin had never seen the problem in doing both, although until recently he'd just moaned and ranted to his wife, Margaret, and anyone in the Seven Stars who was prepared to listen. But he couldn't be arsed to start a campaign against the increasing injustices and disparagement suffered by men over the past twenty years.

Then Margaret had left him, and the blokes in the pub told him to stop moaning and do something, so three weeks ago he'd gone online and started to scroll through men's rights sites on the dark web. Starting a movement was out of his league, but joining one was a real possibility. He eventually found his way to a site named Backlash. It stood out from the others because it was passably literate and well produced. Under the strapline 'Our Purpose', the group set out its aims:

- *To reverse the emasculation, belittling and undermining of men's authority that began in 1970 with the women's liberation movement.*

- *To eradicate the phoney '-ism' of sexism, which is a fiction.*
- *To reverse the gynocentric culture and wave of so-called 'equality legislation' of the past thirty years. This legislation means that men are discriminated against for promotion, labelled as emotionally illiterate, denied the right to see their children after divorce, bled dry by unfair alimony awards and prevented from exercising their rights in the marital bed.*

Having looked up 'gynocentric', Colin had come to the main section of the Backlash website, which highlighted a number of egregious cases in which men had been discriminated against in favour of women. There was a request for like-minded men to join the group, particularly if they'd had similar experiences. He hadn't done anything at the time, but when he read about the lawyer who'd attempted to murder her husband and wasn't even charged, he'd decided to get off his arse. So he'd joined the protests outside Emily Fowler's office, making sure to stay in the background, and made contact with Backlash's Manchester group through the website. He was going to stir things up for Emily Fowler and her supporters.

Leaving her office in central Manchester at the end of the working week in the feeble October sunshine, Emily's heart missed a beat as she saw them across the road. Since she'd gone back to full-time work a month ago, a small group of men – white, forties and above – had tried to intimidate her as she left the building. A call to the police from the head of her chambers had established theoretical restrictions on their intimidating behaviour: no insulting or abusive language, at least ten metres away from the main exit, no defamatory placards. But they clearly used a different dictionary than Emily's to define 'defamatory'.

> *Two attempted murders – only one conviction.*
> *Shame on you, betraying your husband.*

She hated it, but was determined not to show it as she walked on with a thousand-yard stare. Although most of the group appeared harmless, the vile comments shouted by the bolder protesters unsettled her – there was no point denying it. The man she'd seen outside the court on the day the trial ended was sometimes there.

As she drew level with them on the opposite side of the road, one man shouted, "You're going to get what's coming, you bitch. We know where you live."

It was extraordinary. The fact that Robert had also been convicted of murdering another woman didn't count in their warped logic. Neither did the fact that she had been defending herself, and hadn't killed him. No, what really got to them was that she'd been successful in fighting off her husband's attack. That was her crime in their eyes. She'd come out on top against a man, and for some men that was enough to send them into a frenzy of hatred. More worryingly, it seemed that this bunch of inadequates might be the tip of a very big iceberg, judging by the comments appearing on social media.

On top of the personal abuse, other issues were threatening to overwhelm her: her increasingly acrimonious relationship with Lily, her financial situation and her unasked-for fame as a feminist icon.

"So invite me round and we'll sort out your troubles over a glass or two of wine and a takeaway," was Julie's response when Emily had unburdened herself on the phone last week.

Emily walked quickly to Piccadilly Station, trying to forget the protesters and their abuse. She should just make the 4.35 to Macclesfield, which would give her time to drive home, go to her regular Pilates class, have a shower and get the meal started. Julie had given her much-needed time and emotional support in the aftermath of the trial, and they'd become closer. Julie was smart, funny and really good company, but unlike Emily, she was prepared to push boundaries and take a few risks.

She thought about the evening ahead as she settled into her first-class seat for the fifteen-minute journey. Most of the guards turned a blind eye as long as she got off at Macclesfield. She'd pushed Lily to stay over at Tamsin's, as she didn't want to break off halfway through the evening to pick her daughter up. She knew Julie was a lesbian, but she'd clearly signalled that she had always been straight (excepting that brief affair with a friend at university), and was sure Julie was cool about that.

Two hours later she'd had a shower, given the kitchen and lounge a quick hoover and wipe over, and changed into the black dress that Julie had once complimented her on. The Moroccan chicken was simmering gently on the stove and she was just pouring her first glass of Saint-Émilion when her mobile rang. She saw it was Julie, and was surprised to feel the lurch in her stomach at the thought she might be cancelling. "Hi, Julie, is everything OK?"

"Oh yes, I just wanted to let you know I'm running twenty minutes late. Can't wait to see you."

"That's fine, there's no rush."

"I'm getting a taxi so I won't have to drive home."

"You can have Lily's bed; she's at a sleepover."

"Great, I'll bring my toothbrush."

Emily ended the call. *This evening's going to be fun, and I haven't had much of that lately*, she thought.

Towards the end of the meal, and after much indiscreet gossip about colleagues, they began to unpick Emily's issues.

"That's awful, Emily. I had no idea about the level of online hate you've been receiving, or that things had become so strained between you and Lily. Why haven't you told me about this before now?"

"It wasn't something I wanted to dump on you. I've decided to ask Lily to see a family therapist with me, which I see as a first step, and I have got police protection of sorts. But you're right, I should have confided in you sooner. You've been amazing."

"But I haven't even begun to help you sort out the shit going on in your life. If I'm staying over, we could carry on tomorrow morning as long as you don't have to rush off?"

"I haven't got to be anywhere, and Lily isn't due back until the afternoon. Why don't you sit down in the lounge and I'll make us a coffee?"

Julie was distracted as Emily stretched to get the coffee cups from a high shelf, her dress riding up, hugging her figure. *Just my luck you're straight, Emily*, she thought, before reining herself in. *Forget it; she's never sent out the right signals. Stick to your uncomplicated Tinder dates with young women looking for the 'older woman' experience.* "There's something I want to say before the evening gets any older, Emily."

Emily turned, and Julie stepped towards her, taking hold of her hand.

"You don't realise what a special, inspirational person you are. The way you've dealt with all this shit coming at you is amazing."

"That's a wonderful thing to say. And it really means a lot. I think *you're* the special one, keeping me sane, supporting me when things got overwhelming. I couldn't have held it together without you. The coffee can wait; let's toast a wonderful friendship."

Julie woke slowly to half-light filtering through a gap in the curtains and the sound of Emily in the kitchen. She let her thoughts drift a moment before going downstairs.

From the moment she'd read the lurid reports of the incident that had taken place at Robert and Emily's home fifteen months ago, she'd been determined to represent Emily. Although the facts seemed clear-cut – Robert had attempted to strangle Emily when she'd told him she'd worked out that he'd murdered Sue Goodall – domestic violence is rarely that simple. Robert had almost died when Emily had fought back, and Julie knew that the defence would use that to point blame at Emily. And they had. She knew one of the solicitors at Emily's firm, so had let it be known that she'd be interested in representing her. Her own colleagues had cautioned against it – "If Fowler underperforms in the witness box, you'll carry the can" – but Julie had been insistent.

They'd gradually become friends, but nothing more. There couldn't possibly be, given the rules about client/lawyer liaisons. And when Emily's life had become more difficult after the trial and her relationship with her daughter had deteriorated amidst the harassment, Julie had been there to support her.

After their toast last night, they'd carried on exchanging increasingly lurid and inappropriate stories about clients they'd dealt with in the past, frequently breaking into raucous laughter. At half past midnight, Julie had called it a night and crashed into Lily's bed. Eight hours later, she awoke to the sound of the dishwasher being emptied.

"Good morning, Emily, you're up nice and early."

"Morning, Julie. Why don't you have the first shower and I'll get some coffee and croissants together? How long have you got until you have to leave?"

"I'm fine for a couple of hours."

Emily watched Julie drive off and checked her watch. Lily would be back in an hour and Emily needed to assemble her thoughts and regain her composure before she returned.

The conversation with Julie had helped her to begin to find a way through the seemingly intractable, constantly evolving mess that was her life at the moment. The trouble was, Emily realised, solving one of her problems could make the others worse. Pushing ahead with divorcing Robert would damage things with Lily; changing her job could further damage her financially; going public about the harassment could increase threats in the short term.

So much of their discussion had kept returning to Emily's worsening relationship with her daughter, so that had to be her priority. Lily's confused feelings for her father were at the heart of the issues between mother and daughter. It would be amazing if twelve-year-old Lily hadn't had to struggle with the enormity of the situation: her dad had tried to kill her mum, having previously murdered another woman. Emily could see that she wasn't going to begin to help Lily if she kept fighting her over Robert's culpability and preventing her from visiting him. She had to begin again, put herself in her daughter's place and slowly rebuild their relationship.

For the first time since the end of the trial, the stone in Lily's heart had disappeared. She was almost happy. Not in the way she'd been before her dad had attacked her mum, but she now had an optimistic hope that she hadn't felt for a long time. Such a difference to two hours ago, when Tamsin's mum dropped her outside her house. She'd been dreading walking in and having another row with her mum; either that or not speaking for days on end, save letting her mum know what she wanted to eat or asking if she could visit a friend.

Mum had refused to allow her to visit Dad in prison when Lily had first asked a couple of months ago, and every time she'd raised it since they'd argued. She'd said horrible stuff to her mum, things she knew would really hurt her. That used to make Mum mad, but now she just went quiet, which was worse, almost. But this time, when Lily had walked in, instead of a curt 'Hello. Have you had lunch, or do you want something to eat?', Mum had smiled one of her old, lovely smiles and said, "I know I haven't been the best mum to you over the past few months, Lily. I've been having a horrible time with some very nasty people, but that's got nothing to do with you. I've let my anger towards your dad get in the way of doing what's right and supporting you. So I want to say I'm sorry, sorrier than you could ever know. Easy to say, but I want to prove it. Can we sit in the front room and talk, please? I love you so much, my beautiful girl."

They'd talked for over an hour, maybe two; Lily had lost track of time from the moment her mum said, "If you want to see your dad, I'm not going to stop you. I only ask one thing: that we talk with a family therapist about your expectations and my concerns before you go." She had promised to make arranging the session a priority, and Lily knew she would. Something had clearly happened to give her mum such a change of heart – she didn't care what it was, just so long as she could see her dad.

But her upbeat mood plummeted later that afternoon when she looked on her Facebook page and read a vicious new message:

Hi, slut. I s'pose you're getting off on your slag bitch mother stirring up hatred against blokes and rubbing our faces in the dirt. Enjoy it while it lasts; some of us have got plans to teach her a lesson she won't forget, and while we're about it we'll give you a taste too.

She'd received horrible messages about her mum before, but nothing like this; nothing that threatened her too. The room started to swim, and she grabbed a chair just in time to break her fall as she almost passed out. She knew she'd be sick unless she remained still on the floor, which was where her mum found her when she came up to her room on hearing the thump on the kitchen ceiling.

"God, Lily, are you OK? What happened?" Emily saw her daughter's tears well up as she knelt down and put her arm around her.

"I'm OK; I just came over faint when I read a message on my phone saying horrible things about us. Why are so many people out there full of hate?"

Emily looked at the last message on her daughter's Facebook page and decided to contact Deepak Singh. She'd hesitated to involve him further up to now, but these sick bastards had crossed a line when they'd threatened her daughter.

Deepak checked his phone. No message from Emily, though she was only ten minutes late. Not that there weren't worse places to spend time on a chilly November evening than in front of an open fire at the Old Spotted Dog near Prestbury. Then, as if she were reading his thoughts, a message pinged through on his phone:

> *Sorry, running late – be with you in ten mins. I'll have a large glass of Sauvignon Blanc, please!*

Deepak chuckled aloud at her chutzpah, causing the couple at the next table to glance over. He and Emily had met at a conference on prison reform about eighteen months ago, immediately realised they shared a bone-dry sense of humour and a passion to see justice done, and had become friends. That friendship was tested to the limit when her husband became a suspect in Sue Goodall's murder – an investigation led by Deepak. As his team focused on Mason as their main suspect, Emily had had to make an invidious choice: whom did she believe and trust more – her husband or her friend? In spite of the unspoken loyalty between a husband and wife that, in Deepak's experience, could result in misbehaviour being hastily brushed over, she'd chosen to trust him; a decision that had nearly cost her life. He wouldn't forget the faith she'd placed in him.

They'd kept in touch during Mason's trial and had spoken a few times since it ended, so Deepak knew she'd been having a hard time with a bunch of idiots outside her office, and was delighted by her request to meet:

> *Lunch at the Old Spotted Dog on me – now there's an offer you can't refuse.*

He hadn't seen her in person since she'd given her evidence in court nearly three months ago, when he'd watched from the visitors' gallery. Unsurprisingly, she'd looked tired and anxious at the beginning of the trial, but she'd become increasingly assured as she gave her account of her horrific experience when Mason had tried to strangle her. Her confident rebuttal of the defence barrister's aggressive questioning had left no reasonable doubt in the minds of the jury.

Deepak had a few seconds to observe her after she walked in and stood looking around for him. She'd lost some weight and her hair was noticeably greyer, but he still found her an attractive woman. Given the circumstances of this meeting – she was seeking his advice on countering the physical and online hate coming her way – he hadn't known what to expect. He got up and gave her a warm, platonic hug as she reached the table.

"Hi, Deepak, you're looking well. Thanks so much for agreeing to see me. It's nice to meet in such pleasant surroundings; certainly makes a change from our previous meetings. And thanks for my wine – cheers."

They clinked their glasses together, and Deepak said, "There was no commitment I wouldn't have cancelled in order to meet after I'd got your message. Luckily, it seems that both our diaries are a little clearer now, so I didn't have to shift much around. Silly question, but how have you been – honestly?"

Emily spent thirty minutes giving him an abridged version of the past twelve months, including her low moods, stomach-churning court appearances and confrontations with hostile men. It was surprisingly cathartic; she hadn't ever recounted her experience over the last year from start to finish before. Deepak listened intently, interrupting only occasionally to check a date, a name or a place.

"My firm have been great, agreeing to let me take on only the cases I can handle, and of course I can work from home some days. But I'd expected the hostility to be dying away by now, and if anything it's getting worse. The final straw was when some vile specimen sent Lily a threatening message on Facebook. I've told the police about the online hate and the group of men standing around near my office, of course. They're sympathetic, mostly, but say they're doing everything possible with the resources they've got. I know you're busy – I was so pleased to hear that your disciplinary was dropped – but I just need to talk through the legal means available to shut this down, or at least reduce it."

Deepak had seen where Emily was heading halfway through her story. Taking a swig of his pint, he said, "I'm glad you asked to meet, Emily. I knew about some of what you've told me – the protesters outside your office have been in the local news – but I didn't realise how serious it was, particularly the online stuff. I won't underplay this; it's difficult to quickly put a lid on this kind of thing. The problem is twofold: crack down too heavily on protesters and you risk blowing things up into a freedom-of-speech issue, which is probably what they'd like. And tracing the real source of the worst online abuse is very difficult. The two areas are interlinked, of course. The online stuff amplifies the street protests, and the abusers get a disproportionate sense of power and influence when they read the online posts."

"You're saying there's no way of preventing this?"

"I'm not, but there's no quick solution. You need to decide how much time you can give to this, and whether you're prepared to go public and accept that things could get worse before they get better."

"Can you spare any time? I know it's a big ask."

"Of course I'll help you, but I need to be careful. Although I was cleared of any negligence, unfortunately mud sticks and I can't afford to be seen to be running a parallel private investigation. To stop this completely, we'll need evidence that laws have been broken and to get those responsible identified, charged and issued with restraining orders – or even sent down."

"So where should we begin?"

"I suggest we try to identify whether the abuse is random, or an organised campaign. If it's the latter, we need to identify who's behind it. The police have discovered surprisingly influential figures behind groups like this in the past – people with a lot to lose if they're exposed. Then we check if there's been increased online activity among far-right groups, and if so, is there a correlation with the campaign against you? Realistically, I think the most valuable thing you can do in the next few weeks will be to keep a log of the most offensive online abuse and any direct harassment in the street. Then we'll see if there are any obvious patterns or connections. Is there anything else I should know?"

"I've heard a rumour from a colleague who's representing a client on remand in Robert's prison that he's got an unofficial support group inside, which could include sympathetic prison officers. If you've got any contacts there, could you check whether that's just a rumour?"

4
—

THREE WEEKS LATER

Robert put down the copy of *Nineteen Eighty-Four* he'd requested from the prison library the previous week. He'd thought he'd empathise with Winston Smith as the courageous dissenter fighting Big Brother, but he'd become increasingly disappointed with the book and the character. By the end, Smith had been tortured into loving Big Brother.

It was coming up to three in the afternoon, an hour before the prisoners were let out of their cells. Robert had been clock-watching, something many other inmates had warned him about. Three months into his twenty-year sentence, he'd finally got into a routine that made the days bearable, dividing them into time slots devoted to reading fiction and writing letters to his supporters, solicitor and daughter. He'd been surprised by the number of semi-literate letters he received from men telling him to stay strong and fight 'that fucking bitch' to prove his innocence. Even *he* didn't think he was completely innocent.

Two weeks ago he'd been surprised to learn from a screw on his wing that there was a 'Free Robert Mason' group online. Most of those posting used pseudonyms, but the screw had told him that one of them was a prison officer based in this prison, and he should expect a letter from the guy when his weekly mail was delivered, any time now.

He heard keys in the lock, then a prison officer he'd not seen before put six letters on his small steel cabinet and left. Getting off the bed, Robert flicked through them until he saw one without a stamp. It was a serious offence for officers to write personal messages to prisoners, and it had been made clear to Robert how bad his life would become if he told anyone about the communication. For a start, the decision made two weeks ago to transfer him to a single-occupancy cell would be immediately reversed.

He opened the letter.

I'm taking a big risk by writing to you, so say nothing about this to anyone – screw or prisoner. The consequences for both of us will be very painful. You've got more supporters in this prison than you know. One of them belongs to a group that's been fighting for men's rights for years. He's asked me to get your approval for them to start a campaign around your case. I will be around during your time in the yard today, so give me your answer then. Stay strong and flush this down the bog.

Robert felt a surge of optimism; something he hadn't experienced for a long time. It was early days – the earliest of days – but at last there was hope that his case could reach a wider, more sympathetic audience. He didn't want to know how this group intended to get publicity for his case, and he didn't care. He'd give the screw the go-ahead in the next half-hour.

He put the other letters on the tiny table and lay back on the bed, relishing the thought of his case being reviewed and his sentence reduced. Emily might finally be charged for attempting to kill him. He still had the conviction for Sue Goodall's murder hanging over him, but his lawyer seemed confident that they could win an appeal to reduce that charge to manslaughter.

Outside in the yard, he gave the prison officer a nod as they passed each other, taking care to check that they weren't being watched. Back in his cell, he picked up his letters again and saw that one was from Lily.

Dear Dad,

Since I last wrote, Mum has agreed that I can visit you. As she doesn't want to see you, someone else has to come with me. Mum is hoping to persuade Grandma Joyce to do it. I hope she agrees because I'm longing to see you – I've got so much I want to say.

It must be nearly a year since we last spoke to each other and I've changed a lot since then. I've been unhappy since you and Mum had that fight and both of you ended up in hospital. I thought you loved each other and were going to be around for me. Now you're probably going to be in prison until I'm nearly thirty and Mum is unhappy most of the time because of the nasty people who are writing horrible things about her. Some of them say they support you, but it doesn't help me if they're making Mum depressed. Do you know any of them? If you do, can you please ask them to stop?

Sorry if this letter has turned into a moan – I didn't mean to do that. I'm sure we will be able to persuade Grandma Joyce to come to the prison with me, and I will write to you soon with the date. I'm dying to tell you all my news.

I hope you're OK in prison and I love you very much,

Lily xx

Robert's mood deflated. He desperately wanted to see Lily, but the thought that it depended on Emily persuading his mother to accompany her, and to sit next to her in the visitors' room, enraged him. His wife had him where she wanted, able to dictate the terms. He despised her.

Colin walked slowly along Euston Road, trying to follow directions on his phone provided by Todd, a curt, unfriendly man with severe halitosis he'd met two weeks ago in a pub in Chorlton. He was apprehensive and excited, the late November sun taking some of the chill out of the air.

After he'd contacted Backlash, he'd been told to meet Stinky Breath with documents proving his identity, address, workplace and financial status. He'd bridled at that final request, only to be told, "Get real – do you think we let anyone join without vetting them? You can walk away now if you want to." That meeting involved a lot more than handing over copies of the aforementioned documentation, as Stinky Breath quizzed him persistently on his work, his failed marriage and his views on a range of political and social issues. All very obvious stuff, like, "Are men inherently intellectually superior to women? Are patriarchal societies the natural order of things? Can a husband ever rape his wife? What's the worst piece of anti-male legislation that the Labour government brought in?" He'd felt disappointed by the banality of the questions, although he was more impressed at the end when Todd told him that this was just the preliminary screening and he'd hear by the end of the week if he'd got through to the next stage.

He'd read that parts of Kings Cross were being rejuvenated, but clearly the developers had forgotten about the tacky, rubbish-strewn street he was currently walking down. He was heading for a house in Cromer Street, which was the next turning but one, although he was beginning to have doubts about joining an organisation based in a run-down area like this. Those thoughts vanished as he turned into Cromer Street and took in the smartly painted terraced houses, the church and the '60s office blocks. He did a rapid check of his tie, shoes and shirt front as he stood waiting for the bell to be answered.

The door was opened by a man in his late thirties, around six feet tall and casually smart. Probably ex-services, Colin guessed, from his body language and posture. "Mr Stroud? Please follow me; we're on the second floor."

Two hours later, in the Skinners Arms around the corner from Cromer Street, already on his second pint, Colin sat digesting the implications of the information that had been shared with him, trying to take it all in.

Walking into the room on the second floor, he'd been confronted by two men – one late fifties or early sixties, the other probably mid-forties – sitting behind a mahogany desk, each with a folder of papers in front of him. His escort sat on a chair to the left side of the room, as the older man indicated that Colin should take the chair in front of the desk. He introduced himself as Geoffrey. "That's all you need to know about me at this stage, Mr Stroud. Thomas here will take a record of our meeting, and Ben you've already met. I would like to begin by asking why you made contact with our little group three weeks ago?"

At that point, he'd given serious thought to making a run for it. The whole set-up freaked him out, especially Ben sitting rigid in the chair to his left, staring at him. He realised he'd come here without thinking this through – no one knew he was here. But bolting for the exit seemed even riskier, particularly with Ben ready to pounce. So he began to tell his tragic backstory of a crumbling marriage, a divorce that had left his wife with the house, and regularly being passed over for promotion in favour of women with less experience and ability.

After five minutes, Geoffrey interrupted him. "I'm sorry to interrupt you, Mr Stroud. Your story is an appalling but by no means unfamiliar one, as I'm sure you know. What we'd really like to know, though, is what you were hoping to achieve – to change – by contacting us?"

"My apologies for going on. As I delved into your website, I became enthused by Backlash's aim of reversing the legal changes that have advantaged women at men's expense over the past forty years, particularly the strategy of winning a succession of small but emblematic victories in the fight for men's rights that bring about fundamental change under the radar. There's a recent high-profile court case where a woman was given preferential justice over a man, and I would love to be involved in a campaign to challenge that verdict. I believe it's a perfect fit for your strategy."

"Please go on, Mr Stroud."

Colin saw that he'd got their attention, and quickly summarised the case of Robert Mason and Emily Fowler, finishing with their vastly different outcomes at the end of the trial.

Geoffrey listened carefully, waited for him to finish, then said, "Are you confident that this case provides a good opportunity to further our cause?"

"I am, because I've seen how it has already generated significant online attention and a following among men's rights activists."

"Then I would like you to work up a campaign plan around this case, Mr Stroud – two sides of A4 maximum – and send it to me. Please leave the information you've collected on Fowler with us. We may be able to initiate a little surprise for her in the meantime.

"There is one more thing. Our actions are considered unacceptable by some people, even by some who support our overall aim. If you're with us, then innocent people, perhaps even her daughter, are fair game if we're going to win. Do you understand that?"

"Completely, Geoffrey."

"Good. Ben will give you the passcodes to access the dark part of the Backlash site as you leave."

Although Colin's sense of his own importance had received a huge boost from his audience with Sir Geoffrey Granby, he remained unaware of its real purpose, which was to assess his suitability as a cadre in the far-right party Granby was trying to build.

After Ben had returned from escorting Colin off the premises, Granby turned to the other two men. "How would you assess Stroud's suitability for a future role in the party, gentlemen?"

Ben spoke first. "As a back-room worker, perhaps. As a front-line activist on the streets, confronting the opposition, no chance."

"I agree with Ben, sir," said Thomas.

"And I agree with you, up to a point. But our party's at a turning point. I've brought a number of very wealthy and well-connected backers on board, and we're recruiting well within the police, the prison service and men's organisations around the issue of men's rights. We'll continue to do that, of course, but the current political situation in the country will soon provide an advantageous opportunity to appeal to a wider spectrum of the population with far-right sympathies. Cameron's government has signalled years of austerity ahead, unemployment is already starting to rise and immigration is featuring regularly at the top of people's concerns. All this will provide the perfect conditions for grievances to grow and be exploited. On top of that, the Labour Party is becoming a liberal middle-class talking shop and is losing support among white working-class men, UKIP is full of old guys who hate the French and the Germans, and the BNP is a busted flush now that their leader's become an MEP. So we're going to need people to come up with ideas to exploit and direct the growing unrest, as well as street fighters. Let's see what Stroud comes back with."

Preparations for Christmas were only a partial distraction from the abuse Emily was receiving on a daily basis. She'd begun to log the worst online abuse (to record everything would be a full-time job) and keep a diary of harassment in the street. She'd even taken pictures of the protesters outside her office, which had only increased the intensity and ugliness of their comments. One Sunday afternoon, having made herself go to her Pilates class after missing the previous two, she'd braced herself and gone through her records, looking for patterns and recurring names. The protests were mostly random, occurring at various times of the day and on different days of the week, but there always seemed to be a larger group after work on Thursday evenings. They included the smartly dressed man she'd seen standing apart from the main group of blokes outside the court three months ago. He featured in one of her images.

After she'd agreed that Lily could visit Robert, her bond with her daughter was slowly returning, helped by the general pre-Christmas bonhomie and a constructive session with the family therapist. But Emily was increasingly concerned about her daughter's waning social life. She'd noticed that Lily had been getting fewer invitations from friends; her Christmas party invites were a fraction of last year's. There'd also been some particularly spiteful Facebook posts.

"It's horrible, Mum. Girls who used to be friends have either stopped 'liking' me or just ignore me. Others who I thought were OK have started saying nasty stuff like, 'Your dad's a murderer and you've got his genes so you must have that in you too.' Tamsin is great and says to ignore them, but I'm worried that some of the nasty ones will start on her because she's friends with me, and then she'll stop being my friend too. It's like they get pleasure from making me unhappy."

Emily couldn't bear to see her daughter suffering, yet she knew she had to tread carefully. "If they're from school, I could see the head teacher before you break up for Christmas and discuss what she can do about this?"

"Mum, you mustn't. Promise me you won't. It could make things ten times worse, everyone knows that. It will wind the nasty ones up even more, and they'll find other ways to hurt me."

Emily promised Lily that she wouldn't meet the head teacher; a promise she had little intention of keeping.

Deepak looked at the images on Emily's phone of the protesters on the street outside her office. They'd met in a small brasserie in Chorlton High Street, frequented by academics and postgrad students. Emily liked the chilled atmosphere and the veggie menu.

"God, look at them – eight human beings with four brain cells between them. Which is the one you think you saw outside the court?"

"The one second from the left, in the background. He's there every Thursday evening, trying to keep a low profile, but I've never seen him during the daytime. Could be he has a job that wouldn't tolerate his involvement in such a protest – teacher, social worker?"

"I'll discreetly circulate his image and see what comes back. I haven't got anything concrete from my research into far-right groups yet, although there's one focused on men's rights that seems to be raising its profile. I've asked a guy I know in the Greater Manchester Counterterrorism Unit for his view." Deepak paused, looking serious, then said, "There's something I've been wanting to raise with you, Emily, and that's your personal security, at home and outside it. What additional precautions are you taking?"

Emily chuckled. "Given the state of my love life over the past eighteen months, there's no need to take precautions, believe me."

Deepak smiled, a little embarrassed.

"Sorry, large glass of wine talking. I appreciate you raising it, and I've been thinking about Lily's safety, too. I suppose I thought that the group outside my office would get bored and go away, but there's no sign of that. I do get scared sometimes, at night. If they're prepared to protest in public, why not come round to our house and do God knows what? Lily is getting caught up in it, receiving nasty messages on Facebook from so-called friends. I'm going to raise it with the school. Do you have any advice?"

"I'll ask the officer who heads up the unit responsible for witness protection what she thinks is appropriate in your case. I'm also happy to come round and look over your house. In terms of personal protection on the street, the law is quite restrictive. There's a big grey area somewhere in between a pump-action shotgun and a rolled-up newspaper."

She smiled. "That's a deal – consider yourself invited round for a meal soon after the New Year. Are you working over the holiday?"

"I've volunteered to work over Christmas, Boxing Day and New Year. Mum and Dad have gone to India and my adult son is staying with his mum this year – we divorced two years ago – so I can stand in for colleagues with families."

"I'm sorry about your marriage; I didn't know. Was it an amicable break-up – not that it's my business?" *Of course it's none of your bloody business*, she thought.

"That's OK. It was difficult at the time. Gill left me to begin a new life with another man, which sounds clichéd, I know. Our son, Palvinder, had one more year before he went to university, so he stayed with me initially and now divides his time between us. It's all very civilised now, but I can't stand her new bloke, which created tensions at first. Now I'm more careful about what I say about him to Palvinder."

As Deepak walked with Emily to the tram station, she realised how relaxed she felt in his company. He was charming, interesting and actually listened to what she was saying. Not bad to look at, either. But starting a relationship with the man who had arrested Lily's father for her mother's attempted murder? The timing and circumstances couldn't be worse.

She desperately missed the physical intimacy of her marriage, which had remained satisfying, if not exciting, up to that summer fifteen months ago. There'd been nights since then when she'd lain in bed longing to experience the touch of another human being, of a man making love to her, selfishly satisfying her own desires with someone who was doing exactly the same. She realised, for the first time, that she'd hardly spent any time grieving for the loss of her marriage after it ended so shockingly in carnage on the kitchen floor.

"You seem far away all of a sudden. Is everything OK?"

"Sorry; I still sometimes find myself going over those last weeks when Robert and I were together, reflecting on whether I could have done anything to help him. He'd clearly gone to a crazy, dark place, and I no longer recognised the man I'd lived with for fifteen years. But this is probably a conversation for another time."

"Understood. Send me some dates when I can come round and check over your house. I'll be in touch if I have any news about the man at the protest. Until then, please don't take any chances, either in public or at home. Have a good Christmas." He leaned forward and kissed her on the cheek.

Emily hid her surprise at this development – they'd been strictly on handshaking terms up to now. The kiss hadn't made her uncomfortable, but it was a reminder not to send out any wrong messages. "And I hope life doesn't get too exciting on your duty days over the holiday. Take care, Deepak."

5

A CHRISTMAS PRESENT

Julie had thought hard about whether to invite Emily to her chambers' Christmas party. She was on her own and needed some fun in her life. But Julie would be the only person at the party she knew, and Emily might feel awkward. In the end, she'd invited her. When a good friend was going to be on their own over Christmas, it was the right thing to do. Were her motives entirely honourable? Of course not.

"I'd love to come, Julie, thank you. Of course, I'll have to check that I haven't got anything else in my diary!"

"That's great; I'll assume you can come unless you tell me otherwise. How have things been between you and Lily since we last spoke?"

"I wanted to thank you for your advice about Lily. I told her that I would be OK with her seeing her dad and that seems to have brought about something close to a reconciliation between us. However, she has to be accompanied by a responsible adult, and as I can't be in the same room as Robert, we're still trying to solve that problem. His mother could be a possibility, but apparently Robert hates that idea."

"Do you think Lily would be OK with me going in with her? She does know me, after all."

"Would you really be prepared to do that, Julie? That's an amazing offer. Obviously Robert regards you as the enemy, but if Lily's OK with it then he'll have no option if he wants to see his daughter. I'll talk to her about it and let you know."

"How is she coping generally? You know, with the protests and the media exposure?"

"I'm concerned, to tell you the truth. The level of personal abuse she's getting online from girls at her school and more widely is awful. Can you imagine how we'd feel if our friends suddenly started slagging us off publicly with horrible personal comments? We'd be mortified, so think what it's like for a twelve-year-old girl. I think she's being pretty amazing, but it's obviously taking a toll."

Julie thought for a moment. "Why don't you come round to my place before the party and we'll talk briefly about the arrangements for taking Lily to see her dad? Let's say 7.30."

"What should I wear? Smart, fun or casual?"

There was a hint of hesitation, then Julie said, "Wear that black dress you wore when I came round for dinner. That would be perfect."

Emily parked her Golf on the drive in front of Julie's semi-detached house in West Didsbury. She'd been undecided about whether to go since they'd spoken last week. Julie's remark about wearing her black dress had triggered a question that had lain dormant since Julie had come round for a meal. *Did she make a pass at me that evening? Was I sending out signals without being conscious of it?*

"Hi there, come on in. You look great, Emily; let me take your coat. We can sit in the lounge and do a little preloading while you tell me about Lily's decision. What would you like?"

Emily went through to the lounge and looked around while Julie got their drinks. The house was a classically designed semi, built between the wars, spacious, with a big hallway and a grand staircase lit by a tall stained-glass window from top to bottom. The furniture was eclectic – a mixture of '60s Scandinavian, antique and modern British – but the sum of the parts worked well.

Emily was studying four framed photos on the mantelpiece when Julie came in with two large glasses of chilled white wine, one already emptier than the other. "Here you go. Cheers – here's to better times in 2012. I see you've been checking out the mantelpiece hall of fame. That's my parents, of course, both still fit and well; my younger sister Jane and her husband; their two children, my nieces; then me and my ex-partner Claire on a skiing holiday in the Alps two years ago. We were both keen skiers and went on at least two trips to the Alps every year. I really miss it."

Do I ask? thought Emily. "Do you see much of your nieces?"

"As much as I can, but they live in London, and Barry is a bit of a chauvinist plonker."

"So you and Claire aren't still together?"

"No, we split up shortly after that holiday, in fact."

As Julie fought back tears, Emily instinctively reached out and put her hand on her arm. "I'm sorry, Julie."

"Thank you, but I'm the one who should say sorry for welling up like this. It was very painful at the time. Claire was five years younger than me and wanted to have children. I just couldn't face taking on such a life-changing responsibility coming up to forty, so we broke up. She's now in a relationship with a much younger woman, who I'm told is expecting a baby. Oh fuck, not again…"

Julie was weeping now, tears running down her cheeks. Emily put her glass on the mantelpiece and held her, feeling Julie's warm, wet cheek against hers. She was surprised that she felt no urge to end their embrace.

Julie released herself, went to the kitchen and came back dabbing her eyes with a tissue. "Right, that's set the mood for a party! Well done, me. Let's talk about Lily before I embarrass myself further."

"Julie, you've seen me in far worse states over the past year. There's nothing to be embarrassed about, and I'm glad to be the one supporting you for a change. Claire made a big mistake; you're an amazing woman.

"The good news is that Lily thought it was a cool idea to go with you; far preferable to her grandma. So if your offer still stands, what's the procedure from here?"

"I'm so pleased; I'd love to get to know Lily better. You should write to the prison governor, requesting a visit on Lily's behalf and stating that you wish me to accompany her."

Emily agreed that she'd write to Robert, even though she hated the idea, to try and convince him that this was the only way that Lily could see him.

"He'll just have to swallow his objections to me being there. Now, let's order a minicab. Time to have fun."

The clock next to the bed showed 3.30. Emily had been awake for over an hour, but sleep wasn't a prospect any time soon. She'd been mulling over the past few hours since Julie had fallen asleep.

The party was well under way by the time they arrived – chaotic dancing and a big crowd around the bar. They handed in their coats, Julie got them both a cocktail – 'Mojito for me, please' – then they mingled with the crowd, Julie introducing Emily to her colleagues and friends.

Robert's trial came up just once, when an obviously drunk barrister colleague of Julie's turned to Emily and said, "Are you the wife of that head teacher who was recently sent down for your attempted murder? Quite a case; he sounds like a real bastard. I never understand why women stay with men like that for so long – you must have known what he was like all along, surely?"

The two women looked at each other. Before Emily could reply, Julie turned to the man, leant towards him and whispered in his ear.

"What did you say, Julie? He looked furious."

"I told him to ask his ex-wife and I'm sure she'll enlighten him."

Emily hadn't danced for over two years, and as soon as she heard the opening beat to 'Billie Jean', she took hold of Julie's hand and said, "I love this, fancy a dance?", and pulled her onto the dance floor. The two of them immediately picked up the rhythm, sensing each other's moves. They stayed on the dance floor as 'Billie Jean' was followed by 'Into the Groove' and a succession of '80s dance classics.

"Time to slow the pace for a while," broke in the DJ, as he brought up the volume on 'Hey Jude'.

Emily and Julie moved slowly round the floor, holding each other, sweat trickling down their backs. Emily didn't care; it just felt so good holding and being held by her irrepressible friend, alive in the moment.

"God, we're classy!" laughed Julie. "Sometimes I think dancing can be even better than sex."

Emily looked her in the eyes and smiled. She felt what was unfolding between them, and wanted it. "That's pitching it a bit high. Mind you, it's so long since I've done either, I'm not in a position to judge. It might be interesting to test it out, though."

Julie returned her gaze, searching for irony, but finding none. "We could get our coats and go back to my place, if you'd like to."

"That sounds like a good idea."

In the back of the cab, sitting close, Julie put her hand on Emily's. "You mustn't think you can't—"

But she didn't finish the sentence, because Emily was tentatively pressing an exploratory kiss between her lips.

"Would you like a drink?" Julie asked when they were back in the house.

"No thanks, I think I've had enough. Alcohol, I mean."

Watching Julie as she undressed in the bedroom, Emily's confidence of ten minutes ago melted away. "You're beautiful, Julie. I need you to take the lead at this point."

"You weren't doing too badly in the taxi," Julie laughed as she unzipped Emily's dress and slipped it from her shoulders.

Emily took off her underwear and got into bed, heart thumping. They kissed again, embracing each other, then Emily gasped as she felt Julie slipping a hand between her legs.

"Say if you're not comfortable with anything I'm doing."

"That feels good. Don't stop."

Julie looked at Emily's face on the pillow, hair dishevelled, lipstick and mascara smudged. *I'm more than a little besotted with you,* she thought, *but what the fuck am I getting myself into? My last relationship with a straight woman didn't end well for either of us, and we have to talk this through before she leaves this morning.*

Julie quietly got up and went to the bathroom, then downstairs to make two cups of tea. She smiled to herself when she thought about last night; compared to the string of young(ish) lovers she'd had in the past two years, the sex had been less intense, less exciting, even. But she couldn't ever remember feeling this happy the morning after with any of them. Her thoughts were interrupted by the creak of floorboards above.

Emily opened her eyes and slowly focused on her surroundings. A large, white-shuttered bay window, a circular modern ceiling light and a tall pine wardrobe. And that smell. She recognised it at once. The smell of sex; her first time (as good as) having sex with a woman. It had felt good. *So, after over twenty years as a straight woman, you discover your bisexuality. You certainly took your time, Emily.* She got up to pee, went to pull her knickers down, then realised she wasn't wearing any. *Shameless,* she thought, and laughed.

"Good morning. I thought you'd like a cup of tea."

"That's lovely. Thank you."

Julie hesitated, unsure whether to get back into bed.

Emily read her thoughts, pulled back the duvet and said, "You're not getting up just yet, are you?"

"I wasn't planning to; I've got a free day ahead."

As she got into bed, Emily pulled off the spare nightdress that Julie had given her. In the years to come, when she thought about Julie, this scene – Julie laughing, taking her nightdress off, lying next to her, kissing her – would be the image that came into her head.

They were sitting in the kitchen, having coffee and scrambled eggs on toast, when Julie looked at Emily and said, "I think we should talk about last night, don't you? Where does it leave me, you... and us? I don't want to get hurt or to hurt you, and I don't want to mess up a lovely friendship. To state the blooming obvious, I'm a lesbian and you're basically straight. I've had a couple of relationships with straight women and they've ended badly for me emotionally. I don't want that to happen to us. What do *you* want, Emily?"

Emily wished she'd managed to arrive at a clear answer to this question as she'd lain awake at 3am that morning. She owed that to both of them. "At this moment, I feel better about myself, more loved, than I have for at least two years. You're right, I've always thought of myself as straight, and I haven't ever been seriously attracted to a woman before. But I've no doubts about my desire for you. Last night and this morning felt wonderful."

Julie looked at her, waiting for her to carry on.

"I want us to be lovers, but we should take things one step at a time. I'll have to learn how to be with a woman. We'll have to be really sensitive around Lily, and of course you can't be my solicitor any more. But I don't think those things are insurmountable. What do you say?"

6

UNHAPPY NEW YEAR

The last time she'd seen Robert Mason was seven months ago, in court, on the final day of his trial. As she'd walked into the visiting room with Lily, Julie had noticed immediately the toll that prison life had taken on him. Not only did he look several years older, he looked diminished, stooped. But fifty minutes into their visit, she couldn't believe it had gone so well. Robert clearly loved Lily, and she him.

Lily hadn't let the cold, unfriendly process of entering the prison, being searched and lingering in a rank-smelling waiting room dampen her happiness. The thought that she was about to see her father again after more than five months had kept her mood positive ever since she'd learned the date of the visit. She had so many things to tell him and ask him. Julie had promised that she would stay as distant from them as the rules allowed.

Lily saw him as soon as she walked in, and couldn't resist half-running over to his table. She knew the rules about touching, and earned a harsh rebuke from the prison officer when she gave her dad a hug before sitting down. His handsome face had lines at the corners of his eyes, his skin was grey and pallid, and he looked much older than Lily remembered. Tears came into her eyes as he began to speak, haltingly at first. They were both overcome.

"It's so wonderful to see you, Lily, thank you for coming. I've missed you so much. Tell me all your news – how's school? Have you made many good friends there yet? Do you have a favourite teacher?"

Questions poured from both of them; Lily was crying her eyes out and her dad's weren't much drier. The visit would only last an hour and they both kept asking questions over each other, desperate to get as much information as possible, trying to make up for the past eighteen months.

Fifty minutes in, the visit had gone without incident and Julie was thinking about future visits and how much she was looking forward to supporting Lily and, through her, Emily.

And then he switched. The prison officer on duty gave everyone the ten-minute warning, the spell was broken and Robert launched a verbal attack on Julie. "Ten fucking minutes! You're sitting there enjoying this, aren't you, you bitch? Seeing my torment, only being able to see my daughter for one hour a month. Look how upset she is. You're the main reason I'm here, and I hope you and my grass of a wife get what's coming to you."

Lily immediately got very upset, telling her dad not to say horrible stuff like that about her mum, because she loved her too. The prison officer came striding over, stood over Robert and told him bluntly that visitor privileges would be withdrawn unless he calmed down immediately. Which he did. But only then did he realise the damage he'd done to his relationship with his daughter, who was looking at him, aghast.

"Why did you have to spoil everything? Please can we go now, Julie?" Lily got up and walked out, Julie hurrying after her.

The prison officer shook his head. "You handled that well, didn't you, Mason? What a fucking idiot."

Deepak hadn't been keen on Emily's suggestion that Julie should join them for their continuing discussion. "The more people who are part of this informal investigation, the more uneasy I am about it." But Emily had persuaded him to have a joint meeting to share what they'd learned so far, as it made no sense for her to have separate conversations with him and Julie. She had deliberately arranged the meeting to take place following Julie's visit to the prison with Lily.

The three of them were in a quiet café in Didsbury. Having got the 'happy New Year' preliminaries over with, Deepak began. "I've identified the man in the picture of the group outside your office, Emily. He's called Colin Stroud, teaches maths at a large comprehensive school in Bolton; same job for twelve years, no promotion. He's divorced, no children as far as we know, and no record of a current partner. Doesn't have a criminal record, but he was arrested once for a breach of the peace after a Fathers 4 Justice demonstration. Never charged, but he's on the Police National Computer.

"We checked out his Facebook page. There were a few posts moaning about promotion in teaching being limited to women these days, the usual stuff you find from disgruntled men online. However, there was an interesting mention of a site called Backlash that he'd visited frequently and was recommending to his fellow wingnuts."

Julie jumped in. "Did you manage to check out the site?"

"They're not on our list of proscribed organisations, but I got someone in my team to check their website history for any increase in activity. I told her that it was information required for another ongoing investigation. The site appeared a year ago, under the radar at the time. However, there's been a significant increase in subscribers over the past nine months, with a resultant upswing in online posts. The content stays just within the law regarding online hate speech, but I would describe it as a platform for ultra-misogynists to vent their hatred of women. My colleague has agreed to find out if there's an active organisation behind the site."

The two women had listened intently as Deepak was talking, and now looked at each other. Not for the first time since the meeting began, he found himself wondering if there was more than friendship behind their eye contact.

Julie spoke next. "I've already told Emily the details of my visit to the prison with Lily, Deepak, but so you're in the picture, it was both moving and awful, in a way. Robert obviously misses his daughter dreadfully and was overcome with emotion when she walked in. The visits last an hour, and neither of them could get a word in edgeways. But when the prison officer announced that there were only ten minutes left, Robert's mood changed, and he launched a horrible diatribe against me and Emily. Lily became really upset, shouting, 'Don't say horrible things about Mum; she's a good person. Why did you have to spoil everything?', then walked out, leaving Robert in a fury.

"The deputy governor had agreed to speak to me before we left about possible support for Robert inside the prison. He confirmed that a group of men have formed an unofficial support group, calling themselves 'Justice for Mason'. They're following the news stories about the group protesting outside Emily's office. When I asked if he thought that any of the prison staff could be sympathetic to that point of view, he clammed up. I was left feeling that I'd touched a nerve."

Emily had listened quietly throughout Julie's account, but now said, "So how significant is the level of support for Robert inside the prison?"

"Based on the deputy governor's remarks about prisoners who are into men's rights politics, and the fact that he got very cagey when I asked if any officers are sympathetic to those views, Robert may have a way of communicating with groups on the outside. We should probably assume that he can encourage harassment of you from inside the prison. What do you think, Deepak?"

"On the evidence, it's definitely a possibility. As Emily's solicitor, I think you should contact the governor and ask him to monitor the situation and keep you informed."

The two women looked at each other again, and this time Deepak knew.

Emily got there before Julie. "I've had to instruct another solicitor, Deepak, as Julie and I have recently begun seeing each other. No one else knows yet, and apart from a couple of Julie's closest friends, we're not intending to tell anyone. Not because we're ashamed, obviously, but because we realise that it will only give the hatemongers more ammunition to fire at me."

Deepak's stomach lurched. *Maybe if I'd made a move two months ago, who knows?* But he just said, "That's marvellous; I wondered if you two lovely people would ever get together. Congratulations!

"Summing up," he continued, "I think we agree that we've found enough evidence to indicate that these attacks could be part of a wider campaign. I will keep pushing my colleague to dig deeper into Backlash. Julie will brief Emily's new solicitor on Lily's next visit and ask him to chase the governor about a potential group of hostile prison officers. Emily will covertly monitor the group outside her office for any new members and increased activity. Are you two OK to meet again in two weeks and see what we've got?"

But those plans were to be overshadowed by a shocking incident.

She'd taken her usual route from the station to the car park. As she walked under the bridge carrying the mainline from London to Manchester, she didn't notice anything unusual about the Toyota pickup parked down a side street, even as she heard two vehicle doors slam in rapid succession. Her equanimity faded when she heard footsteps approaching quickly from behind, but her instinct in these situations – stupidly, it turned out – was to keep up a brisk pace without running and assume that ninety-nine times out of a hundred there was nothing to be alarmed about. She put her hand in her pocket, checking for her rape alarm, then realised that she'd changed coats but hadn't transferred it. *Shit – you idiot.*

And then, having somehow covered over thirty metres in seconds, they were behind her. A hand closed tightly around her left arm, gripping and spinning her round. She screamed louder than she'd thought possible. She couldn't see their faces, only their eyes, but that was enough for her to take in their hate, their exultation at their sense of power.

"Shut up, you posh bitch," the taller one shouted as he slapped her shockingly hard across the face; hard enough to stun her momentarily. The second man punched her in the stomach, winding her and doubling her up as she struggled to get air into her lungs. She could see traffic on the main road less than fifty metres away, but she knew she'd have to hurt these men to get there.

"This is a present from your husband, the guy you betrayed to the cops. And a warning to stop your feminist cheerleading shit."

With air in her lungs again, she screamed and kicked the shorter one as hard as she could on his shin.

"Shit, that hurt! You fucking slag – now it's personal."

His mate grabbed her hair and pulled her head back hard. Yelling in pain as clumps of her hair came out, she half-turned and jabbed her fingers through the holes of his balaclava, feeling two nails break off as she gouged his eyes as hard as she could. His scream sounded primeval. For a moment she was free of them, and she ran towards the traffic on the main road, screaming, "Help me, someone, please!"

She heard them behind her, stumbling, cursing, slower than they'd been before. Two young men came running around the corner of the bridge support ahead, followed by a third, older and much bigger. "What the fuck's going on? Leave her alone, you bastards! We're calling the police."

As her three heroes ran towards her, she heard her attackers stop, shout something unintelligible and run back to their pickup.

Deepak's dream about a failed attempt to save a woman from drowning was interrupted by his *Pulp Fiction* ringtone. He snatched his mobile from the bedside table; it was Emily.

"Deepak, I'm sorry to ring you so late, but I can't reach Julie. I was attacked earlier this evening."

He felt as if he'd been stabbed in the chest. It was a physical pain. "Are you hurt? Where are you? I can come now if you need me."

"I'm at home now. It happened as I walked to my car from the station. There were two of them, wearing balaclavas; I've no idea who they were. I'm bruised, shocked and sore, but otherwise OK, I think. I called the police and an ambulance, the paramedics checked me out and the police drove me back here – they wouldn't let me drive. I gave them a statement, all the details I could remember, and they said they'd check the CCTV in the area. I was shaken, but the sedative the paramedics gave me has kicked in and I feel calmer now. I just needed to talk to someone and hear a friendly voice. I'm feeling better, so you don't need to come, really. But thank you for asking."

"How about Lily?"

"Luckily, Lily is on a sleepover. Sorry, Deepak, I'm feeling really sleepy, so I'm going to ring off."

Emily put the phone down. She'd really wanted to talk to Julie, to hear her say, "I'll come over right now," and be taken to bed and held in her arms. Strange that she hadn't picked up her calls. She'd lied to Deepak about feeling sleepy. The events of the past few hours were still far too intense, her mind running over the ordeal on a loop.

Her call to Deepak had only just finished when her phone rang. It was Julie. "Emily, is everything OK? I've just seen your missed calls, I'm sorry."

"Julie, I'm so glad you rang, I've been longing to speak to you. I was attacked in the street by two guys this evening and—"

"You've been attacked?! How badly? Are you hurt?"

"My face is bruised, I've got a splitting headache and lost some of my hair. Three blokes heard me screaming and chased them off; I called the police and an ambulance and the paramedics checked me over. The police drove me home. I'm sore but OK."

"Don't say any more now; I'm coming over. I'll be there in half an hour. Is there anything you want me to bring?"

"Just yourself. I can't wait to see you."

The twenty-something PE teacher lying across Julie's stomach looked up quizzically.

"I'm sorry, Zoe, my girlfriend has been badly beaten up. This will have to be a case of carnal interruptus, I'm afraid."

"Eh?"

When Emily opened the door in her pyjamas, Julie couldn't hide her shock.

"I know, it looks bad, but you should see the other guy."

They both forced a laugh. Julie embraced her, then kissed her very gently.

"God, it's good to see you. I was so proud of myself for fighting back, but since the attack I've realised what might have been and I'm fucking angry at what they've done to me."

As Emily took Julie through the attack, she interrupted several times, asking questions the police should have asked about the attackers and the events: did the men have accents, what was their clothing like, had Emily damaged the guy's eyes enough to send him to hospital? "Those fucking bastards. Your case attracted support because of men like that. Where else did they hit you? You're going to have a nasty black eye."

"One of them pulled a big chunk of my hair out as he wrenched my head back."

"Why don't you go back to bed and let me take care of you? Is there anything I can get you?"

"The paramedics gave me a good checking over and luckily the damage is superficial. But you could get me a new ice pack, some hot tea and sit with me for a while."

Lying awake in bed, listening to Julie's breathing beside her, Emily went over each moment of the attack. She'd always thought she'd be too scared to fight back in such a situation, afraid of encouraging further violence. But that hadn't happened. Yes, she'd felt fear, but from the moment one of them grabbed her arm, her instinct had been to fight back hard, inflict maximum damage and get away. She knew that a hard kick to the tibia could be shockingly painful, and nobody likes to feel fingernails scooping their eyes out. She pushed aside the uncomfortable memory of slashing at Robert with the food-processor blade; was she really only aiming to cut his tie? The second assailant might well need hospital treatment for his eyes, so she'd contact the police with her crime number early the following morning and suggest they inquire at local hospitals.

What to tell Lily when she came back that afternoon? She needed to know the truth, or at least most of it. Emily would play down the seriousness of the attack, reassure her that she had nothing to fear, but let her know that the men had said they were acting on Robert's behalf.

Some days were bearable, like when Robert had been on duty in the library and helped another prisoner read a passage that had been frustrating him. Some were hell, like yesterday, when the inmates had been locked down the whole day because a prison officer was assaulted, and Robert didn't have a book so he was stuck in his cell with his mind going over and over what might have been. And some, like today, were suddenly transformed from shit to brilliant by an unexpected event.

Robert was out in the exercise yard, going through his circuit of exercises, when the prison officer who'd left him the note about the men's rights group walked past him. "Good exercise routine you've got there, Mason." Then, in a lower voice, "Brought you some good news. I heard that wife of yours had a bit of an accident a few days ago. She got into an argument with a couple of our blokes outside and it didn't end well. Mashed her up a bit, I heard. Would have been even worse if three do-gooders hadn't turned up, but the warning's been given. Have a nice day."

Robert carried on with his routine, jubilant.

Their next meeting was held in Emily's house, as agreed. Deepak had arrived early, inspected the place thoroughly and given her a list of immediate changes to make.

"I can't believe you've been so casual: no deadlocks, no alarm, no cameras. Not even a trapdoor with pointed stakes underneath! I'll give you the details of a reliable company, so please promise me you'll get them tomorrow. Give them my name and say it's an emergency."

Once Julie arrived, Emily updated them on her attack. She'd given a statement to the police the day after and had asked them to check local hospitals for anyone admitted with an eye injury. Nothing had yet shown up on the CCTV, so Deepak promised he would chase them to keep checking for images of her attackers. His colleague in Cyber Surveillance had confirmed that the increased traffic on Backlash's dark site indicated that the group was probably planning something; it could have started already. The site was well designed to obstruct anyone attempting to hack in and identify the URLs.

"Do you think they were behind the attack on Emily?"

"It's an obvious assumption to make, Julie, but too early to say. Cyber Surveillance has more avenues to try and get through the site's security, but it will take time," said Deepak.

Julie confirmed that Emily's new solicitor, James, had already spoken with the deputy governor at Robert's prison, who's putting out feelers to trusted prison officers.

Then Emily spoke. "I can't thank you two enough for the support you're giving me. The attack has given me a sense of urgency and time to think about our next steps. I'd like to share those with you, if that's OK?"

"Great, let's hear it," said Julie.

Emily looked at her notepad. "First, it seems likely that the campaign against me is organised and not just a few disparate misogynists, and if that's correct then I suspect there are probably other women in the news like me being targeted. So we need to talk to them. Second, judging by the evidence from Robert's prison, his trial has sparked support among some prison officers, who may also be getting involved with Backlash. Finally, the Backlash website states that their core aim is to roll back the gains made by the women's movement over the past thirty years, which is a big project. Attacks like mine could be part of building a national men's rights movement, and that would need leadership and funding. Discovering who's behind Backlash is key to uncovering what's really going on. What do you think?"

"Impressive – you should take sick leave more often. But it's ambitious – can the three of us take all that on?" Deepak asked.

"I agree, we've all got day jobs. But I think it's feasible if we concentrate on those three areas: researching other cases like mine across the country and contacting the women involved; persuading the deputy governor to look for further evidence of support for Robert's case; and finding out who's really behind Backlash. You should also know that the partners have agreed that I can go part time and work from home, which means fewer opportunities for protesters to harass me and I'll have more time to be with Lily and pick her up from school. Any thoughts?"

Julie and Deepak looked at each other, then Deepak said, "I agree with everything you've set out. I'll keep pushing my contact at Cyber Surveillance to come up with a lead on Backlash, and I'm sure I'll be able to do some research of my own on top."

"I've already set up regular meetings with James, Emily," Julie added. "He'll tell me if there's anything more concrete from the governor about support for Robert. I'll also contact friends involved with the prison service in London and Leeds. Uncovering the involvement of prison officers in Backlash or other violent men's rights groups would be explosive."

"I can't expect more from either of you; you've both been brilliant. I've now got the time to research recent cases like mine and contact the women involved, so between us we've got the three areas covered. I've set up a WhatsApp group we can use to communicate from now on. It's supposed to be secure, as you know."

"Promise me you will follow through with all the security advice you've been given, and don't walk down any more deserted dark alleys. You're very dear to us both."

"Thank you, Deepak. I've arranged a meeting with a chief superintendent tomorrow to discuss improving my personal protection."

7

—

FALSE HOPES

Colin had decided that his commitment to the cause of men's rights was far more important to him than his teaching career – if that's what you could call it. He'd do just enough in the day job to keep the head of department off his back, which wouldn't be difficult given the lesson plans and materials he'd accumulated over the years. Teaching about quadratic equations never changed – his pupils would still get a better deal with him than with most of his colleagues. He'd also found time to alert the head teacher to the affair between Shirley Hazlitt and Roy Milton – "I'm concerned it could bring the school into disrepute, Head."

But he was getting impatient. When he'd contacted Geoffrey six weeks ago to tell him that his plan to bring down Emily Fowler was ready, he assumed he'd be asked to present it in person. But he'd been told to send it to a box number and wait to be contacted. Two weeks later, Stinky Breath – Colin knew him now as Darren – got in contact and invited him to a meeting at a private address in Fallowfield. When he'd got there, Darren had asked him to wait in the narrow hallway while he filled him in about the meeting. He'd explained that Colin would be joining a meeting of the Manchester Backlash group.

"We've got about twenty members meeting monthly, including twelve regulars who turn up every time. Most were driven to get involved in direct action by one of three things: losing custody rights to their kids, trumped-up charges of sexual harassment or being passed over for promotion at work in favour of a woman. Some just hate women, full stop.

"The agenda's pretty simple. Review any action that's taken place, agree on action for the coming month, hear news from other groups around the country. If there's a speaker, they'll usually start the meeting. So after I introduce you, the floor's yours for five minutes to say a few words about your plan for Fowler. Just one more thing. We've checked you out pretty thoroughly – you wouldn't be here otherwise."

The front room was really too small to take twelve people; Darren apologised that there wasn't even a chair for Colin to sit on. Colin made his way across the room, stepping gingerly in between the sullen-looking men, and perched on a windowsill. He looked round at the assembled group as Darren introduced him. All white, mostly in their thirties or forties, all but two with a bottle of beer on the go. One, a tall guy wearing a cheap suit, had a patch over one eye, and stared at Colin for an uncomfortably long time with the good one. Although, Colin noticed, the good eye didn't look too great either.

Darren finished introducing him and said, "Colin will now go through an idea for an action he's proposed to the leadership."

Once Colin had finished, instead of inviting questions, Darren quickly moved the agenda on. "Let's start by hearing about any successful actions undertaken since our last meeting."

The man with the eyepatch began to speak. "Soon after our last meeting, as agreed, Dave and I set up an ambush for the slag Fowler. We jumped her in Macclesfield on her way home from work as she walked to her car. The plan was to slap her around, scare her and have a bit of naughty fun with her, if you know what I mean. We roughed her up, but she went berserk, kicked Dave in the balls and nearly blinded me in one eye. It's worked, though. I understand she hardly ever goes to work any more, and leaves early when she does. But don't worry, Emily Fowler and I will have a reckoning before much longer, no danger."

Slowly, it sunk in. Geoffrey must have sent Colin's plan for a surprise attack on Fowler to the Manchester group, who'd already carried it out. He didn't recall advocating serious sexual assault, but wasn't going to lose any sleep if it happened. He felt a sense of achievement that he'd never felt as a teacher – an idea he'd been responsible for was now being put into practice, and changing things.

There'd been little else to interest him at that first meeting, and the following month's was cancelled as it clashed with a Manchester United home game. So an update from Geoffrey, or his second in command, on any further success was definitely due.

The following day, a WhatsApp message was delivered to the members of the Manchester group. It was brief and to the point:

Hi, guys, good news. As those of you who were at the meeting will know, the slag Fowler was badly beaten up by two of the group, and the online petition for Robert Mason's retrial is starting to take off. We've recruited a second screw in his nick, they've made contact with Mason and he's agreed to do whatever he can to boost the campaign.

As he read the message, Colin became increasingly irritated. Yes, there was good news, but he'd been sent the same communication as the rest of the group. As the brains behind the plan, he should have received a personal mention. Geoffrey owed him that.

Emily's life was calmer than it had been in months. She rarely commuted to the office now, and on the days she went in there were fewer, if any, protesters. The police were taking a harder line, and she guessed that with no one to shout at on most days, the fun had gone out of it.

Using nothing more than a browser, local newspaper websites and her own privileged access to court reports, she had quickly found six other cases of women who'd had similar experiences to hers. They'd all been involved in a high-profile court case with an ex-partner who'd assaulted them, only to find it being used to whip up a campaign about discrimination against men. She'd made contact with four of them.

Spending more time working from home meant that her relationship with her daughter was back to where it had been before Robert's attack; this had brought her more happiness than anything, even her developing relationship with Julie. She'd been dreading telling Lily that Julie was now more than a friend; not because she feared that Lily would be outraged that her mum had 'become a lesbian' – she was pretty sure her daughter would be cool about that as she approached her thirteenth birthday – but because she couldn't accept anyone replacing her dad. She'd been right on both counts, but to her surprise Lily rapidly came to terms with the knowledge that her mum and dad would never get back together, so her sadness about her dad's 'replacement' was short-lived. Emily suspected that the fact that his replacement wasn't a man helped, in a way.

But there was a cloud. She was still concerned about the impact that being targeted on social media was having on her daughter's well-being. Emily's meeting with Lily's head teacher had been productive. Ms Walton had empathised, then reached an agreement with the offending girls and their parents. Upsetting posts from Lily's 'friends' had virtually stopped. Yet poisonous messages from complete strangers sometimes got through to her

Facebook account, and every time she blocked one, another would get through a few days later. Emily too had noticed an increase in her own hate mail following an online petition calling for a retrial for Robert that had been launched around four weeks ago. The petition stayed within the guidelines for such campaigns and didn't attack Emily directly, but many of the comments attached to it did. Always the same themes: 'You're going to be raped', 'Wives don't shop their husbands' and 'Get back in your box, slag'. She tried to brush it off, but these were sentient human beings, walking around out there, consumed by hatred for women. It was scary. Her solicitor was monitoring the petition to ensure that they kept to the guidelines.

Her feelings for Julie were growing stronger; something she'd never expected. At first, Emily had just delighted in discovering such a strong emotional connection with a warm, loving human being; someone with whom she could share her thoughts, fears and hopes. She began to relish their physical intimacy. Sex was fulfilling, possibly down to the novelty of a lesbian relationship, but she hadn't stopped fancying men. Only last week she'd looked a moment too long at a good-looking man on the train who must have been ten years her junior. She'd sent the wrong message and spent the rest of the journey trying not to make eye contact.

Julie was happy; she found Emily's guileless delight in exploring sex with a woman a flattering and, at times, hilarious turn-on. But she found that she still needed the occasional Tinder hook-up to satisfy her need for uncomplicated, exciting sex with a younger woman. Emily could never know about that part of her life.

There'd already been a near miss. One weekday afternoon, relaxing on the bed after making love, Julie's phone had pinged. As Emily went to pass it over, Julie launched herself across the bed, grabbed her phone and intercepted the message on the screen.

Last night was incredible!! When can we do that again?

Lily had guessed what was coming the moment Emily had asked to have a chat "because I've got something to tell you". The past two years had been an overwhelming emotional roller coaster for her mum, including the months leading up to her dad's arrest, when her parents had started to argue more with each other. As a result, her mum clearly hadn't realised how much she'd matured in that time, enabling her to notice signs between adults that she wouldn't have registered, let alone understood, as an eleven-year-old. So when Emily had told her that she and Julie had become more than just friends and Julie would be staying the night sometimes, Lily's reaction had surprised her.

"Mum, that's been pretty obvious since Christmas. You've seemed happier recently, so I'm pleased for you. Tamsin and I sometimes talk about the number of our friends' parents who began a gay relationship after they'd split up. I like Julie and understand that she's your new partner, but please accept that she can never replace Dad in my life, even when he's being horrible."

Julie had gone with her for her second visit to see her dad. The thought that she was being taken by her mum's girlfriend had amused Lily, and unlike other adults who didn't have children, Julie didn't talk down to her.

"Are you looking forward to seeing your dad again? It's been over a month since your last visit, hasn't it?"

"I still love him, but it upsets me so much when he goes for Mum. I understand that he's still angry and it must be awful being locked up in prison, but he knows that I hate it when he does that, so why can't he control himself when he's with me? It's not as if we've got all the time in the world to make up again afterwards – the visit's spoilt and that's it for a month or more."

"I've arranged with the governor that I can sit at the back of the room, so hopefully that should help."

The second visit was more disastrous than the first. It broke Julie's heart to see Lily's hopes for a happy reunion ripped to pieces by this angry, vicious man and his all-consuming sense of injustice. Where had that come from? He'd murdered one woman in cold blood and tried to kill his wife! The deputy governor had been as good as his word, and Julie was allowed to sit on the perimeter of the room, behind Robert and facing Lily. The visit repeated the pattern of the first one: father and daughter greeted each other warmly and talked animatedly for half an hour. Then Julie noticed a change in Lily's body language, the conversation stopped for a moment, and she heard Lily say, "Please don't say things like that; you know it spoilt our last visit."

Robert had erupted, shouting, "I'll say what I like about your mother – she's a fucking whore."

As the prison officer strode over to their table, Lily simply got up, quietly told her dad that she wouldn't be coming back again for a long time and walked away. As she left the room with Julie, they heard Robert shouting and the officer bellowing at him to shut up.

"Julie, promise me that you will remind me how horrible this was if I ever want to visit him again."

Lily had stopped looking at social media, but her friends told her that recently they'd noticed a change in the comments about her. The number of posts was slowly going down, but there seemed to be a small group continuing to post vile, hateful stuff about her and her mum. It was as if the idiots who had jumped on the bandwagon had got bored, leaving a core group of real haters. But thanks to Tamsin, she now had a wider circle of friends in her year at school; girls and boys who were supporting her.

8
—

REFLECTIONS AND DECISIONS

Driving away from the prison, with Lily in tears beside her, Julie
struggled to think of a single good reason for not locking up men
like Robert Mason and throwing away the key. As a lawyer she
believed that incarceration for its own sake achieved nothing, but
for Robert she'd make an exception. Of course he was capable of
controlling himself; he'd been a teacher for nearly twenty years.
Julie had pushed the question of how Emily had lived with him
for fourteen years, apparently unaware of his true character, out of
her mind. She convinced herself that dramatic circumstances can
change people dramatically, and left it there.

Since her relationship with Claire had ended two years before,
Julie had assumed that she'd never have anything that fulfilling
again: the feeling that the other person wasn't just part of your
life, but almost a part of you, and your life could no longer be
whole unless they were in it. That's why the break-up had been
so devastating. Julie had lost part of who she was. After their
split, she'd been celibate for months, wary of online dating. But
following a couple of disastrous experiences, she'd worked out her

ideal type for a one-night hook-up – athletic, late twenties and up for anything – and embraced the lesbian dating scene.

Then Emily had come into her life and it had been hard to keep her feelings for her separate from their professional relationship, particularly when Emily was almost overwhelmed by the strain and ugliness of the trial. Julie had just wanted to hug her and make everything all right, which would have spelt the end of her career and any chance with Emily. Emily was clearly straight – or, rather, had led a straight life and been content with that, up to now – but Julie had noticed her looking at women occasionally in a way that signalled only one thing. She'd almost blown it when she'd gone to Emily's for a meal, misjudged the moment and came close to overplaying her hand. She'd been determined not to make that mistake at the Christmas party; if anything happened, then Emily would have to make the first move. She'd certainly done that.

Since the morning after their first night together, when she'd asked Emily outright what she wanted and she'd replied, "I want us to be lovers," Julie's feelings had deepened. It wasn't the life-changing bond that she'd had with Claire; Emily was a remarkable human being but yearned for a settled life, unlike Claire, who lived in the moment, which had made their relationship so exciting. And Julie had soon realised that while sex with Emily could be fulfilling and pleasurable, it wasn't enough; she needed the occasional thrill of sex with no ties. She'd just have to make sure that Emily never found out.

Julie had arranged to see the deputy governor again before Lily met her dad. He'd agreed to give her ten minutes to update her on his inquiries into a Backlash presence among his prison officers.

"The officer in charge on Mason's wing, who I trust completely, has noticed that one of his officers has recently been talking to Mason in the exercise yard more than usual. The same officer also asked to be moved to Mason's corridor for what turned out to be spurious reasons. Furthermore, he's close friends with two other officers; they all joined us around the same time five years ago, live near each other and drink in the same pub. This pub is well known in the area as a meeting point for National Action, a far-right group that's been linked in the past to assaults on Muslims and Jews. Although the evidence is circumstantial, there's enough for me to continue to monitor the situation for a few more weeks. As soon as I have anything more concrete, I'll be in touch."

As they pulled up outside Emily's house, Lily ran ahead to tell Emily about her visit. "It was awful again, Mum. Dad lost it, just like last time. But I'm OK; Julie has been great. I think I'll go up to my room for a bit."

Emily gave her a hug, waited until Lily had gone upstairs and then turned to Julie. "Thank you so much for going with her, Julie. I was so worried when I first told her about us, but I needn't have been. She really likes you."

"And I really like her, Emily. Come here."

Deepak's involvement with Mason's case had begun almost two years ago, when a woman's body had risen to the surface of a local reservoir. Identification of the body had taken a frustratingly long time, but it eventually proved to be that of schoolteacher Sue Goodall, who'd gone missing two months earlier. A past connection with Mason – teaching at the same London school in the early 1990s – eventually unearthed increasingly incriminating evidence. Deepak had arrived to arrest Mason at the moment when he was attempting to strangle his wife, whom he blamed for informing on him. In the end, ironically, it was Mason's life he'd saved, as he lay on the kitchen floor haemorrhaging from a deep wound inflicted by Emily as she'd fought back.

Since then, and especially after the trial, Deepak had felt the need to support Emily; protect her, even. He was honest enough to admit that his motives weren't entirely altruistic – he'd been attracted to her from the moment they'd met. He now accepted that nothing was going to happen between them, but as a detective he'd become absorbed by the challenge to discover if there was a deeper right-wing conspiracy behind the campaign against Emily and other women victims.

After his first meeting with Emily and Julie two months ago, Deepak had gone back to his flat, poured a whisky, put Dvořák on the hi-fi and slumped on the sofa to think. He was about to commit time and emotional involvement to uncovering the truth behind the campaign against Emily. The risks to his career were obvious. If his off-the-books inquiries into Backlash came to the attention of his superiors, it would probably spell the end of his career – a greater risk than either Emily or Julie was taking. If he was going to drop out, or simply adopt a background role, he had to do it now. He'd already helped Emily by improving her personal security and initiating the trail to unearth a Backlash connection. She would understand how serious the consequences for him could be, should his superiors discover that he was diverting police resources to a freelance investigation. *So get the hell out now, then, Singh.* But this was an existential, fork-in-the-road decision that would partially define him for the rest of his life. Play safe and secure, withdraw meaningful involvement, and enjoy a successful career; or take a risk and play a part in uncovering a conspiracy that probably involved prison officers in a nasty far-right movement to reverse women's equality by thirty years.

As the *New World Symphony* came to an end, he'd made his decision. Emily had believed him over her husband when he was trying to catch Sue Goodall's murderer, and it was payback time. He was a Sikh, for fuck's sake. It was a no-brainer.

Since he'd taken that decision, progress uncovering names behind the Backlash group had been slow. He couldn't push his IT Surveillance source any harder, so he'd decided to do some old-fashioned detective work in his spare time. One lead from the hack into the Backlash website was an address in Cromer

Street in central London. Then there was the pub in Fallowfield that the prison governor had said was a meeting place for the far right, including officers he suspected of liaising with Mason. A five-minute check confirmed that CCTV covered both premises; comparing the footage might identify an individual who frequented both the pub and the Cromer Street house. Such a person would definitely be a subject of interest, and possibly involved in the Backlash plot. Deepak had been lucky: the CCTV covering both places was functioning and well defined. The big problem was finding someone to analyse facial recognition scans of the footage, particularly when this wasn't officially a police operation.

On most evenings, whenever his journey took him close to Emily's house in Bollington, he would divert his route, drive into the close and slowly circle around, checking that there was nothing suspicious or out of place. It used to get to him a little if Julie's car was there, but he was over that now.

9
−

UNCOVERING A CONSPIRACY

"Can I ask you something?"

Julie looked at Emily quizzically. Halfway through the evening news, they'd impulsively gone to bed and made love. Emily was now abstractedly stroking Julie's body as she lay beside her. "What can I say, except 'Yes'?"

"That evening when you came round to my place for dinner, before we became an item, were you planning to seduce me that night?"

"I'll know not to say, 'Yes' the next time! OK, I was confused. I thought there might be a chance, but I was also telling myself not to be ridiculous. I fancied you, as you know, but you hadn't given me any reason to believe you were interested. So 'No' is the answer; I wasn't intending to make any moves on you that evening."

"I hope you weren't frustrated by the end of the evening."

"I managed."

Emily laughed and said, "We did say earlier, before we had a better idea, that we'd update each other on the Backlash developments."

"I'm afraid I can't give that question my full attention, if you keep doing that."

Before Julie went to work the following morning, they updated each other over fresh fruit salad, yoghurt and coffee. Julie relayed the recent conversation she'd had with James about the situation in Robert's prison. "There's good news and bad news. The good news is, there's clear evidence that Robert has been receiving and sending messages out of the prison via one of the prison officers. He hasn't actually been caught red-handed with a letter in his possession, but the evidence is overwhelming. The bad news is that the governor is going to charge the officer in question, who will be suspended and face a disciplinary. This could trigger suspicion within the Backlash network that someone is on to them, which will put them on their guard in the future. How about you?"

"I'm now in contact with four women around the country who've had a similar experience to mine, and their accounts are fascinating. In every case, there was a well-publicised court case in which a man was accused of a serious assault or worse on his wife or girlfriend, which he fought to the end before being found guilty. A campaign against the women began almost immediately, portraying the men as the victims. Those campaigns have all the hallmarks of the one against me – physical assault, online hate, demands for a retrial and demonstrations. I'm writing a summary of the four cases. The five of us have established a real bond; it's lovely."

"Not too much of a bond, I hope?"

"Ha ha. I adore you, you know that. We need to meet with Deepak again and put his findings into the mix; see if there's a picture emerging."

Two days later, Emily, Julie and Deepak were becoming increasingly excited about the picture that was falling into place. Emily summed up their discussion.

"The question we're trying to answer is simple: is there a coordinated and orchestrated campaign by a far-right organisation with links to the prison service to exploit recent trials of violent men convicted of assaulting their partners and use them as a springboard to launch a campaign against women's rights? I think the answer is 'Yes.'"

The other two both said, "I agree," as one, so Emily carried on.

"OK, but interrupt at any point if you need to. We've found enough evidence to show that the Backlash site is a front for a group that's orchestrating and coordinating the attacks on me and the abuse Lily's receiving. The evidence comes from analysing posts on the Backlash site, finding links to the Cromer Street address on the site and observing one of the demonstrators outside my office, Colin Stroud, visiting Cromer Street twice. These attacks aren't just aimed at me, but part of a wider campaign against women. That evidence comes from the testimonies of the four women I've contacted, and the fact that their cases have all been highlighted on the Backlash site. They've all suffered a similar pattern of abuse to me.

"With respect to the connection between Backlash, prison officers and Robert, we know that two officers are providing a communication channel for him to the outside. Those same officers also appeared on CCTV at both Cromer Street and the Fallowfield pub.

"When we join the dots, I think it's clear that we've uncovered an operation that's using the Backlash website as a front to establish a far-right group aiming to roll back women's rights. These people are prepared to use violence. Crudely, their appeal is basically 'Men have no rights any more, women are running things, it's time for blokes to fight back'. Deepak, can you now say more about the other figure identified on the Cromer Street CCTV, please?"

"Thanks, Emily. When I first thought of analysing the images outside the Fallowfield pub and Cromer Street, I was stumped as to how to take it forward – I've no authority to ask for the footage to be analysed. Then I remembered an ex-colleague who used to be an inspector in Special Branch. I thought she might be particularly interested in uncovering a plot to roll back women's rights, and she was. The big surprise was discovering footage of an establishment figure with a dodgy backstory entering the Cromer Street address, which bringing an ominous new dimension to the picture."

"How ominous? Who are we talking about?" said Julie.

"A knight of the realm, no less. Sir Geoffrey Granby, ex-Guards officer and merchant banker. If he is linked to Backlash and this operation, then we must expect some serious kickback if we rattle their cage. There were rumours linking him to that attempted coup in 2004 involving a group of mercenaries plotting to overthrow the leader of an African state."

Emily gasped. "I remember. Wasn't Mark Thatcher allegedly involved in that, too?"

"The very same."

"Granby must know there's a CCTV camera near his building. How come he's not taking steps to hide his identity?"

"He does. He uses a huge golfing umbrella, in all weathers, believe it or not, to cover his face as he moves from his taxi to the front door. His bad luck that on one of the days when we were reviewing the CCTV, it was blowing a gale, the brolly blew inside out and his hat blew off. We got a very clear image of Granby and his two companions; one turns out to be a former SAS soldier and the other's a young woman. We're guessing she's an escort – an expensive sex worker, in other words."

"Thank you, Deepak, I think Emily and I both know what an escort is. Do you have still images of their faces?"

"Yes, I'll send them now."

Julie and Emily waited while Deepak sent the images via WhatsApp. As they heard the ping, a startled look crossed Julie's face.

"He looks like hundreds of others from the higher echelons of the English upper class. She's stunning, though. You could find out who she is and fix an evening out with her, Deepak," said Emily, grinning.

"I've a feeling I couldn't afford even five minutes of that young woman's time."

Emily glanced at Julie to make sure she was in on the joke and saw her face and neck colouring. Julie tried to force a smile, and said, "If prison officers are involved, and ex-soldiers, and a knight of the realm, then who else? High-ranking police officers, politicians, lawyers? How far has this group of men who hate women and are determined to take us back to the 1950s penetrated the establishment? In the light of this new information, I think we should take a moment to discuss what we're getting into and ask ourselves what our goal is now."

"What are you saying, Julie? Do you want to drop this, just as we seem to be getting somewhere?"

Julie looked at Emily almost disparagingly. Emily hadn't seen that look before. "I hope you know me better than that, Emily. I'm not saying that at all; no way should we drop this investigation. But this is now looking bigger than we realised, with far-reaching consequences. So we need to be honest with ourselves, and each other, about the risks and make sure we're prepared for what might come our way."

"Sorry, you're right, but I'm too tired to thrash this out now. Can we give Julie's question serious thought over the next two days, then Skype each other? How does that sound to you, Deepak?"

"I agree, we all need a break. Whatever we decide, uncovering the people behind Backlash should be our priority."

"And I will get back to my four sisters and see if they can give me any further clues to identify the bastards harassing them."

"I understand, Geoffrey. You want me to liaise with Darren and identify a couple of capable members to attack our target's house within the next two weeks. Is there a reason for the tight timescale?"

"Obviously, Colin. I want the recipient to link the attack to recent events in our friend's prison. Some people have been stirring things up with the governor, who's set up an unhelpful internal investigation as a result. So speed is of the essence. Sort it out with Darren then report back to me when it's over."

The line went dead. Colin would normally feel furious and humiliated after being spoken to like that, but the adrenaline rush from being tasked by Sir Geoffrey with organising an attack on Fowler's house pushed such pettiness aside.

By the end of the evening he'd contacted Darren and agreed on the names of two members who would be dying to have a crack at Fowler again.

Emily tried to hide her apprehension. "I've been meaning to ask you something. When Deepak showed us the CCTV pictures from the Cromer Street house, you seemed shocked for a moment. Was I imagining it, or did you notice something that I didn't?"

Julie had been dreading this moment. Dreading Emily's reaction when she knew the truth – and she would have to know the truth, or at least some of it. "You're right, I was completely taken aback by one of the pictures, and I've been scared to tell you why. But we promised each other the truth, and I've been plucking up the courage to tell you for days. I'm going to pour myself a large gin and tonic first. Can I get you one? I recommend it."

"God, Julie, what the fuck is it? OK, I'd better join you."

Emily watched Julie go through the routine of collecting ice from the freezer, cutting the lemon, and pouring gin and tonic into two glasses. She couldn't believe her luck that someone so loving, funny and smart had come into her life. As Julie approached with their drinks, looking apprehensive, Emily's heart melted. She just wanted to give her a hug and reassure her that there was nothing she could say that would damage their relationship.

Julie took a large mouthful of her drink. The words came tumbling out. "I know the woman in that picture. In the biblical sense. We met through a dating app about a year ago, and saw each other a dozen times or so. After Claire and I split up, I eventually began to want a sex life again. Nothing more than that – I never thought I'd have a relationship like mine and Claire's again." She looked directly at Emily. "But then I met you. Never say never.

"So I went on a couple of apps, saw this woman – she's called Marion – and we met up. She's almost ten years younger than me and I thought she'd lose interest the minute she saw me, but she didn't. Part of me was flattered that this stunning younger woman fancied me. We didn't have much in common, except in bed. That was very good, but she's materialistic, probably votes Tory and lives in London.

"After several months I found out, by chance, that she worked as an escort for wealthy businessmen wanting female company for a night in London. Sex would be part of the deal for most of those dates. We'd sometimes meet in London, sometimes in Manchester, but that was becoming a hassle so I was thinking of finishing it. Then one evening we were having drinks in a bar in Islington and this bloke came up to her – late thirties, aura of superiority, obviously loaded, face like a gargoyle – and started talking to her, completely ignoring me. She was hanging on his every word, not bothering to introduce me. After about five minutes of this, I excused myself and went to the loo. I wasn't sure she'd be there when I got back, but she was, on her own. When I sat down, she had a go at me for leaving her! That was it; I lost it and told her what I thought of her blanking me completely, not even introducing me to her friend. Things got pretty heated, and she gave a sneering laugh and said, 'Don't be stupid; he's not a friend, he's a client.' From the way she said it, along with what I'd observed of their exchange, I knew exactly what kind of client he was.

"I said, 'So you're telling me you're a sex worker? Don't you think I had a right to know that, given our regular exchange of bodily fluids?'

"I thought she was going to hit me, but she just said, 'Oh, am I not good enough for Ms Stuck-Up Lawyer, then? Don't worry, Julie, I'm clean. Fuck you and goodbye.' She walked out crying.

"I got myself checked for every STI possible – there was nothing, thank goodness – and until I looked at that picture, I hadn't seen or thought about her for months. So it was a shock, and now you know about my sordid dating experience. There's been no one else, until we slept together."

If Emily had been paying attention, she would have seen Julie's eyes move down to the left at that moment; a sign that she had just erased over twenty Tinder dates from her recent (and current) sexual history. "You didn't think for one second that that would change my feelings for you, I hope? But you realise what it means; she's our link to Granby. You could get back in touch and find out more about him."

"Oh, sure. We could be in bed, scissoring each other, and I'd casually ask, 'Have you ever escorted any really important men, like Sir Geoffrey Granby? Did he tell you about Backlash?' I can't see that working, somehow."

"I said get back in touch, not sleep with her again. And what's scissoring?"

Julie smiled and kissed her softly on the lips. "My wonderful straight girlfriend. So much to learn."

10

CONSEQUENCES

Deepak hadn't intended to drive past Emily's house on his way home, but he wanted an excuse to test-drive his new car around the winding roads near Whaley Bridge. When he'd seen the silver two-year-old BMW 3 Series on the forecourt, he'd just thought, *Why not?* He'd never had anything as cool as this before – and just wait till Palvinder saw it! So as he was going to be passing within a mile of Emily's house, he thought he might as well drive into the close and out again. He wasn't going to stop, as he didn't want Emily to know he did this. She'd probably be annoyed with him. He also knew that she'd be home alone with Lily, as during their Skype call yesterday to decide on their next moves Julie had mentioned that she was going to London for a two-day conference.

He'd felt buoyed up after their call. It was important for the three of them to keep reinforcing their successes, their little breakthroughs. They were all taking risks with their futures, and mutual reassurance that their goal was worth it was important. And they needed to keep focused on the big prize – uncovering the key players behind Backlash and shining a light on the wider conspiracy. The challenge was how to achieve that without risking their jobs and their personal safety.

Emily's assiduous cultivation of the four women who'd suffered similar abuse and attacks after their partners had been jailed was paying off. The cases had all occurred in different parts of the country, but the patterns of abuse were remarkably similar. Linking the names of the men involved with Backlash cells in those areas would be a breakthrough.

As their Skype conversation continued, Deepak had had a mad idea; so crazy he'd kept it to himself, to raise the next time they met. Colin Stroud probably kept lots of information on Backlash around his house. Deepak could easily break in and search for lists of names, minutes of meetings, etc. Julie could be his lookout and stage a distraction if she saw Colin coming home.

He took the turn-off for Emily's village. As he turned into the road that led to her close, he saw a Toyota pickup parked nearby and instinctively memorised its registration. He remembered Emily saying that the vehicle used by the two men who'd attacked her had been a pickup. If they were here to attack her house, he had an opportunity to apprehend them. But they would have to attempt an attack first. He drove into the close, past Emily's house, parked out of sight and rang her.

"Emily, it's Deepak. I'm round the corner from your house. Don't ask why, but I believe that the men who attacked you may be parked at the entrance to the close. If they attack your house, this is my chance to arrest them, but I have to let them make the first move. How do you feel about that?"

"Christ, Deepak, this is a lot to take in. Luckily, Lily is out this evening, or I wouldn't risk it. Tell me what I should do."

"Make sure you've got the house secured. Have the fire extinguisher to hand, and the Mace spray that I gave you ready. Dial 999 the second they try to break in. Good luck."

"Don't take stupid chances, Deepak. Be careful, please."

Deepak put on his stab vest, took out his taser, handcuffs and baton, and walked back around the close. He knelt down behind a telephone exchange box, and waited.

Just as he thought that they might only be scouting the house, the two men appeared wearing balaclavas, walking purposefully. One of them was carrying two bottles with rags stuffed in the top, and the taller one had a baseball bat. Deepak's heart thumped faster in his chest. What was he thinking? Emily could be in real danger. But he had to let them make the first move; if he arrested them now, the maximum charge would be carrying an offensive weapon. Fifteen metres from the house, the one with the baseball bat started running towards it while the other lit one of the petrol bombs. Their plan was now obvious. Smash the windows, throw in the Molotov cocktails, and drive Emily out of the house and give her a beating, before getting out fast.

Holding the taser in one hand and his ID in the other, Deepak moved as soon as the taller man swung his bat hard at the lounge window and the other brought his throwing arm back. The glass cracked but the window held, as Deepak knew it would. The shorter man had already released the petrol bomb, which smashed against the damaged window and burst into flames. Panicking, he lit the second bottle and threw it at the front door.

Deepak ran towards them, holding the taser in front of him, shouting, "Police. Drop your weapons and lie on the ground."

They both turned and looked at him, motionless for a second, then fled. Deepak levelled the taser and fired at the nearest man, who stopped in his tracks and fell to the ground, screaming and convulsing. He ran over to handcuff him, extending his baton in case the other one returned, but he'd carried on running. There came the hiss of a fire extinguisher going off; Emily was covering the flames around the front door with foam.

Having secured one prisoner, Deepak headed after the second assailant, who'd run out of the close. The pickup was already reversing into the main road as he turned the corner. He ran back to the cuffed suspect, who swore at him. As he read him his rights, he checked that Emily had got the two fires under control, took the taser barbs out and told the man to, "Shut the fuck up." He radioed in the details about the driver, vehicle, place and possible direction of travel, then walked over to Emily. "Are you all right, madam; is the fire completely out?"

"Yes, thank you. You're a police officer?"

"Detective Inspector Singh. Have you called 999?"

"Yes, as soon as I heard the window smash. They said a car should be here in five minutes."

"Brilliant."

The man had been trying to stand up, so Deepak roughly applied a hold and pushed him into a sitting position, taking his balaclava off at the same time.

"Don't touch me, you Paki bastard."

"Shut your racist mouth, or I'll make sure the judge adds a hate crime to the charges. What happened to your eye?"

The man looked at Emily. "That bitch tried to blind me. Ask her."

"You're a real piece of work, aren't you? Arson, attempted murder, assault on a police officer... I'd say minimum ten years after parole."

"Fuck off."

Deepak heard the police sirens – three cars, judging by the sound – and quickly went over to Emily. "Are you sure you're OK?"

"I'm fine, really. A little shaken. Thanks for your advice about shatterproof covering for the windows. You were amazing; a real action man to my rescue once again. How on earth did you just happen to be here?"

"Let's talk later. My story to the police will be that I sometimes drive past your house on my way home as I know you've been receiving threats. This time, luckily, I surprised an attack in progress."

"I presume we're open about the fact that we know each other, if it comes up?"

"Definitely. It would look as if we've got something to hide if we kept that back, and there's no reason to. Here they are now."

Three cars swept into the close, past the occupants of the other houses standing outside their front doors.

"We know one of them also attacked me a few weeks ago, so I think we can assume that the same group is behind this attack."

"The police will want to talk to both of us now, then the Crime Squad will interview you at the station as soon as possible. We'll be in touch before that. You did well, Emily. Oh yes – and please get your letter box blocked up and a mailbox put outside."

"Thanks, Deepak. I'm going to try and clean up the front of the house before Lily gets back. Thank goodness she wasn't here; I'll have to think of something to explain the blackened paint on the door."

Colin was shitting himself. He'd been summoned to Cromer Street the day after Dave and Graham had been arrested, following their disastrous attack on Emily Fowler's house. He could understand Geoffrey's fury – at this moment, the police were interrogating the two Manchester members about the attack, and they were too stupid not to let slip information about Backlash. Dave had bolted but been stopped by a police patrol within a mile, taken back to the scene and identified by the copper. *How could I have known that a Paki inspector would happen to be around at the same time?* Colin thought.

"This balls-up could cause us big problems, Colin. Those two idiots know very little about the deeper organisation, but they know enough for the police to begin to suspect that they weren't acting alone. How were they chosen, and what went wrong yesterday evening?"

"They volunteered for the job immediately after Darren and I put the word out. They carried out the first attack on Fowler, which left them both injured, and wanted revenge."

"That was a very stupid mistake on your part. You should have insisted on giving this job to someone else, not the fools who had already botched one attack. Carry on."

"Information about yesterday's events is still hard to come by. Our member on the inside isn't part of the police investigation – he's in another division – so he's only going on rumour, but it seems likely that either this copper had been tipped off, or was checking Fowler's house on a random visit."

"Maybe the police have someone watching the house every night?"

"Our man on the inside says he's sure there was no permanent presence."

"There will be now, that's for sure, so we're now in a worse position with respect to Fowler than before. How much do you know about our chap on the inside?"

"According to other members of the Manchester group he's completely reliable and trusted."

"In that case, it looks to me as if Dave or Graham was too loose with his tongue in a pub and someone overheard and then earned themselves a few quid with the information. The chance that this copper just happened by at exactly that moment is too far-fetched. Tell Darren to warn the group, from me, to keep their mouths shut about our operations in future. They won't be asked to leave nicely if it happens again."

"This won't happen again."

"You're right, it won't."

Two days after the attack on her house, Emily reported to Greater Manchester Police headquarters for an interview with DCs Jacob Shaw and Mandy Trot. Shaw had politely made clear on the phone that the invitation was one she couldn't refuse.

"Just routine, Ms Fowler. DI Singh has given us a full statement and it's basically a matter of ensuring that your recollection matches his. Shall we say tomorrow at 11am here at police headquarters?"

Looking around the interview room, she thought of the times when she'd sat in near-identical surroundings with her clients. Some nervous, some full of false confidence and others boiling with rage at the system, at 'them', at her. Because, to some of her clients, she'd represented the system, even if she was representing them. She'd studied hard to gain the right to represent clients in court when Lily was still a toddler, which had been tough. To be fair, Robert had pulled his weight in those days; she couldn't have done it otherwise. *Christ, what happened to us? To him? Don't go there – no point.*

Her musings were interrupted as Shaw and Trot made an entrance. *DCs are definitely getting younger,* Emily thought, and smiled at her cliché. *They're dressing more appropriately, too.*

"Thanks for coming in, Ms Fowler. I'm DC Trot and this is DC Shaw. I hope you're feeling OK now. The firebomb attack must have been very scary."

"I'm fine now, thank you. More importantly, my daughter wasn't home at the time, and I had a chance to clean up some of the damage before she got back. She knows something was thrown at the house, but not that it was an arson attack."

"Could you take us through the events of that evening, please? Take your time, and don't leave anything out, even if you think it's trivial."

Emily had gone over her account with Deepak yesterday, just to be clear about the aspects he didn't want her to include.

"Please omit my phone call informing you that they were outside; don't say I ran after the other suspect – I shouldn't have left the first one unattended; and obviously don't say anything about the unofficial investigations the three of us have been pursuing."

"So I shouldn't say you left me guarding him with my can of Mace, then?"

"Probably best not to."

Shaw and Trot sat listening politely, stopping her only once for clarification. "How would you describe your relationship with Inspector Singh?" Shaw asked.

"We have the occasional drink, we know each other well, but not in the biblical sense."

"What does that me—"

"I'll tell you later, Jacob," Trot interjected.

When Emily had finished, they both continued to take notes for half a minute or so, then Trot said, "How sure are you that this was the man who attacked you over two months ago?"

"Given his build and voice and the damage to his right eye, I was pretty sure. When he blurted out that I was the bitch who gouged his eye, that seemed conclusive."

"Do you have any idea why these two men attacked you twice, Ms Fowler?"

Emily looked at Trot and then at Shaw as she said, "Most probably because I've got a vagina. I'm sure you know I'm Robert Mason's wife. Since his trial, I've been subjected to harassment, hate mail, street protests and physical assault. Why? Because he went to prison for murder, but I wasn't charged for defending myself. Some men – a small minority, I hope – can't accept this, and are using the verdict to campaign for men's rights at the expense of the gains made by women over the past three decades. Apologies – here ends the sermon."

"No apologies needed, Ms Fowler. Thank you for coming in. Hopefully they'll both plead guilty and you won't have to give evidence in court."

11

DEPTHS OF DEPRAVITY

"I've checked out Stroud's address and assessed the risk. I believe the potential gains are worth it, as long as Julie is my lookout."

The three of them were Skyping. Julie and Emily looked at each other, then Emily said, "So you're intending to go ahead with this, Deepak? Have you really thought through all the possible things that could go wrong?"

"I think so, but there will always be surprises with a job like this. But if we can get hold of Backlash membership lists, and minutes of board meetings, that could be a game changer."

"Why Julie and not me?" Emily asked.

"This guy has seen you many times; he'd recognise you however you disguised yourself. He's so obsessed he's probably got your picture stuck above his bed."

Emily shrieked. "Deepak! That's such a revolting thought. It'll stay with me now."

"You mean short, balding schoolteachers in their mid-forties aren't your type?"

Julie decided the banter had gone far enough. "Deepak's right; it has to be me. We need to visit the address beforehand to check out the house and its surroundings. When were you thinking of carrying this out?"

"Within the next few days. I'll send you possible dates and times. The Easter holidays are late this year, so he'll still be at work for another week."

"I've got his address, so I'll go tomorrow. Let me know the date and time as soon as possible. Bye, Deepak." Julie switched off Skype and took a sip from her wine glass. "This is lovely – what is it?"

"Picpoul de Pinet. My local sommelier recommended it. Such a confident yet subtle bouquet," Emily replied.

"You're so convincing when you talk shit like that; it's scary."

"Do you ever feel guilty that we have something so good together? It doesn't seem fair to everyone else out there, passing time in perfectly serviceable, but unfulfilling, relationships."

"Now you mention it, no. But I never stop marvelling at how I've managed to luck out with Emily Fowler, who I've fancied since we first met.

"Actually, there is something I need to talk through with you. Since Deepak is prepared to risk burgling Stroud's house, which is pretty 'out there', I wondered about trying to arrange another date with Marion. I still have her number, and we know she's been in contact with this Geoffrey creep."

Emily said nothing for a few seconds. Several thoughts went through her mind at once, particularly, *Why does she still have her number?* "You can forget that; I don't want you taking such a risk."

"Hold on, Emily. This isn't really your decision to make, though obviously I don't want to hurt you. But the potential gain is very high. If she begins to suspect anything, I'll bring the date to a halt. I think it's unlikely she'll want to meet anyway, but I'd like to try it."

"How far will you go with this? Would you have sex with her if you thought it would help you get more juicy details?"

Julie burst out laughing. "I wasn't intending to go anywhere near her juicy details!" Then she started laughing again, more hysterically.

"Very funny, but I'm serious. I don't think you'll be tempted, but I know you. If you think that going to bed might get us the information we need, you might be prepared to do that. I admit that I'm finding the idea of my partner playing the role of some sapphic Mata Hari difficult to handle."

"OK, I understand, but please calm down. I love you to bits. Will you please agree to me making contact and trying to arrange a date? If I sense real hostility then I'll back off."

"I'm behaving like a jealous idiot, sorry. Please contact her. Actually, there's something I've been meaning to mention to you as well. It's Lily's thirteenth birthday during the Easter holidays, and I've said I'll take her and her friends out to Pizza Express in Poynton. I'd love you to come – please?"

"Lily told me it's her birthday in a couple of weeks, so I've been presumptuously holding the date. Thank you, I'd love to."

"I've booked a minibus taxi; if you're able to take your car as well, that should be enough space for all of them."

"Your daughter, a teenager! What have you bought her?"

"I've told her that I'll take her into Manchester for a mum-and-daughter shopping trip, but I want to get her something special as well. She's had so much to deal with over the past year, she deserves it."

"Hello."

"Hello, Marion, it's Julie. I've been feeling increasingly guilty about the way we left things all those months ago. I want to apologise; I completely overreacted."

There was silence at the other end. *But at least she hasn't put the phone down*, thought Julie.

"So what's brought on this sudden bout of contrition? I thought I was too sullied for you? We both do things in our jobs that we'd rather not do, Julie, it's just that our hypocritical society judges my work to be muckier than yours."

"I was upset because you hadn't told me, not because you sleep with men for money. But I should have trusted you, instead of assuming you'd put me at risk. I'm sorry. How have you been?"

"I'm getting by. I've had some awful clients since we split, absolute pigs. One experience was particularly horrible. When I tried to resist his sick demands, he carried on hurting me until I couldn't take any more, and gave in. The fact that I was obviously in pain just turned him on more. For men like that it's about having the power to degrade women. I informed the agency, but the boss just told me to suck it up."

"That's awful. I'm so sorry to hear that, Marion," said Julie, meaning it. "Fucking bastards."

"How about you? Are you seeing anybody?"

"No. I saw someone on and off for a couple of months after we split up, but there's been no one for a while." *I'm becoming a serial liar*, Julie thought. "What about you, are you seeing anyone?"

"No, believe it or not. My experience with that client has shaken my confidence generally, not just with men, which is bloody unfair. I'm having counselling, which is helping a little."

Julie left a silence.

"I don't suppose you fancy a drink sometime?" Marion asked. "Just for a chat? It might help me on my journey back to normality."

"I'd like that. I'm coming to London in a couple of days; we could meet for lunch."

"Great – I'll find somewhere cosy and text you the address."

Julie should have felt pleased with herself after the call, but the feeling that she was using Marion – who was clearly not in a good place – made her uneasy. She had to keep reminding herself of the bigger prize. If she, Emily and Deepak helped to break up Backlash and reduce the rise in violence against women, it could help women like Marion in the long run. Maybe.

The small trattoria in Bloomsbury was certainly cosy, and surprisingly quiet. Marion was already there, sitting at a table for two near the back. She'd put on a couple of kilos and looked five years older, but Julie had time to wipe the surprised look from her face before Marion saw her. She was a different person psychologically, too. She'd been fun, confident and full of life, in spite of their political differences. That Marion was no longer apparent.

Julie didn't have to probe for information about Geoffrey Granby. To her astonishment, it came tumbling out over the next hour and a half, from the minute she asked if Marion knew the man who'd abused her, and if she'd thought of reporting him to the police?

"For a smart lawyer, you ask some stupid questions, Julie. His name is Geoffrey Granby; *Sir* Geoffrey Granby. I'd say he has a hatred of women verging on the psychopathic. In my line of work you quickly find out that there's a side to some men that they hide very well in everyday life. Let's call it getting a sick pleasure from exerting sadistic, perverted power over women. Geoffrey Granby took that to a level I hadn't experienced before, and never want to again.

"Our date began normally. He'd paid the top rate, making it clear at the start that he wanted sex, which makes things easier, in a way. There's no facade that we're just like other couples, having a romantic evening out. He explained that we would be dining at his London home, which I believe also serves as his office address. That wasn't particularly unusual, but alarm bells should have rung when his driver came into the house with us.

"He took me through to a beautiful dining room, with a huge chandelier hanging over a large, polished oval table. Our places were already laid at one end, and I was shown to my seat. As soon as the decanted wine had been poured – which I later suspected had been spiked with a muscle relaxant – he deliberately started a confrontation, goading me about my views on feminism. When I didn't give him the answers he wanted, his tone changed. 'I presume you're not a feminist? I mean, we're clearly not equals here, as you're providing me with a service, at my bidding. And yet you make a very good living through this unequal situation by satisfying men's desires. The inequality of the sexes suits you very well.'

"I should have seen the question for what it was – a nasty attempt to belittle me even further – and ducked it. But I stupidly decided to challenge him. 'If by "feminism" you mean the belief that in many societies women have less power than men to determine their lives, that men decide what is acceptable for women to do and say, and that situation has to be challenged, then yes, I am a feminist. It doesn't mean I hate men, or don't enjoy their company.'

"'But that makes you a hypocrite, doesn't it? You're not challenging the "power imbalance", as you would call it, by whoring for money, but reinforcing it. And you're earning more than most men in this country. Eight hundred pounds for a few hours' work is more than I earn; you can be sure that I'm going to get my money's worth.'

"'I don't think it's hypocrisy to want to change part of the system and work in it at the same time. Historically, women's choices have always been much narrower than men's. Many women feel that the work I do is simply another example of how patriarchy distorts relations between the sexes.'

"Alarm bells were going off by this time, so I tried to change the subject. I complimented him on his lovely home and asked him what he did for a living.

"'I deal in property – buying, selling and managing. I'm also involved in politics. Not party politics – I lost faith in the Tory Party a long time ago – but helping to build a movement for real change. Most people in this country have lost faith in our democracy and the ability of the main parties to improve their lives – they feel they're not being listened to. The movement I'm building will speak their language – which, let's face it, needs to be kept pretty simple for the average man and woman.'

"'What's this movement about?'

"We'd finished the main course and I could see he was keen to get to the dessert – me. But he couldn't resist puffing himself up once more. 'Let me put it like this. If the campaign is successful, all of you feminists, lefties, liberal do-gooders and hangers-on will get the shock of your cosseted lives. Now, we must go through to the bedroom.'

"Usually, at this moment on a date I'm pretty calm, moving into performance mode and thinking of the money that's going into my account. Not this time. I really didn't like this guy; something about him repulsed me and the thought of having sex with him made me feel sick. But that's why I'm paid eight hundred quid for three hours' work, so I got up with a smile on my face.

"Two things happened as we went into the bedroom. I had to hand my phone over, and his driver appeared from a door to the left and came in behind me. At that point I realised my instincts had been right. I was in the kind of situation that escorts hope never happens. I told Granby that our agreement didn't include a threesome and I was entitled under the terms of our arrangement to leave now. But in situations like this, sex workers have very few cards to play.

"'We both know that your only safe course of action now is to accept what's coming and pretend to enjoy it, so please drop the bravado. Don't be surprised if I use certain aids on occasion. First, we're going to watch a movie, so undress down to your bra and knickers and sit down there.'

"As I undressed, a screen came down from the ceiling and a video projector began to play a porn movie. I've obviously seen porn before, it's a feature in around fifty per cent of my dates, but this was extreme; revolting. There were women, men, children and even a dog involved; the women and children were subjected to every kind of degradation and sex act, including violence. I was terrified, which was obviously the point. That, and helping to get them aroused, although his driver didn't need any assistance in that direction. He gestured towards the bed. 'On the bed, love. Just do what we tell you and you won't get hurt.'

"Something about him puzzled me. His eyes were telling me that his heart wasn't in this, so as I went over to the bed, I looked at him and said, 'What kind of bloke enjoys having sex with a woman when she's scared out of her wits? A rapist. Is that what you are, a rapist?'

"He grabbed my upper arms, bent me over and began to fuck me. I'm not going to say what happened in the next couple of hours, Julie, because I forced my mind to disconnect from what was happening to my body. But when I went to A&E later that evening I was treated for injuries to my vagina, anus and throat, had faecal matter removed from my mouth, and was given a prescription for strong antibiotics."

Marion began weeping uncontrollably, so much so that her whole body was shaking. A couple on another table looked over to check she was OK, and Julie instinctively got up, hugged her and remained holding her.

"Thank you, that's lovely. Believe it or not, that's the first time I've told anyone other than my shrink what happened. The A&E doctor wanted to inform the police, but I persuaded him that I'd be in more danger if he did."

"Have you healed up, physically?"

"Pretty much. I sometimes pass blood when I have a crap. Sorry, too much information."

"Don't be silly, I asked. What happened afterwards? Did they threaten you not to go to the police?"

"The driver got dressed, turned to me and said, 'Don't suppose you'll be sitting down for a while', then left the room.

"Geoffrey cleaned himself up – the bed was soiled – put on a ridiculous smoking jacket and said, 'Don't think of going to the police. I've made sure that Ben and I have alibis from some very important people, a number of whom are connected to law enforcement. And if you do put me to the inconvenience of using them, I can easily find out where you live. You noticed that we both wore gloves and condoms throughout, so there won't be any DNA. All of the bed linen and implements will be destroyed and the whole room professionally cleaned. The film is on a DVD, not the web. I will wait outside while you get dressed, then return your phone and escort you out.'

"I wanted to get out of there as quickly as possible, but I was sore and bruised and had to dress very gingerly. Sitting on the bed, I noticed a piece of folded paper under the chair where Ben had thrown his trousers. Maybe it had fallen out of his pocket when he'd removed the condoms. I quickly stuffed it in my bag without thinking. As I walked out I realised how stupid that was – they'd almost certainly been watching on CCTV. But no – Geoffrey gave me my phone and showed me out without saying a word."

"What was on the paper?" Julie tried to keep her tone as casual as possible.

"It looked like a list of contact numbers and email addresses from around the country. Probably something to do with that movement Granby was talking about."

"What did you do with it?"

"I almost threw it away – I didn't want any reminders of that experience. Then I thought that it could be useful in the future – you never know, do you? – so I kept it."

Julie felt her heart rate increasing. The list, if it was what Marion thought it was, could provide them with a goldmine of information about Backlash.

As she was thinking of a way to get invited back to her flat, Marion said, "I don't suppose you remember, but my flat's not far from here. I wondered if you have time to come back for tea and cake? Talking to you has done me good; I'd like to carry on."

Julie hesitated, giving the impression of working out how to rearrange the non-existent arrangements she'd supposedly made for that afternoon and evening. "I'd love to. I'll just need to ring a friend and change our meeting to tomorrow lunchtime. I'm sure that'll be OK with her."

Marion wasn't exaggerating when she'd said that her flat was nearby. It was in the Brunswick Centre near Russell Square; a famous modernist block of flats built in the 1960s. Julie had been there before when she and Marion were dating; she admired the architecture from that period, though parts of the Brunswick were now looking shabby.

"Come in. Nothing's changed since you were last here, except I've repainted the lounge and kitchen."

"I've always admired this building, but I know some people loathe the style."

"You'll find a number of the residents loathe it too. Too hot in the summer, freezing in the winter. Remind me – how do you like your tea?"

"White, no sugar, please."

12

BREAKING AND ENTERING

Julie made the 9pm train to Manchester with three minutes to spare; luckily Euston Station was only a ten-minute walk from Marion's flat. She'd booked an open return, but treated herself to a first-class upgrade for fifteen quid when she saw the state of the rest of the train. *A window seat on my own, free wine and a Virgin snack – la dolce vita.* She smiled as she felt the piece of paper in her jacket pocket and reflected on the past four hours.

Marion's invitation to go to bed as soon as she'd served the tea had caught Julie by surprise. She'd stammered something about it not being a good idea, and couldn't they just carry on talking? Marion had apologised for making a pass and said she'd love to talk. They'd talked increasingly openly about what had been happening in their lives since they'd split up, and at an opportune moment, Julie had asked Marion if she could see the list of contacts.

"Sure, I'll get it."

Marion went to her desk, came back with a scruffy piece of folded A5, sat on the sofa next to Julie and gave it to her. It was a Word document listing areas of the country, names, email addresses and phone numbers. Julie realised that she was probably showing more interest than would be normal, which Marion noticed immediately.

"Why are you so interested in this?"

Julie had seen so many bad attempts at lying in her work that she knew that she wouldn't be able to lie convincingly. She didn't have to tell the whole truth, though, so she explained that she currently had a client who was being harassed by her ex-husband. The client was convinced that her ex had got in with an extremist men's group who were coordinating the attacks. "He's not smart enough to do it himself." Julie added that her case was one of a number of similar cases which she was researching to see if they were linked.

And then the inevitable happened.

"And you're wondering whether Geoffrey Granby's movement could be connected to the cases you're looking at?"

"It crossed my mind, yes."

"Would you like a copy of the list?"

"That would be very useful, thank you."

"How badly do you want one?"

Before Julie could answer, Marion leant towards her and kissed her softly on the lips. She pulled back slightly; then they kissed again, but harder this time.

"That was nice. It's a long time since I've been kissed like that by anyone. I need to make love with a woman again, Julie. Don't make me plead with you."

"Aren't you still too tender?"

"There's just one way to find out."

The guard came down the carriage checking tickets, interrupting Julie's thoughts. She didn't feel guilty, just upset. Upset because she knew that it would cause Emily pain if she told her, and the thought of that brought a lump to her throat. But she had to put this evening's events behind her for now. Downing the rest of her glass of barely passable Sauvignon, she focused on her meeting with Deepak near Stroud's house tomorrow at 10am. She'd agreed to keep watch while he carried out the break-in. *We're fucking crazy*, she thought, and smiled to herself.

Deepak had scrounged a white van from a friend, which he'd told Julie would be parked two roads away from Stroud's house. They were meeting there to finalise arrangements for the break-in. She hardly recognised him as she opened the door, disguised as a bespectacled, hirsute meter reader.

"Good morning, Deepak. Has anything come out of the interviews with the two arsonists yet?"

"Yes and no. They're not denying that they set out to attack Emily's house, nor that they were the men who attacked her previously. They could hardly do otherwise. However, they're sticking to their story that this was their own idea and there's no one else involved. We won't get anything more from them – they're too frightened of what will happen if they grass."

"That's a pity. Now, are you really sure about this?"

"Completely, so no more discussion, please. Let's just go over everything one more time. The rule for this kind of operation is to be as visible as possible and hide in plain sight. I'll ring the bell once, just to confirm that he's at work, stand obviously at the front door while I use the skeleton keys, make a show of saying hello when I open it, then walk in. I'll give myself fifteen minutes – should anyone notice me and report it, any longer risks the police arriving. If you see Stroud coming, phone me, let it ring three times, then end the call. What's your idea for delaying him, should you need to?"

"I'll keep it simple. I'll ask him if he knows my friend Susan Beech who lives in the road. I've forgotten her number, etc, etc, and she's not answering her phone. And I've bought myself a wig and glasses. How do I look?"

"Blonde suits you, you should try it on Emily. I'll drive the van round, it's time."

"I'll walk from here. Good luck, Deepak."

He slowed as he approached Stroud's house, checking and checking again, then parked the van two hundred metres down the road, hung the meter reader's equipment round his neck, put a miniature camera in his pocket and walked towards Stroud's terraced house. Everything looked as it had on the last two occasions he'd surveyed the place. He pushed open the gate, walked up the unkempt path and pressed the bell. Seconds later he saw movement behind the glass door pane; the door was opened by a middle-aged woman with her coat on and a bag in her hand.

"Hello, luv, you come to read the meter? I'm just leaving; do you have some ID?"

Deepak showed her his forged ID card (he owed so many favours, he'd be paying them back until retirement) and said, "I don't think that's wise; I won't be able to lock up afterwards."

"Don't worry, I don't lock up when I leave on Tuesdays; it's Colin's half-day and he'll be back soon. Just slam the door behind you. Bye, luv."

The cleaner left, pulling the door to. Deepak texted Emily:

Just went in, met cleaner leaving and she said he'll be back soon, so you may be needed.

He quickly went round the house to identify the likely locations – he now knew that he didn't have long – and decided to focus on the study, bedroom and kitchen. The house was an unattractive, dispiriting and charmless place, lacking colour, art or ornament of any kind. Utilitarian in the extreme – Stroud had made no effort to make his home a place to enjoy living in.

Deepak took out his camera, put on his surgical gloves and went upstairs to the study. He channelled the nervous energy running through his body into uncovering any document, note, list or pamphlet that might contain information or clues about the clandestine group behind Backlash. He took pictures of the noticeboard hanging to one side of the desk, documents in the in-tray and recent pages of a desk diary, taking care to put everything back exactly as he'd found it. He easily picked the simple lock on the filing cabinet, which initially appeared to contain only teaching-related documents. But why bother to lock up such innocuous stuff? He quickly flicked through each hanging file, returned it and moved on. The last file in the bottom drawer contained the mother lode: minutes of the last two meetings of Backlash's Manchester group, lists of names and email addresses, and scribbled notes that Stroud had apparently taken down from phone calls.

He looked at his watch and was shocked to see that he'd already been in the house for eight minutes. As he moved through to the bedroom, the gloomy feel continued; it was far from a romantic setting. The chest of drawers contained nothing but pullovers, casual shirts, underwear and socks in bland, neutral colours. There was one bedside table, and this time the drawer was unlocked. Inside was a diary, with entries dated as recently as yesterday. He went back two months, photographed every page with entries, and stepped out of the bedroom just as he heard the front door being opened.

His heart stopped, then began to race madly. *Why the fuck hasn't Julie rung?* He heard hurried footsteps in the hall and chanced a look over the landing banister in time to see the cleaner going into the kitchen. He stepped back into the bedroom doorway and heard keys being scooped up, more steps and the front door closing. He looked at his watch; it was now fifteen minutes since he'd entered the house.

The kitchen clearly had a distant relationship with cordon bleu, judging by the lack of cookery books and the pizza boxes piled in the waste bin. Based on Deepak's years as a junior DC searching properties, kitchens seemed to be the room of choice for hiding stuff that people really wanted to stay hidden. After drawing a blank inside the relatively small number of pasta, sugar, tea and coffee jars, he pulled out the three drawers under the kitchen table. Taped underneath the final drawer was a plastic pocket with two pages of A4 inside. He carefully slid the pages out, photographed the four sides of paper and put them back. Twenty-five minutes; he had to go.

He looked around one last time, remembered to open the meter cupboard door slightly, and walked to the front door just as his phone rang. Once, twice, three times. Stroud could be at the end of the road or standing outside. *Hide in plain sight. Step outside, close the door normally, walk down the path unhurriedly, look straight ahead.* To his left, out of the corner of his eye, Deepak saw Julie talking to an obviously impatient Stroud about ten houses down. Neither was looking in his direction, although he sensed Stroud starting to turn his head as Deepak pulled the gate shut and walked towards the van, in the opposite direction to the odd couple.

"Lily! We're talking to you. How are we getting to Pizza Express next Thursday?"

Lily smiled at the group of friends sitting around the two desks they'd pulled together. It was the final session with her tutor group on the last day of the Easter term, and Ms Ross was indulging them as usual. The best bit was always when Mr Marshall, the head teacher, put his head round the door to check that every group was engaged in productive work, and Ms Ross just gave him a big smile and said, "Tell Mr Marshall what we've been discussing, everyone."

"Everyone meet at my house at 6.30, then we'll go in a minibus. I'll text you all a reminder."

Lily had been shocked at first when Tamsin's mum had turned into the close and she'd seen the black marks on the front door and a huge crack across the lounge window. But her mum had sat down with her straight away and explained that two horrible men had been immediately arrested and would now be in prison for a long time. They didn't want to harm Lily or her mum; it was a stupid prank that had gone too far. She'd chosen to believe her. That was a conversation she'd had with her counsellor: if you know someone loves you, then trust them until they let you down.

She'd suggested to Mum that they invite Julie to the party, as she was now living at their house every weekend and for a day or two in the middle of the week. Most pupils in Year 8 knew that Lily's mum was going out with a woman and either thought it was cool or not worthy of comment. A couple of boys had called out, "Your mum's a lezzy," in the playground, but Ms Ross had spoken to their parents and they'd stopped it.

There had been times during the autumn term when Lily had felt so unhappy, so low, that she'd even thought about cutting herself to mask the pain of disliking herself, like some other girls she knew did. She'd really believed that she must have been partly to blame for her dad trying to kill her mum. Mum was also unhappy because of the revolting men shouting at and messaging her, and she and Lily had argued about Lily wanting to see her dad. Then Lily had worried that she'd lose some of her friends at school, but Tamsin made it clear that she wasn't going anywhere and made sure the others all stayed on Lily's side, and her counsellor had helped her to understand that she wasn't to blame for what had happened between her mum and dad. The breakthrough had come when Mum agreed that she could see her dad.

Her mum was also in a much better place since she'd started seeing Julie. In fact, Lily couldn't remember the last time she'd seen her so at ease and comfortable with herself. She was obviously still getting abuse – and worse – but Lily had worked out that Julie, Deepak and her mum were plotting ways to stop it.

She'd decided to write to her dad and tell him that she wasn't going to visit him again for a long time. The second visit had confirmed what the first one had suggested – that he was so full of anger towards her mum that they'd never have a friendly, loving encounter until he got over that. Lily had begun to suspect that he was sending messages to encourage the men attacking her mum. She couldn't forgive him for that, or for being horrible to Julie. If Julie hadn't agreed to come with her, her dad wouldn't have seen her at all!

She'd write to him tomorrow.

13

A PICTURE EMERGES

Deepak downloaded the pictures from Stroud's house and sent them to Julie and Emily, with the suggestion that they start analysing the data, as his off-the-books visit as a meter reader meant he had no time over the following days. He then wiped them from his laptop – he couldn't take a chance that they'd be viewed accidentally.

After her lookout duties Julie had worked solidly from midday until late afternoon the following day, preparing papers for a contested divorce. She'd arranged to go over to Emily's that evening and start pulling together everything they had on Granby and Backlash, particularly Deepak's pictures and data. They'd spoken quickly on the phone and Julie had given Emily only the briefest feedback about her meeting with Marion, pleading pressure of work.

"You and Deepak have been amazing, Julie. I'm longing to hear how everything went, but in the meantime I'll make a start on Deepak's stuff. I can't wait to see you."

Julie had keys to Emily's house, but she still rang the bell. She'd been dreading this moment since the train journey from London.

Emily would want to know if anything had happened between her and Marion, and would probably work out the answer from the guilty look on Julie's face the moment she saw her. *I'll have to tell her at the earliest opportunity,* she thought; *it will be at the front of my mind all evening otherwise.*

Emily came out of the kitchen as Julie walked into the hall and gave her a massive hug and a kiss. They stood embracing until Emily finally said, "I can't tell you how relieved I was to hear from Deepak that you two had got away with the break-in at Stroud's place. I've had a look at the images, and I think we're really getting somewhere. If I'm right, police and prison officers are embedded in this group of men's rights activists. First things first, though – the wine is poured, so come and sit down and tell me about your meeting with Marion."

They went through to the lounge and sat together on the sofa. Julie took a long swig of her wine. *This will either make us or break us,* she thought, then turned to Emily and said, "There's no easy way to say this, and anyway, you mean far too much to me for me to sugar-coat it. I had sex with Marion, in her flat, after we'd had lunch. I'm so sorry, Emily, I know how much this will hurt you, but please hear me out."

She paused and looked at Emily, whose face gave away surprisingly little, other than her increasingly watery eyes.

"She'd told me over the meal what had happened with Granby and his driver/bodyguard that evening when we saw a picture of them going into his house. It was horrendous; he's clearly a misogynistic psychopath who enjoys humiliating women. She's completely broken by the experience. But she also told me that she found a list of names and addresses before she left the house. When she invited me back to her flat for tea, I was hoping to persuade her to give me a copy. She showed it to me, but made it clear that I could only have a copy if we went to bed. I thought it could unlock so much about this organisation that we've been struggling to uncover, so I did. I'm so sorry; I hope I never have to make a decision like that again."

Emily had tried to prepare herself for this news. *But you can't, really, can you?* she realised, as the implications of Julie's words sunk in. *How could she do this so casually?* She felt sick at the thought of the two of them together, and needed to ask a question before she heard any more. "I feel sick, Julie. Whatever you thought, however you justify your decision, I can tell you it was the wrong one as far as our relationship is concerned. Before you say any more, I want to know if you're intending to end it between us."

Julie felt relieved. The worst part was over, and now she could begin to reassure Emily with the little speech she'd prepared. The necessarily edited little speech. "God, no! It was totally transactional, and meant nothing. I did feel sorry for her, so there was an element of pity mixed in somewhere, but no loving feelings. I love *you*, and saying yes to her was an awful choice to make. I knew it would hurt you, but I thought we were strong enough; I wouldn't have done it otherwise. If this breaks us up, I don't know what I'll do. You're the best thing that's happened to me since Claire."

Emily looked her in the eyes. "So, what happened?"

Julie described a soulless and sad sexual experience with Marion, feeling exposed, a sense of shame.

Emily asked a few questions – "Was it like the last time? Did you stay around talking afterwards?" – but quickly decided that she didn't want to hear any more. "I know I asked you, but I've heard enough now. I appreciate you telling me – you didn't have to, and that means a lot. We're strong enough to survive this, I know that, but it's going to take time to get my head around it. My wanton lover, come here. And don't ever do this again."

Julie promised herself that she'd give Tinder a miss for a few weeks.

Emily had her worst night's sleep in weeks, but they hadn't looked at any documents last night so she forced herself out of bed, into the shower and downstairs.

"Good morning, Emily, I was going to bring you a cup of tea if you hadn't shown up in the next five minutes. Are you up to making a start on Marion's list and the documents from Stroud's place?"

"I will be after a big cup of coffee." Emily had downloaded and printed all the documents Deepak had sent her and spread them out over the kitchen table; she'd even sorted the documents from Stroud's house by location – study, kitchen, bedroom. "I only had time yesterday to give them a cursory look, but it was enough to realise that we've got some really valuable material here. Some of the data is obvious – lists of names and email addresses, etc. – while other pages contain entry codes and passwords. With some expert assistance, these could unlock Granby's leading role in this conspiracy, and reveal the possible involvement of other members of the establishment."

"Let's do what we can for now, then pass our findings on to Deepak."

They set to work in an atmosphere that was unusually reserved.

"What are you guys doing?" Lily came down for breakfast around 11.30 (it was the Easter holiday) to see them poring over sheets of paper and notebooks scattered across the table. "How can I get my breakfast together? This isn't the place to do stuff like this; it's not fair."

Emily and Julie glanced at each other. Quickly, Emily said, "Sorry, Lily, this is a one-off, I promise. Do you mind having your breakfast in the lounge, just for today? Julie and I are trying to solve a mystery, and the answers could be somewhere here."

"OK, if it's important. Could I speak to you for a moment, Mum?"

Emily followed Lily out into the hall and closed the door.

"I've decided that I don't want to see Dad again for a while, so it's only fair to write and tell him. Would you have a look at the letter, please, and let me know what you think? I want to be as sensitive as possible."

"Of course I will, as long as you've thought about this and made your mind up."

"Thanks, Mum. Is everything OK between you and Julie?"

"Yes, sweetheart, we're fine, why?"

"Just that there seems to be a bit of an atmosphere this morning."

Back in her room after breakfast, Lily checked over her letter again, made a couple of changes and gave it to her mum.

Ben Trafford felt well out of his comfort zone. Granby had invited him to his London club in St James, "just for a chat", and he knew that it wasn't going to be good news. Ben had visited a few servicemen's clubs, but as an NCO he only got into the rougher ones. He assumed Sir Geoffrey's would bear no relation to those, and he was right. As he walked up the carpeted steps outside and through the brass-framed glass doors, the sight reminded him of the interiors he'd seen depicted in numerous British films from a certain era. Dark wood panelling, carpet thick enough to swim in, obsequious staff in ridiculously braided uniforms. He noted the discreet 'Gentlemen Only' sign, just as one of the flunkeys approached him.

"I'm here to meet Sir Geoffrey Granby."

"Of course, sir – please wait here while I inform Sir Geoffrey that you're here."

Ben had been Granby's driver, bodyguard, gofer and procurer of sex workers for over a year. He was well aware that he had a nice little number; the job even included the occasional bonus, such as spending an evening with a high-class 'escort'. That last session had gone too far, though; she'd really taken a beating. He'd had no choice, without arousing suspicion. Granby had made clear from their first meeting that he used prostitutes and that Ben would be expected to join him. "Most women aren't worth having anything to do with, Ben. They have their uses as vessels for satisfying men's needs, but little more. Men are the only companions a man can trust. Never trust a woman, Ben."

He was shown to a discreet corner of the dining room, where Sir Geoffrey was already seated at a table laid for two people. He was talking with a waiter, who left as Ben was shown to his seat.

"Good morning, Ben. I'm glad you could come. Please sit down."

"Nice place you've got here, sir." Ben wasn't expecting – and didn't get – any acknowledgement of his little joke. Sir Geoffrey didn't do irony.

"I wanted your view about a situation that's developed at Mason's prison. The deputy governor is being pressured by Fowler to uncover how Mason has been communicating with us. Our man in the prison believes they're getting close to gathering enough circumstantial evidence to suspend him, and the union is advising him to take an early retirement deal if he can get one. What do you think?"

"Any idea why they suspect him?"

"He's got careless, both in the prison and in a pub he frequents with two other officers. The officer in charge of his wing saw him talking to Mason once too often, and a busybody with nothing better to do overheard them in the pub and reported what he'd heard to the authorities."

"Fucking idiots. It's no wonder Britain's never had a coup; we're just too fucking nosy. Is there any chance that the uncovering of our prison service members could spread to other cells? I'm asking because Fowler seems to be on a mission to expose our project, and I wouldn't put it past her and her friends to check if we're recruiting in prisons around the country."

"I see. Coming back to my question, what would you advise us to do?"

"Tell our bloke in Mason's prison to take the retirement offer and lie low. No more meeting up with the other two, except in private.

Inform the Manchester branch to suspend all meetings until further notice. Instruct the regional leaders to stand down all serving prison and police officer comrades, again until further notice."

"That sounds like panic, Ben. Not like you."

"Taking action before things get to a stage where our work is under threat isn't panicking, sir, it's smart. It wouldn't involve a huge amount of work."

"I take your point. Will you contact the appropriate people and ensure that it's done? Through the secure channels, of course."

"What about Fowler, sir? I've got a feeling she's not going to drop her campaign any time soon."

"I believe you're right about the risk she poses. Please give that some thought and come back to me with some options by Wednesday. On another matter of interest to both of us, I think it's time for a repeat of our little threesome. I so enjoyed the last one. We gave that whore a seeing-to she'll remember for a long time."

"We did. The look on her face when she realised her circumstances was a picture."

"Shall we eat?"

But as Granby went through the menu, the question that had been nagging at Ben since their 'threesome' came back to him. What had happened to his copy of the list with the names and email addresses of the board? The thought that the information could be out there somewhere unsettled him. He couldn't risk asking anyone to change their passwords and codes, as he'd have to explain why, and then Granby would find out how incompetent he'd been – or worse.

"You two have done an amazing job, assembling all this information from different sources and highlighting the connections between them; I think we may have enough on your five slides to unlock the structure of Backlash and its reach into the establishment and the prison and police services."

They were in Julie's front room, as she was the only one with a projector. This was pointing at the only blank wall in the room, and hooked up to Emily's laptop.

Emily clicked the mouse and brought up the first slide. "Thanks, Deepak – we got really excited about what we were seeing. We'll look at them in turn, agree the key findings and decide what we're going to do next."

The first slide showed the piece of paper Marion had picked up at Granby's house. The words 'Inner Circle' were typed across the top, above a list of twenty-two sets of initials; next to each were details of occupation and/or rank, emergency contact numbers and code names. The next slide, 'Northern Contacts', set out the information Emily had got from conversations with the four women who'd been targeted following a case like hers, including the names of suspects. Slides three and four summarised the information from Stroud's house; the pages concealed under his kitchen table contained names of the central committee in each of the nine English regions. Next to each name was an email address, a contact number, a password and an abbreviation denoting occupation, e.g. 'PO' for police, 'PrO' for prison officer or 'A' for army. Stroud's diary listed dates and addresses of meetings with 'GG' and the Manchester branch, and the attack on Emily's house. There were also dates and locations for possible future actions. The last slide showed the connections between the information from the previous four. For example, some of the abusers named by Emily's contacts on slide two corresponded to regional organisers from slide three.

After two hours of intense discussion, they agreed on the way forward. Emily summed up. "So we agree that the priority is to uncover the names of everyone in the inner circle, using the knowledge that four of them are regional organisers. This means logging into their accounts, then hacking them to get the inner circle's names. After that, we check the dates of past meetings and actions in Stroud's diary with what we know actually happened, then communicate the dates and locations of proposed future actions and attacks to all relevant agencies. Then further scrutinise the Cromer Street CCTV on the date of the last board meeting, if it hasn't been wiped, and match the images to the names of the inner circle. Finally, uncover the identities of every member who's a police or prison officer by hacking the regional committee accounts to get their membership lists. Agreed?"

Deepak nodded decisively. "Spot on. I'll approach my IT colleague again about hacking the inner circle and regional organiser sites. If I tell her that there are important establishment figures involved in this organisation, she'll get enthused and put more effort into it. Now, what does a bloke have to do to get a beer around here?"

Robert held the unopened letter from his daughter in his hand. It was the first one he'd received since her visit weeks ago, when she'd angrily walked out. He was dreading the message inside.

Dear Dad,

I hope that life in prison isn't too bad. That's easy for me to say, I know. I was very upset for days after my last visit. I don't understand why you have to get so angry; we only have an hour and it's such a shame to waste any of that time being horrible to Julie or Mum. Someone has to come with me, and it can't be Mum – you'd go crazy if she was with me. Julie is practically living with us these days and I like her a lot, so it made sense for her to come.

I will visit you again, Dad, but not for a long time. I need to believe that you're capable of behaving like the dad I used to know, and I don't believe that at the moment.

I think of you every day.

Love,

Lily xx

Robert's head throbbed as he fought to control the rage. He knew there would be serious consequences if he lost it again – his card was already marked after his two eruptions in the visitors' room. Taking several slow, deep breaths, he gradually regained some control. Lily's decision to stop visiting him wasn't the issue; he'd prepared himself for that, and she wasn't ruling it out forever. No, it was the words that his daughter had seemingly innocently dropped into her letter – 'Julie is practically living with us these days' – that had sent him heading for the edge. *The final humiliation. My role as Emily's husband and lover taken by a woman.*

14

CROSSING A LINE

Following the attack on her house, Deepak had arranged for Emily to meet with a specialist police officer to go through additional security measures that she'd now need to adopt and build into her routines.

"How long will I need to keep these up, Sergeant?"

"For as long as you don't want any harm to befall you or your daughter, Ms Fowler."

"Please call me Emily. You have my full attention."

Emily memorised every routine and precaution that Detective Sergeant Louise Crisp took her through, including checking all the windows and outside doors before entering the house, looking at the CCTV immediately, and varying her route to and from the train station. She was intrigued by one measure in particular, which was to check her rear-view mirror to see if she was being followed by another vehicle. It had a touch of James Bond about it.

Louise immediately dispelled such thoughts. "It's not like the movies. Just remember to glance behind every two hundred metres or so and remember the colour and last two letters of the reg number of any car following you. If you recognise the make, even better. Under no circumstances try to get away from them."

"Cool, as my daughter would say."

"I'd say it's pretty cool, too," said Louise, smiling.

Two weeks after her briefing with Sergeant Crisp, and three days after her meeting with Julie and Deepak, Emily was feeling almost disappointed not to have been followed by any suspicious vehicles. Then it happened. Driving back from Macclesfield Station after work, she clocked a metallic blue Mondeo that had fallen in behind her as she'd driven out of the car park. When the same car was still there after a kilometre, she thought it was highly likely to be suspicious, and when it followed her as she overtook another car she was certain.

She rang the number she'd memorised, then decided to take a longer route home to make time for the hard stop to be put in place. Mondeo Man – she could see it was a man but couldn't make out any more, as he wore glasses and a baseball cap – stayed about five car-lengths behind. What would happen if she tried to lose him, she wondered? Just for the thrill, she dropped two gears and floored it as she made a sharp left and opened up a gap of over one hundred metres before he could respond. Keeping her speed through the next two corners, she saw him almost lose control round the last bend in his desperate attempt to shorten the gap.

She was now certain this was offensive action, and felt a twinge of anxiety. What if the plan failed? But as she snaked into Bollington around a tight bend, a police BMW X5 and two officers were taking up her side of the road and a bit more. As she pulled in behind the BMW, she just caught the look of indecision on Mondeo Man's face in her mirror before he swung round her Golf, ignored a police officer's raised hand and carried on. Fifty metres further on, the Mondeo went over a stinger laid across the road, burst two tyres and swerved into a drystone wall.

The two officers in charge of the stinger, one holding a taser, ran to the driver's door, shouting at him to "Get out of the car slowly", which he did. By now, Emily was out of the Golf and had taken his picture. He was about six foot tall and solidly built, with an angular face, hair in a brush cut. *Surprisingly plump lips*, she thought. He didn't look happy, and as their eyes met she sensed his malevolence. The two officers from the BMW walked up to him, joining their colleagues. As the five of them stood around the car, Mondeo Man began shouting at the police officers.

"What the fuck did you stop me for? You'll pay for that damage."

"I'd calm down if I were you, unless you want to be arrested for threatening behaviour. You ignored an instruction from my colleague to stop, almost hitting him. Could you tell me why you've been following this lady's car for the past four miles from Macclesfield Station, sir?"

"That's ridiculous. I haven't been to Macclesfield. I came up behind her a mile or so back, and couldn't get past. I've been waiting for an opportunity to overtake."

"Is that true, madam?"

"I'm afraid he's lying, Officer. The rear-facing camera in my car will show exactly how long this man has been following me, and from where. He could have overtaken me on a number of occasions."

At the words 'rear-facing camera', Mondeo Man's features crumpled in anger and despair. He vainly attempted to recover. "OK, so I was behind her from Macclesfield. That's not a crime, is it?"

"Perhaps not, but failing to stop when instructed and reckless driving are. Is this your car, sir?"

Mondeo Man's expression changed from pissed off to *I'm fucked*. The car wasn't his; a fact being confirmed at that very moment by the officer who'd been checking the number plate.

"I presume you're not Sir Geoffrey Granby, sir?" he said with a smirk. "What's your name, please, and can I see your driving licence?"

"Ben Trafford. I work for Sir Geoffrey."

Opportunities like this don't come round very often. Emily walked up to Trafford and looked him in the eye. "If this is the best your hate-filled little outfit can do, then maybe you should reconsider your career plan. You lot are utterly pathetic."

Trafford moved towards Emily, who stood her ground. The officer with the taser shifted slightly, and Trafford stepped back. "You'll regret this."

"Right. Ben Trafford, I'm charging you with failing to stop when instructed, threatening behaviour and dangerous driving. You will receive a summons to appear in court within fourteen days."

Emily took note of his name and thanked the police officers, one of whom she'd realised was Louise Crisp. As she drove home, she recalled Louise's advice from two weeks ago, which had worked like a dream.

"What do I do if I'm being followed, Louise?"

"As long as you're ninety per cent sure, ring this number. There's a tracker on your car that works throughout the Greater Manchester and East Cheshire areas; plus we've fitted front- and rear-facing dashcams. You'll be asked for a description of the vehicle following you. Try to give us fifteen minutes, then we'll intercept you and set up a police stop. Would you like my number, in case you think of further questions?"

"I think I've got the station number."

"I meant my mobile number, just in case the station can't reach me. Don't forget to make an appointment to give your statement about this incident to the police."

15

PRESENTING THE EVIDENCE

"Hi, Deepak, I hope this isn't a bad time? Something dramatic happened on my drive home this evening, which may affect the timescale we agreed on a few days ago for revealing our information about Backlash to the authorities. I've already told Julie; she's listening on speakerphone."

"I'm all ears."

Towards the end of a slightly embellished account of her car chase, Emily said, "The best bit was when the cops checked the registration and discovered that the car was registered to Geoffrey Granby! The driver gave his name as Ben Trafford, and I'm positive that he's the bloke we saw going into Cromer Street with Granby and Marion."

"Fantastic! What did the police do?"

"They arrested him for failing to stop when instructed, threatening behaviour and dangerous driving – though I've no doubt that Granby will dispatch his lawyers as soon as possible to get any charges reduced. The thing is, we now have a window of opportunity. We're holding information that could potentially turbocharge what would otherwise just be an embarrassing inconvenience for Granby."

"Go on."

"I've been worried about how we can approach the police with our evidence regarding Backlash, given its dodgy provenance. We could be perceived as delusional conspiracy theorists. But this attempted assault gives us a great opportunity to build on. We now have a choice. I could give my statement, keeping largely to the facts surrounding yesterday's incident. In other words, as a result of several threatening and violent incidents, the police put a number of measures in place to protect me, one of which was triggered yesterday when I realised I was being followed. The man arrested for stalking me was driving a car registered to Sir Geoffrey Granby, his boss. Backlash, the men's rights website that's encouraged threats against me, uses the London address that I understand to be Granby's office. CCTV shows the man arrested walking into Cromer Street with Granby."

"That's all provable, and pretty damning," interjected Deepak.

"It is, but it doesn't conclusively tie Granby to Backlash. He will no doubt convince Ben Trafford to claim to be a lone wolf, and that Granby knew nothing of his escapade. It'll be an offer he can't refuse – Trafford could say that he was driven by some terrible wrong committed against him in the past by a cheating woman, and he only meant to scare me, etc., etc. Outcome: brief spell in prison for Trafford – maybe just a suspended sentence; Granby suspends all Backlash activities for six months, and then it all starts again."

"Go on."

"I could delay the interview until we've got the names of the inner circle, details of Backlash members who are serving police and prison officers, plus the four similar cases to mine that I've uncovered. That information will be too difficult to ignore even if they want to. But until we've hacked Backlash's site, we don't have that evidence. How far have we got with that?"

"There's good news. Since I told my source exactly what Backlash is really about – aiming to roll back women's rights, involving senior members of the establishment – she's devoting as much time as possible to it. She's confident."

Julie cut in. "So where does this leave your interview tomorrow, Emily? Do you think you should try and push it back a couple of days?"

"Definitely; that's got to be worth doing. I'll get in touch, make up an excuse and try and put it off for two days at least. I'll get back to you when I know their answer."

Elated, Julie said, "Just think, in a few days we could be about to finally expose these misogynistic bastards and bring them down."

Later that evening, on a high thinking about what was in their grasp, Emily remembered something she'd intended to tell Julie. "I meant to tell you; the police sergeant who gave me the personal security briefing asked me if I'd like their mobile number."

"Highly unprofessional, of course. But I'm not too surprised; you're an attractive woman. He obviously fancied you."

"*Her* name was Louise Crisp. I've never been asked by a woman if I'd like her number before. Maybe I'm sending out different signals since I've come over to the other side?"

"Interesting question. Don't think about checking it out."

They had to wait four days for Deepak's source to come back, but the data she handed over – names of the inner circle, including a number of well-known establishment names, names and details of the area leaders responsible for coordinating the infiltration of the prison service, and details of future operations – had dramatic consequences. When she made the appointment to attend the police interview, Emily disclosed that she would be bringing additional incriminating information about Backlash, the organisation to which Trafford belonged. At which point she was asked to "Hold for a minute", which became almost ten. Then a different voice came on the line, insisting that the meeting would be brought forward to the following morning at 9am, and would Emily email through all the relevant documents immediately?

She texted Deepak and Julie at once:

I think we've stirred up a Backlash hornets' nest! I've been instructed to email all documents in my possession related to that organisation and attend an interview tomorrow morning at police headquarters. I'll let you know what happens.

Deepak rang her within minutes: "Hi Emily, I'm not putting this in a text for obvious reasons. It looks like the breakthrough we've been hoping for, but please make sure there's nothing on the documents you send that can identify the sources, especially the ones I got from Stroud's house. Awkward if they're traced back to me, obviously! You can say that I was involved in identifying Stroud from the picture of the street protest. Good luck tomorrow."

"Thanks, Deepak. I'll go through them with a fine-tooth comb."

Julie's text followed immediately:

Yes, we're really getting somewhere. Well done, Emily! Please be careful, though – it sounds like they may have some serious characters in that room who'll be very interested in where you got that information. Love, Julie xx

Emily realised that she could be walking into an exhaustive interrogation. She sat down to prepare and rehearse a plausible story before 9am tomorrow.

Walking into the interview room, she saw that Julie had been right. Her little car chase wasn't going to be the main item on the agenda. In addition to two police detectives, there were two men in suits: one in his late thirties, the other a few years older. The hierarchy was clear: eldest suit number one, younger suit number two, male police inspector number three and female sergeant number four, whom Emily recognised immediately as Louise Crisp. Neither gave anything away as they made eye contact.

Suit Number One introduced the others in order of rank, looked at Emily and said, "Can you tell us how you came by this information, Ms Fowler?"

"Can I assume that everyone here is aware of the physical attacks on me and my home, and the online abuse and threats that my thirteen-year-old daughter and I have been experiencing for nearly a year?"

The four officers nodded, although the expressions on the suits' faces betrayed that much of it was news to them.

"After several months of taking this horrible misogynistic abuse and watching my daughter grow increasingly anxious, I decided to find out more. Specifically, whether these attacks were random, or whether there was a coordinated campaign against me personally. A friend mentioned a men's rights website called Backlash, which was posting updates on my case and veiled threats against me. When I went to the site I noticed that the dates of my attacks closely followed those of posts on the site, so Julie Taylor, my solicitor at the time, and I focused our efforts on hacking into the site to identify the people behind it. We also scoured newspapers for reports of cases similar to mine throughout the country, and followed up stories of collusion between my husband and certain officers in his prison. We're amateurs, but we got lucky."

"Can you be more specific about your methods, please, Ms Fowler?"

"The Backlash regional organisers were revealed through phishing scams on the organisation's website. I'm afraid I'm not prepared to name the person who helped us with that. I personally tracked down and talked with several women who'd suffered similar abuse to mine. Backlash's website also contained an address in Cromer Street, London. The Land Registry gives the owner's name as Sir Geoffrey Granby. This individual has links to far-right organisations, particularly those spreading hatred of women. I'd taken pictures of the protesters outside my office and handed them to the police, who ran them through the computer and came up with a name: Colin Stroud. He's a maths teacher in Manchester, and heavily involved in Backlash, judging by his Facebook page. Finally, an envelope was posted to me anonymously at work containing a list of names headed 'Inner Circle'.

"Julie arranged to speak to the assistant governor at Robert's prison when she took my daughter to see her father. He admitted that there was collaboration between Robert and at least one prison officer suspected of being a member of a far-right group. I believe they're trying to get clear evidence before moving to suspend the officer in question."

"So what made you decide to come to us now?"

"As a lawyer I was aware that all of the above 'evidence' wouldn't get very far in a court of law, so there was little point in bringing it to your attention. However, when the police stopped the car tailing me a week ago, I overheard their exchange with the driver. He was called Ben Trafford, and the car he was driving was registered to one Geoffrey Granby, his boss. Voila! A direct link between Granby and the catalogue of abuse directed at me. Finally, it seemed worthwhile to come forward."

"Thank you, Ms Fowler, you've been most helpful. Do you have any idea who could have sent you that list of names?"

"No, but I presume it's either someone in Backlash who's become disaffected with their methods, or a faction within the organisation that wishes to create problems for the leadership and stage a coup."

"Both interesting speculations. I don't think we have any further questions at this point, do we?" said Suit Number One, looking at the other three in turn and clearly not expecting any.

"Excuse me, sir, but I would like to ask Ms Fowler a question."

Emily and Number One both turned to glare at Louise Crisp, for very different reasons.

"Of course, Sergeant… Crisp, go ahead."

What the fuck is she going to ask me? thought Emily.

"You may remember that I was one of the officers taking part in the operation to apprehend the man chasing you. I may be mistaken, but I got the impression that you might have seen him before?"

Emily felt an immediate jump in her heart rate as adrenaline gushed into her bloodstream. She couldn't possibly reveal how she'd recognised Trafford; it would give away their CCTV surveillance outside Cromer Street, which would drop Deepak in it. "Well spotted, Sergeant. As you know, I was seriously assaulted in Macclesfield by two men, one night in February. They were both wearing balaclavas, so I didn't see their faces, but Trafford's build, height and voice all fitted one of the assailants, so I was suddenly taken back to that night. I think it's called 'triggering' these days, isn't it?"

Louise nodded, said, "Thank you, Ms Fowler, I understand", and indicated that she had no more questions.

"Thank you again, Ms Fowler. My colleague and I will leave now and let the two officers take your statement about the incident when you were tailed."

"Will I be informed about any potential developments occurring as a result of the information I've presented today?"

"That's unlikely, I'm afraid. But you may want to keep an eye on the newspapers in the next week or two."

There was a tangible release of tension as the two suits showed themselves out and closed the door; so much so that the three remaining found themselves smiling at each other. By unspoken agreement, the presence of two members of the Security Service wasn't commented on. The inspector took down Emily's statement, while Louise interjected occasionally for clarification. Nothing more was said about Ben Trafford, and the conversation was over in less than thirty minutes.

"I'll show you out, Ms Fowler; it will help you get through security." As they walked towards the security hoops, Louise looked apologetically at Emily and said, "Sorry to put you on the spot in there. It's just that I wondered about it at the time and thoughtlessly took the opportunity to ask you. Apologies."

"Asking questions is part of your job description, so no problem. I assume those two were spooks of some kind; seems we may have rattled someone's cage."

"Do you think?" said Louise sardonically. After they'd gone through security, she turned to Emily and said, "I still feel bad about my inept question. At least let me buy you a drink to make amends?"

Emily looked at her quizzically. Surprisingly, without missing a beat, she replied, "Sure, I'd like that. What are you doing this evening?"

16

A NEW FRIEND

Louise certainly looks more relaxed out of uniform, thought Emily. Different make-up emphasising her bright blue eyes, wavy hair down to her shoulders and a broad mouth accentuated by deep red lipstick.

"I've not been here before; it's nice. Chilled, and not too serious about itself. I'd guess lesbian couples in the majority, plus a few singles and straight couples. It's good to be able to hear myself think, too, but then I'm probably one of the oldest people here. Cheers!"

"Cheers! I doubt that, Emily; you'd be surprised by the effort a number of women here this evening have put into taking the years off. Please don't mind me being blunt, but I'm guessing you're not looking for anything more than a pleasant evening."

"That's fair, Louise; I hope I didn't mislead you earlier. I'd found you easy to talk to when you were advising me about personal safety and so admired the way you dealt with Trafford when you stopped his car. I remember thinking, *She'd be interesting company.* So when you asked me for a drink, I thought, *Why not?*"

"That's what I thought. I googled you after that hard stop operation, and couldn't believe what I was reading! I'd just been in the presence of a feminist celebrity. I'm a little in awe of what you took on."

"That's very flattering, thank you, but that so-called celebrity status has been a millstone round my neck for over ten months."

"I'm serious. All that amazing sleuthing you've been doing on that vile group – I can't believe you're unaware of your reputation. You don't have a clue, do you?"

"Acclaim can be a curse too, I'm afraid. Changing the subject, what did you make of Pinky and Perky joining the party today?"

"This is where I need to remember that I'm a copper and you're a lawyer – those professions aren't obvious bedfellows."

They both laughed.

"That's a good point," Emily said. "We need some ground rules. Let's say that we can both decline to answer at any point without offence being taken, and we both commit to trusting each other. Agreed?"

Louise nodded. "Agreed. Obviously their presence was related to the documents you sent – which I haven't seen, by the way, so I'm only privy to what was in your verbal account at the interview. Pinky and Perky only came on board once they'd seen them. I'm pretty convinced the Security Service already had suspicions about Granby's outfit. They wanted to see if you knew anything they didn't."

Emily was taken aback. "What makes you think they're already on to Granby?"

"I've got to be careful what I say, as these are just my observations. The station got really stirred up after you'd said you'd be presenting additional evidence, and a couple of senior colleagues let slip things they shouldn't have. Plus, you had an easy time in there; they were deliberately putting you at ease to check you out rather than your information. I've a hunch they knew a lot of that."

"That makes sense; it did seem very softly-softly."

"Some of those blokes think they can tell if someone's lying after thirty seconds. Arrogant pricks."

"Would it be fair to say you don't have a very high opinion of men, Louise?"

"Try being a woman in the police force and not being somewhat jaundiced about men's behaviour. And before you say anything, yes, I did know about that before I joined, so I shouldn't complain."

"I wasn't going to say that – it's only by making a fucking nuisance of ourselves that women have made the progress we have in the past hundred years."

"I'll drink to that. Cheers!"

Emily frowned slightly. "I feel at a disadvantage here. You're acquainted with my backstory from the case file, so tell me a bit about you."

"I like a woman that says what she wants. Get some snacks and another bottle, and my tongue may be loosened."

They left the bar two hours later, having got to know each other considerably better. Emily now knew that Louise was thirty-five going on thirty-six, and had joined the police force eight years ago after languishing in a number of uninspiring jobs following a degree in history from Manchester University. Her police career had survived (just) in spite of the deeply chauvinistic and homophobic environment. She'd successfully applied for detective training after three years and been promoted to sergeant two years ago. She'd come out at nineteen, after realising that she was more attracted to her boyfriend's sister than to him. Her working-class Catholic family from Salford still didn't know what to be more shocked by – that she was a lesbian, or a police officer. Her mum was now speaking to her again, but she'd lost contact with her dad.

"But there's an elephant in this room. Your husband tried to kill you! What the fuck happened there?"

"It was after one of our dinner parties that I began to notice that Robert was behaving strangely. We're talking over two years ago. I'd always believed that we had few secrets – he'd had one affair with a friend of mine when our daughter was a baby, but there'd been no straying after that, as far as I knew, so at first I didn't suspect anything and just put it down to pressures at work. Our marriage was sound, we made each other laugh, fancied each other and enjoyed occasional, comforting sex. But as the unexplained changes to his routine grew, and last-minute invites to unmissable conferences kept cropping up, I started investigating."

"Aha! That's where you honed your sleuthing skills! Carry on; this is brilliant."

"I finally caught him out when he fabricated an Ofsted conference in Stockport. He denied having an affair, but refused to say where he'd been. We stopped speaking, but went ahead with our planned holiday in France for our daughter's sake. One night he said he couldn't stand the lies any longer and told me another story to explain his night away. I believed it at the time, but when I probed some more it too turned out to be a lie. As you know, he'd actually murdered a former colleague who was threatening to go to the police about the fact that the two of them had colluded in covering up the death of a pupil during a school camping trip Robert had led ten years before. His career would have ended in disgrace if Sue had gone ahead, so he strangled her and disposed of her body in a reservoir."

"As you do!" Louise interjected.

"The police were really suspicious by now, and when they asked me to confirm that Robert had been with me on the night of the murder, I said he hadn't. They went to arrest him at the school, but he saw them arrive, realised what was happening and raced home. He flew into a rage when I admitted I hadn't given him an alibi, and started strangling me with his tie. He was strong and I knew

I had seconds before I passed out, so I grabbed a food-processor blade and managed to slash an artery. Blood was pumping out of him, and he would have died if the police hadn't arrived and saved his life. He got twenty years for murder and attempted murder. The rest you know."

Louise was taking in what she'd just heard, looking at Emily in amazement. "It's not that I haven't heard about similar cases in the past eight years, but never a story like that, related so calmly and fluently by the victim, sitting opposite me in a wine bar."

"Believe me, I was traumatised. At the time, I was in no doubt that he was going to kill me. I couldn't stop thinking about it for weeks, or the sight of him slumped on the floor close to me, blood pumping out of him in a rapidly growing pool around us. He was terrified – he knew he was dying."

Louise exhaled. "Wow. Vodka chaser before we go?"

"Just one, then I'd better get back. Lily, my daughter, likes me to be back by ten. Preferably sober, but she can't have everything. I'm guessing you don't have children?"

"No. I probably can't; my tubes are too scarred. I had endometriosis three years ago, which I manage pretty well."

"Oh, I'm really sorry, Louise."

"Thank you. I was devastated at the time, but I've accepted it now. I love being an auntie to my sister's two kids."

Emily smiled. "This has been such a great evening; I'd like to do it again sometime."

"Well, you've got my number."

The moment Colin realised that his life was about to change forever came when he tried to log onto the Backlash site for his weekly fix of stories about women being taught lessons they wouldn't forget. The page was blank, except for one message:

Due to a server error, this site can no longer be reached.

Even though it was to be used only in emergencies, he tried Granby's number – unobtainable – then a couple of the numbers he had for members of the Manchester group. One was unobtainable, but the other picked up.

"Who's this?"

"C. S."

"Don't ring here again, arsehole." The phone went dead.

Three days later, passing a newsagent on his way to work, he saw a headline, stopped the car and bought a copy of *The Times*.

Sir Geoffrey Granby questioned for possession of child pornography

Colin got back into his car and drove off, then after less than a hundred metres swerved towards the kerb, threw open his door and vomited onto the road, much to the amusement of a group of kids on their way to school. He rang in sick, slowly drove home, poured himself a brandy and steeled himself to read the coverage. It took up half of the front page and a double-page spread on pages five and six. It wasn't just as bad as it could be; it was worse.

> *Acting on intelligence from a number of sources, in the past twenty-four hours police have raided a house and offices in central London and found depraved images of adults engaging in sex acts with children as young as nine on hard drives, DVDs and PCs.*

The article went on to outline a connected investigation that had been under way for some time, involving a network of men's rights extremists. These groups were understood to coordinate their activities, including violent attacks on women, their homes and their families, via a sophisticated encrypted website which police experts had managed to break into.

*A police source who wishes to remain anonymous told our reporter
that he believes there are a number of police and prison officers
involved in these groups.*

The Home Secretary had delivered a statement saying that
she'd ordered the Anti-terrorist Squad and MI5 to carry out an
immediate investigation, adding, "Any involvement by police or
prison officers in such groups would be extremely serious and
warrant instant dismissal."

Colin let the newspaper slip onto the kitchen table. It was now
a matter of waiting – but for what? Hammering on the door at
five in the morning? A mid-morning summons to the head's office
about disturbing information she'd received? This had to be the
work of the Fowler bitch. *That fucking woman has ruined my life*,
he thought. For a few seconds, he allowed himself to hope that his
name wouldn't come up. Then he remembered his visit to Granby's
house in Cromer Street, and just made it to the sink before puking
again.

17

TRIUMPH AND DESPAIR

Sir Geoffrey Granby questioned for possession of child pornography and link to violent men's rights groups
A report by our home affairs correspondent, June 2012

At an initial court hearing today at Manchester Crown Court, Sir Geoffrey Granby was granted bail of £100,000 for the possession, circulation and promotion of child pornography.

During their investigation into Granby, police are also believed to have unearthed evidence that a website called Backlash, allegedly funded by Granby, has been promoting attacks against women around the country by members of extremist men's rights groups. This came to light after police were tipped off that Backlash was in reality two sites: one that hosted articles on the supposed erosion of men's rights and promoted 'justice for fathers'; the second an encrypted site that provided names and contact details for Backlash groups around the country, promoted and publicised attacks on individual women, and supported a man's right to rape his wife. Analysis of membership lists revealed the involvement of members of the police, prison service and armed forces.

Police are also reported to be 'keeping an open mind' about the unexplained death last month of an escort living in central London. Earlier this year, the woman was seen on CCTV accompanying Granby and an unidentified man into Granby's office in Kings Cross.

Emily and Deepak stood taking in the view from Deepak's flat on the tenth floor of his block in Castlefield. He'd invited her and Julie round to celebrate the success of their campaign: Granby charged, Backlash being broken up, and countrywide investigations into the penetration of the police and prison service by right-wing extremists. But the mood was sombre, not celebratory.

"I'm sorry; I can't celebrate knowing that I'm responsible for Marion's death. Victory at the expense of an innocent woman's life isn't fucking victory, it's hubris." Julie's voice broke as she tried to hold back her tears.

Deepak and Emily looked at each other. They'd tried to ease Julie's anger, but she wouldn't be moved. Her sadness filled the room. Earlier that afternoon, Emily had tried to talk to her.

"Julie, please, I was the one who suggested that you see her – pressured you to, even. It's equally my fault. We insisted on keeping Marion's name out of it – even when the CPS were threatening us, the bastards, we didn't budge. God knows how Granby found out, but we did everything we could to preserve her anonymity."

"We clearly didn't do everything, or she would still be alive. I was the one who persuaded her to give me a copy of that list, and we handed it over to the police. Nice try, Emily, but you know what I'm saying is true. Sorry, guys, I'm going home. I'll give you a ring tomorrow morning, my love."

Emily stood up and gave Julie a big hug. "Please ring me any time if you need to talk. I love you."

"Let's do this again in a couple of weeks," Deepak suggested. "You'll feel more like talking more by then."

Julie looked at him, started to reply and then thought better of it.

Emily and Deepak sat in silence after she left. When she could bear the silence no longer, Emily said, "I feel terrible about Marion's death, but I can't regret what we did. I think I could lose Julie over this; I can already feel a distance between us."

Deepak sighed. "Look, maybe we're getting ahead of ourselves. As things stand, Marion's death hasn't even been ruled suspicious. It might not be. From what Julie said about meeting up with her again, she didn't seem happy – isolated, still shocked and depressed after her appalling experience, no friends to turn to. She might have killed herself."

"I don't think it will make much difference to Julie, even if it does turn out that way. She'll still blame herself."

Julie let herself into her house, threw down her jacket and went into the lounge. She felt numb; her memory of the route she'd taken from Deepak's flat back to West Didsbury was a blank. She poured herself a large glass of red wine and slumped on the sofa. It was different for her; the other two hadn't been involved with Marion as she had. She'd played down her feelings when she'd told Emily about having sex with Marion in her flat – they were more complicated than she'd let on. Remembering her words now, she felt ashamed of her deceit: *It was totally transactional, and meant nothing. I did feel sorry for her, so there was an element of pity mixed in somewhere, that's all. A soulless and sad experience.*

Of course there'd been feelings between them. She'd dated Marion for six months – had the other two forgotten that when they suggested that she should get over her death so quickly? All right, she and Marion weren't similar; they'd kept their conversation light and they engaged with the world in very different ways. But Marion was ten years younger, fun, passionate and had a kind heart. Julie's feelings had been rekindled when they'd gone to bed again.

Thinking about Marion that afternoon, Julie was consumed by self-loathing. Marion had clearly thought that she was the devious one, plotting ways to lure Julie into bed. The poor woman. Julie had deceived her into revealing information that had almost certainly cost her her life. So maybe Granby would go to prison for a few years, there'd be a cull of those named prison and police officers, Backlash cells would be broken up and more effective vetting procedures introduced to make sure it didn't happen again. But a rather beautiful, if naive, human being had lost her life. *Because of me.*

She woke up on the sofa at two in the morning, wine glass still in hand and bottle on the floor. She went to bed and cried herself to sleep.

Emily woke before six, unable to get back to sleep. The sun had risen to greet a beautiful clear morning, and she had the urge to sit outside on the east-facing patio with a cup of tea, soaking up the June sunshine as it burned off the dew from the fields. Slipping on her dressing gown, she went quietly past Lily's room and downstairs to make her tea.

She'd promised herself for weeks that as soon as their campaign reached a conclusion, successful or not, she would scale back the time and energy she'd been devoting to exposing Granby and Backlash and do two things. Persuade Julie to go away together for a week's break, walking in the Alps. And spend much more time with her daughter. When she'd mentioned this to Julie two weeks ago, she'd responded enthusiastically.

"That's a wonderful idea, I've always wanted to see the Alps in the summer. And you know I adore Lily. I sometimes think that if we ever broke up I'd miss her more than you! She really needs you at this age."

It was nearly a year since Robert's conviction, two since his arrest, and at thirteen years old Lily had coped with more than most people under the age of thirty would have had to deal with. The father she loved sent to prison for murder and attempting to murder her mother, receiving vile messages about her mother and herself, losing friends at school (though most of them were now reconciled), her dad behaving horribly when she finally saw him, adjusting to her mum starting a relationship with a woman, knowing that her mum and then her home had been attacked, sharing her mum with Julie and then with her campaign to expose Granby and Backlash. As Emily went through the list, she felt her eyes filling up and tears running down her face. How could she have been so unknowing? Then she allowed another voice into the 'terrible mother' discourse in her head. Lily's resilience, her genuine affection for Julie, her growing teenage feistiness, confronting the friends who'd melted away and coming back stronger. She had a fantastic daughter, and she allowed herself to believe that some of that was down to her.

"Mum, are you OK? What are you doing sitting out here – have you been crying?"

"Lily! I didn't know you were acquainted with this hour of the morning. Come and sit with me for a moment."

"Same old jokes, Mum. For your information, I'm often awake and out of bed at this time. You haven't answered my question."

"Come here and I will. I've been sitting here on this lovely morning thinking about the horrible time you've had since your dad was convicted, and how strong you've been in confronting the haters, dealing with your disappointment when you saw your dad, and your sensitivity when you found out that your mum's bisexual."

"God, Mum, too much information!"

They both laughed. Emily put her arm around Lily and kissed the top of her head. She smelt of citrus and sleep.

"I know there were times when I should have been there for you and wasn't; I was spending too much time chasing the bad guys. Whatever happens now, I'm dropping out of all that. You're my focus for the next few years."

"What about Julie? She'll need you too. Do you love her like you used to love Dad?"

Lily had got Emily's full attention. If she'd meant what she'd just said to her daughter, she couldn't dodge the question. "That question deserves a serious answer. I've only ever really loved three of the people I've gone out with. There was Sean, a lovely, funny man I met at university before I met your father; then there was your dad; and now Julie. I loved them all in different ways. Sean was my first big love – the relationship swept us up and took over our lives; no one and nothing else existed. When I met your dad, I'd been out with a number of perfectly nice men since Sean, but none with really strong characters, so your dad blew me away. We loved each other very much, and then we had you, whom we both adored, so our shared love for you kept us close. For a while, anyway. We became less close soon after he became a head teacher, but we still had a good relationship until six months from the end. Julie and I became close friends when we spent so much time together before the trial. Slowly we realised our feelings for each other went beyond friendship. To my surprise, when it became obvious that she fancied me, I realised that my feelings for her weren't platonic either. 'Platonic' means—"

"I know what 'platonic' means, Mum. It makes me happy that you and Julie are together. I really like her."

"Thank you for saying that. She really likes you too. Can I get you anything for breakfast, or is it too early?"

"I'm fine, thanks; I think I'll go back to bed for a while. No school today, remember? It's a training day."

Emily waited until Lily had gone upstairs and sent Julie a text.

Darling Julie, I hope you managed to get some sleep last night. Please ring me and let me know how you're feeling. I love you so much. Emily xxx

"Heard anything more about the changes the new governor is supposed to be making?"

Robert had done little else but try to work out what the changes would be, why they were happening and what they meant for him. He'd read about the arrest of a Knight of the Realm for possession of extreme pornography, and a possible connection between said knight and allegations about prison and police officers being linked to an extremist men's rights group. The 'new broom' in the prison had to be connected to that operation, and could only mean a further deterioration in his chances of building a groundswell of public support for his appeal. Lying on his bunk, he thought about ignoring his cellmate, who he'd been told on the prison grapevine had been put into his cell to report on him. Though it looked like the arrangement would be permanent, he might be able to use it to his advantage.

Robert had first realised that something big had happened two weeks ago, on the day 'his' prison officer suddenly disappeared, along with three other officers on his wing. Then he'd been moved to a double-occupancy cell in a different wing. A few days after that, Gorgeous George, as he was known, had joined him. Robert wasn't stupid; in fact, given the competition, he was the apex intellectual in this particular establishment. So within an hour of learning that four officers on his wing had been moved elsewhere, he'd realised that the network outside the prison to which those officers belonged must have been compromised. And that meant no more messages from him to the world outside; no uplifting news about attacks on Emily and how difficult her life had become.

"You not speaking to me anymore? Have I offended you?"

"Sorry, George, I was miles away. The only thing I've picked up is a rumour that every screw is being hauled in for an interview with the governor and two Home Office high-ups. Putting two and two together, I'm assuming they think that corrupt screws were bringing in stuff for prisoners from the outside for money, and they're trying to find out how widespread it was." Robert knew there was more to it than that, but he wasn't about to tell Gorgeous.

"I assumed that too, but I heard a rumour that it might be about more than bent screws."

He's probing again, thought Robert. *Definitely a plant.* "You know more than me, then."

Prisoners sharing a cell quickly sensed when to end conversations without causing offence; those who didn't were either too brutal to care or learned the hard way. George understood that he was being given his cue that the conversation had ended, so he left it. He'd have plenty of time to pursue what the assistant governor had called his 'mission' in the next few months.

Robert went back to thinking about the inequity of the system, and the fact that an upper-class paedophile's predilection for watching young girls being raped and abused had sunk his chances of getting out early. But he couldn't escape another, more unsettling thought. Some of those girls were probably younger than Lily. If Granby was representative of the kind of men who had mounted the campaign in support of Robert and against his wife and daughter, then what kind of people were they? *And what does that say about me?* For the first time since his conviction, Robert reflected on what being locked in a mindset of hate was doing to his soul.

When Julie hadn't called or texted by midday the following day, Emily rang her. She answered on the sixth ring.

"Hi, Emily, sorry for leaving so abruptly last night and not getting back after your lovely message this morning."

"You don't have to apologise, my love; I just wanted to hear your voice and check that you're OK. I understand that Marion's death means far more to you than it does to me, given that you two had a thing. I was insensitive yesterday. But if her death is connected to Granby and Backlash in any way, I'm even more to blame than you are, for persuading you to see her. It's shocking, whatever happened to the poor woman."

She's saying the right things and I know she just wants to make everything better, but she doesn't really get it, thought Julie. *It's not a question of the degree of blame. I was with Marion for four hours in her flat, and there was a deeper and more intimate connection between us in those four hours than there'd ever been during our earlier dates. I know beyond doubt that if I hadn't passed on that list of names, she would still be alive.*

"Julie, are you still there?"

"Sorry, I was thinking about Marion. Thank you for acknowledging that. I don't think I'll find peace until I find out what really happened to her, so until then I'm probably not going to be an easy person to be with."

Emily's stomach lurched. "What are you saying?"

"Sorry. I'm not saying that I don't want to see you. But it's probably better if I have more time on my own until I get myself straightened out. Of course I want to be with you; we're for keeps, I hope you know that. But for the next few weeks, let's not virtually live together, as we have been doing."

As she listened, Emily's nausea began to subside. *Don't be an idiot,* she thought; *nothing is ending, she just needs time to follow this through.* "I get it, really. How do you want to take things forward? I don't want to push you, but would you like to come over this weekend for a bit of pampering?"

"I'd love to. I'll update you on anything I've managed to dig up by then."

"Just be careful where you dig. Better to use a trowel to start with, not a shovel. There will be people out there who won't be keen on you looking into their affairs. You can always run things past me if you need a second opinion."

"I will. Promise. Love you."

"Love you too. Be careful." *Our holiday in the Alps is obviously off the agenda for the foreseeable future*, she thought.

18

A DATE WITH A DIFFERENCE

Julie had no intention of sharing her plans with Emily and Deepak. They would probably think she was crazy, and she wouldn't blame them. But unlike them, she was grieving for Marion. Her plan carried a serious risk to her welfare, and could potentially prove fatal. But she couldn't go through the rest of her life knowing that she'd done nothing to get justice for Marion. She couldn't undo her selfish actions that evening in Marion's flat which had probably contributed to her death – suicide or murder – but she could at least try to make sure that those responsible faced justice.

She had to satisfy herself, beyond reasonable doubt, about the cause of Marion's death. Studying the autopsy findings that Deepak had acquired, she'd learned that her ex had been found dead in her flat by her cleaner, who visited once a week. The pathologist estimated that she'd died three days before the cleaner found her, and had no doubt that the cause of death was a lethal dose of benzodiazepine in her system; 'a level that would kill a man twice her size'. He'd found no obvious signs that the drug hadn't been self-administered, and noted that there was no trace of the usual recreational drugs in her body, which was unusual in cases like this, apparently. Based on the autopsy, the coroner's only options for his verdict were suicide or accidental death. Given the level of the drug in Marion's system, and no apparent evidence of foul play, there was no doubt that it would be suicide.

Julie needed to speak to the pathologist, Anthony Rice, BSc, BM, to satisfy herself that there was no evidence that the overdose had been administered against Marion's will. It didn't take much browsing to find him on LinkedIn. He'd been a pathologist for ten years, felt his job carried huge responsibility and took his work very seriously. He lived in London, but fortuitously *spent as much time as possible in my cottage in Chapel en le Frith exploring the glorious Peak District.* A search of dating sites revealed that he was forty-three years old, divorced and sexually active. It was a long shot, but if she could set up a date with him, she might get the information she needed before the date led anywhere she wasn't prepared to go. Julie updated her details – a euphemism for taking two years off her age and choosing a picture with a younger hairstyle – swiped Anthony's picture and waited.

A day later, having received no reply, she felt an odd combination of relief and regret. Not having to go ahead was a relief – a date with a bloke was not something she looked forward to, obviously – but how else could she get more information about the cause of Marion's death? Then the following day, he responded. They arranged to meet after work in a bar in Didsbury in two days' time, during which time Julie changed her mind several times about what she was doing. *Is this keeping faith with Marion's memory, deceiving him as I did her? What am I becoming?* she thought. But she knew it was her best chance.

As she walked in and saw a slightly older version of Anthony's profile photo, Julie knew that she had to end the deceit sooner rather than later and explain exactly why she wanted to meet. The risk, of course, was that he would simply walk out on the spot.

His eyes met hers as she approached the table, and flickered with recognition. From the unforced smile that followed, Julie could see that he wasn't disappointed with his first impression. After the obligatory but awkward cheek-kissing, ordering of drinks and ten minutes of small talk about traffic on the M60, Julie braced herself and began.

"This is a terrible way to begin our date, and I won't blame you if you walk away, but please hear me out. I understand you're the pathologist who carried out the autopsy on Marion Davies, the woman found dead in her flat by her cleaner three weeks ago. We had a six-month relationship that ended over a year ago; not too serious, but not just a series of date nights either. I was horrified when I read about her death, especially as there were reports in some papers that she might have been involved with that disgusting bloke who's just been arrested for child pornography. Knowing her well, I just can't believe that she would take her own life. I haven't been able to put it out of my mind, so I thought if I could just speak with you, I could put my mind at rest by confirming that her death was definitely suicide."

Anthony had been looking increasingly angry, and now he interrupted her. "Have I got this right? Our date isn't really a date at all, but an opportunity for you to quiz me about an autopsy I carried out recently on a young woman who committed suicide; a verdict you query. Assuming for a moment that your doubts are backed up by some knowledge of forensic pathology, do you really think I would sit here and discuss a post-mortem examination I carried out with a complete stranger? I will give you the benefit of the doubt and assume that her death has temporarily affected the balance of your mind. That wouldn't be good PR for a lawyer, I imagine, so I won't take this any further, but our date is over. Which is a pity, because you're my type – assuming you're even into men as well as women. Enjoy the rest of your evening, Julie. Let me make a contribution towards the wine."

There was clearly no point in trying to change his mind. Julie watched as he took out a ten-pound note, left it on the table and walked out. As he left, Julie noticed that this outward show of taking control seemed to be covering an underlying unease. Despondently, she took a swig of wine, picked up the money and asked for the bill.

At nine o'clock that evening, just as she'd finished her poached egg with cheese on toast, she heard a text come in. It was from Anthony.

If you want an answer to your question, meet me in the Sett Valley car park in Hayfield at 10pm tonight. I'll be in a black Mercedes SLK two-seater, and I won't wait more than five minutes. Please respond immediately and confirm that you can make it.

Julie responded as soon as she'd got over the shock. This had to be good news. Of course, meeting a stranger in a remote location was a risk, especially as she'd revealed to him that she doubted his verdict on Marion's death. But it was more than worth it. Her house was less than thirty minutes from Hayfield at this time of night, but she wanted to get there before him if possible. She was still wearing her date clothes, so changed into a tracksuit, sprayed on deodorant and was reversing her Honda out of her drive by quarter past nine. M60, M67, then skirt Glossop and on to Hayfield. She could drive it without thinking.

As she descended the winding road from the top of Chunal, just minutes from Hayfield, she was passed in a crazy overtake by a black Mercedes SLK. It was still only twelve minutes to ten, so presumably Anthony wanted to be certain that he got there first. *Either that, or he's an adrenaline junkie, overtaking from back there,* she thought. She slowed down for the last mile; she wasn't going to arrive before Anthony anyway, and there was a speed camera on the Hayfield bypass. She felt charged up in a way she hadn't experienced since the train journey back to Manchester after her afternoon in London with Marion.

As she turned into the car park, her lights picked out the Merc in the far corner, near some trees. There were no other cars. Heart beating faster now, she parked alongside and switched off the engine. Anthony got out, walked round to the passenger side of Julie's Civic, opened the door and got in.

"That was a bold overtake back there."

"I haven't driven out to the rural splendour of the High Peak to listen to your views on my driving. In the past few hours I've been getting to know a lot more about you, Julie Taylor. So why don't you tell me all about yourself and why you're so interested in knowing whether Marion Davies killed herself or not? That way I'll check whether you're bullshitting me. The first indication that you're lying, I get out and you won't ever see me again."

"What if I'm right and your sources are wrong?"

"They won't be, not about anything fundamental. I don't need to know what nail varnish you use."

Either I tell this stranger the whole story, including Robert's trial, my relationship with Emily, our mission to uncover Backlash and the connection with Marion, or I lose this opportunity to hear what he knows. Because he clearly knows something. "OK, I'll tell you. But I need to know that I'm not being recorded, so please switch off your phone, get out of the car and let me check that you're not wired. I'll do the same, obviously."

Anyone walking their dog along the Sett Valley Trail that evening would have been intrigued by the sight of two people patting down each other's bodies in a very asexual way, checking for hidden recording devices. Which is not to say that Julie didn't notice Anthony's hands veering slightly off course towards her breasts as he was feeling under her arms.

Back in her car, she took him through everything: the reasons she took on Emily's case, their platonic year-long friendship, the trial, the post-trial traumas, becoming Emily's lover, the way they'd painstakingly unearthed the connections between Backlash and the attacks on Emily and other women, the amazing coincidence of finding that Julie had dated the woman seen going into Granby's house, the horror of Marion's experience, reconnecting with her to find more evidence on Granby, and their joy at the success of their campaign followed by Julie's despair at Marion's death.

"So now you know pretty much everything about my life over the past two years. Emily is moving on, but I can't rest until I've done everything possible to find out what happened to Marion. Did Granby have her killed because he assumed she'd given the police details about his use of child pornography? That's why I contacted you and arranged a date. I'm sorry I deceived you."

As she finished speaking, a car drove into the car park, headlight beams sweeping around as the driver made a turn.

"Come here," snapped Anthony, putting his hand behind Julie's head and pulling her face against his as the headlights briefly lit them up. He smelt of mint gum.

As the driver tooted his horn and drove off, they sat back in their seats and looked at each other.

"You didn't mention accompanying Lily on her prison visits, but otherwise, ten out of ten. I believe what you've told me. Before I say anything more, why don't you tell me why you don't think Marion committed suicide?"

"Obviously I can't be sure. But in my career I've worked for a number of people during desperate periods in their lives, and developed a sense about those who are more or less likely to take their life. I never thought Marion would do that; she'd come through the trauma of Granby's assault and was slowly getting her life back on track. Then there's the fact that her suicide coincided with Granby's potential exposure, and that the list of names she gave me proved vital in exposing some important people who would have wished to remain hidden."

"Circumstantial evidence, then?"

"I agree. But I'm presuming that you must have some doubts too about the cause of Marion's death, or you wouldn't have asked me to drive out to the sticks at this hour."

"What I'm about to tell you must never be repeated or shared with anyone. Not even with Emily. I must have your word on that, because if this gets out, it's not just my job that's at risk; it's my life."

"You have my word. I've already been responsible for one person's death; I won't be responsible for another."

"OK. It's not unusual for pathologists to find the police or the Security Service taking an excessive interest in a particularly sensitive case. A death in police custody, for example. Almost always this takes the form of a chief inspector or equivalent making it clear through back channels that I have to be very sure about my judgement of the cause of death because, 'This will be scrutinised at a senior level and we would have to bring any concerns to the attention of your superior.' In the case of Marion Davies' death, the arm-twisting to amend my initial findings went to a completely different level. I've never experienced anything like it before."

To her surprise, Julie noticed that Anthony's hands had begun to shake slightly. "Are you OK?"

"I'm fine. This is the first time I've told anyone about this, and the memory is still raw. Benzodiazepine can be ingested orally, injected or as a suppository. As I examined the body, which showed the classic signs of a benzodiazepine overdose, it became clear from the stomach lining that the deceased hadn't ingested the drug orally. I couldn't see any signs of recent needle marks. The drug can be administered anally as a suppository, and when I checked, it was obvious from tissue damage that it had been forced into her anus, probably by a fist. There were also signs of recent use of wrist restraints, and bruises on her arms, so by this time my working hypothesis was that the victim had died from a deliberate benzodiazepine overdose administered against her will.

"Shortly after, I was summoned by my boss to a meeting with her and two others: a man and a woman whom I immediately took to be members of the Security Service, presumably MI5." Anthony's hands had stopped shaking, and he paused a moment before carrying on. "I was asked by my boss if I had a preliminary idea about the cause of death, and proceeded to tell them my findings so far and my initial conclusions. I left nothing out, obviously. As I finished, the woman, whom I took to be the senior of the two officers, interjected. I won't go through everything she said, but it can be accurately summarised as: 'This unfortunate woman's death is now a matter of national security. In the light of that, I've agreed with your superior that your autopsy findings will simply state that the cause of death was a self-administered benzodiazepine overdose, with no sign of foul play. This isn't a request, Dr Rice, it's an instruction. Do I make myself clear?'

"I looked at my boss, who nodded and made it clear that this order came from way above her pay grade. I turned back to the MI5 woman and said, 'As I'm about to lie to protect state security, can I please be given a reason?' At which point the two spooks informed my boss that they were going and would leave her to apprise me of the implications of the Official Secrets Act. I'm no Sarah Tisdall, Julie, so I complied, obviously."

Julie had remained quiet throughout Anthony's explanation, hardly able to believe what she was hearing. She had one question above all others. "Why would the state be so desperate to hide the truth about Marion's death? I mean, she was an escort, and we know that – tragically – it's not unusual for sex workers to be seriously assaulted or even murdered. People wouldn't be suspicious."

"True. But you're thinking too rationally. Try to consider the steps the state would be prepared to take to keep its own operations secret."

"I'm not sure I follow."

"Like protecting the identity of one of its own, for example."

"Fucking hell, you mean she was killed on the orders of the Security Service? What possible risk could Marion pose to state security that would justify killing her, given that they seem determined to send Granby and his upper-class cronies down?"

"Now you're getting close. The Security Service are relaxed about Granby going down because they've been working to expose his neo-fascist network and break up the cells of prison and police officers for over a year. That includes agents working on the inside, close to Granby. I've been told that you and your chums were beginning to really piss them off with your amateur sleuthing. They didn't pay much attention at first, but apparently they hadn't reckoned with your success in persuading key people to listen to you. You would know much more about that than I do, of course. I'm just telling you what my source felt able to share with me, when I decided I had to know why I'd been so humiliated in front of my boss by those arseholes. He owed me a favour from a couple of years ago when I gave him some information on a murder that helped him to get noticed."

Finally, Julie began to understand the shattering implications of what Anthony was saying. Over the past year, she, Emily and Deepak had probably been risking their careers and their lives for nothing. The Security Service had been on Granby's case all the time, building up evidence against him. As that thought sank in, countless pathways in her cerebral cortex fired off and the final piece of the puzzle dropped into place. It was as if she'd had a mild electric shock.

"So if I've understood you, your source told you that Marion was killed by the Security Service to ensure that she could never give evidence in Granby's trial, with the risk that in doing so she might reveal that one of their agents had been working undercover within Backlash. So presumably the agent and Marion must have met, somehow. But there's no way he would have revealed himself to Marion, who wasn't connected to Backlash at all, except via Granby's sick sexual activities."

"I think I've told you everything I know; anything else would be speculation. Presumably someone in the Service was sufficiently concerned that if there was a trial, Marion could identify the undercover agent, either deliberately or by accident."

Julie had trouble taking this in. What had Marion got herself into? Maybe there was more to know about her connection with Granby than Marion had been prepared to tell her that afternoon? Thinking about her last hours with Marion, then the horror she must have experienced in her final moments, Julie felt an overwhelming sorrow. Tears ran down her face, silently at first, then accompanied by loud, anguished sobbing. She sensed Anthony shift his position, then felt his arms around her.

"Let it out, Julie. You've had a massive shock." He pulled her head onto his shoulder, holding her tight. Julie went to wipe away her tears, but Anthony gently pulled her hand away and cleaned her face with a tissue. "You mustn't blame yourself for her death. Once they'd decided she posed a risk, no other ending was possible."

The warmth of Anthony's cheek against hers had felt wonderfully comforting, but as he began tentatively to go further, she took control.

"Stop, please, Anthony."

He quickly removed his hand. "I'm sorry. It sounds corny, but I got carried away in the moment there."

"Me too. We might have been reported to the parish council."

"I don't know, I hear this is a very broad-minded community. We might be asked to liven up the annual May Queen parade with a re-enactment on the back of a lorry."

They both laughed, then Anthony was serious once more.

"Please remember that you can't share anything I've told you with Emily or anyone else. It would be too dangerous for both of us."

"I understand, and you have my word. But why did you decide to tell me about MI5's involvement and take this risk?"

Anthony was quiet for a while, then said, "I got married in haste at the end of university, as we didn't want to face going our separate ways. I couldn't stand the thought of not being coupled up. It was pathetic, really. After that, the usual story – we both grew up, realised that we were different people who wanted different things, and each had a couple of affairs before we accepted the inevitable and got a divorce. But we remained good friends and kept in touch. After about eighteen months, she meets this guy, and the next thing I hear, they're getting married and I'm invited. So I turn up with my then-girlfriend, hoping to have a great time. But it's clear from the moment I meet the guy that my ex is marrying a controlling arsehole who sees me as a threat. He ends up with his face in mine, telling me that he'll fucking kill me if I ever see her again. From that moment I carried this awful certainty around with me that this marriage would end horribly for her. He's now inside for twenty years for choking her to death, and I can't forgive myself for not doing more to get her away from him. When I researched you this afternoon after our date, and read about your campaign to help women fighting back against these misogynists, I had to help you."

"Thank you, Anthony. I think I should probably be getting back now."

"I'm glad you contacted me, Julie. Good luck, but please remember that these people are completely amoral; they don't think twice about ruining people's lives or killing them if they decide it's in the interests of the state – which, funnily enough, almost always seem to coincide with their own interests. I don't want to know what you intend to do now, but please be very careful. If you're not absolutely sure that something won't be traced back to you, then don't do it. If in doubt, I'm here for a second opinion."

They hugged again, then Anthony got into his car and drove off, rear wheels spinning as he turned out of the car park.

19

JULIE GOES HER OWN WAY

The closure that Emily had hoped Granby's arrest would bring was proving elusive; she hadn't stopped worrying about what Julie might be getting into. Over the past twelve months, Emily had experienced how tenacious and bold Julie could be, whether she was getting vital evidence from Marion or staying calm as Deepak's lookout. Still, it was difficult to see what possible route she could take to uncover the cause of Marion's death. What was she planning to do – kidnap the pathologist and lock him up until he confessed the truth? And that was just the start – if she did manage to uncover evidence that the pathologist had overlooked, what then? Try to bring the culprits to justice on her own, like Superwoman? She had to hope that Julie would see how impossible the odds were, and leave it. But she couldn't bank on it.

Her thoughts were interrupted as Lily wandered into the garden, holding her phone in front of her. She'd got into FaceTime recently. Emily studied her daughter as she paused and carried on a conversation with Daisy, who'd recently joined her Year 8 tutor group. The two were becoming inseparable, if phone time was any indication of the strength of female friendship. Emily made a mental note to remind Lily not to exclude Tamsin, who'd been her rock for nearly two years.

Since Lily had turned thirteen five months ago, Emily had noticed the changes taking place in her daughter's poise and appearance, and could now clearly imagine her at twenty-five. Her mum's green eyes, full, wide mouth and high cheekbones; her dad's square face and perfect straight nose. *Could be worse*, Emily thought. The change in her looks had already given Lily a boost in confidence, and hopefully the extra time she and Emily were spending together had helped, too.

Finishing her call, Lily suddenly seemed to remember why she'd come into the garden, and walked over to Emily. "Hi, Mum. Is Julie OK? I miss her – is she coming round this weekend? I'd love to see her."

Last weekend, Emily had asked Lily to go for a walk with her along the Macclesfield Canal "to bring you up to date about what's happening in our lives". After getting over the shock of being asked to go walking with her mum – in spite of living close to Lyme Park, they'd rarely done that since her dad had gone to prison – they'd chatted without a break for nearly two hours. Even so, Emily had only given her daughter an abridged explanation of why Julie wouldn't be around so much in the coming weeks. She could tell that Lily had been left wanting more, so wasn't surprised by her concern.

"She's coming to stay with us this weekend, and I'm sure she'd love to talk to you about her plans over the next few weeks. Just give her a bit of space at the start so she doesn't feel like she's facing an inquisition from the moment she gets here. But I don't have to say that, as you've become really sensitive about reading people's moods lately. I'm very proud of you, Lily."

"Thanks, Mum. I promise I won't overwhelm her."

Lily took Emily's request to heart and didn't push Julie for information. Emily had made a mushroom risotto, and after an hour Lily went to hang out with a friend from two streets away.

"Make sure you've got your key, sweetheart; text me when you get there and again when you leave."

Later, in bed, Emily turned to Julie. "Is everything OK? You should have said if you weren't in the mood."

"I'm sorry, I'm just distracted by the unanswered questions over Marion's death. That's not fair on you." Julie knew why she'd been distracted. It was linked to Marion, but not in the way she'd told Emily. She was feeling guilty about sleeping with Marion, but she'd be deceiving herself if she thought that was all it was. Sex with Emily had lost some of its spark over the past couple of months. "Let's walk along the Middlewood Way after breakfast tomorrow. I'd like to share what I think may have happened to Marion, and get your opinion."

"Lovely idea. Goodnight, Julie."

Julie turned over and kissed her. *I'd better decide what I can and can't say*, she thought.

The next day they set off along the canal early, before the sun was high enough to really warm the air. Julie had quickly given Emily a summary of the events leading up to Marion's death.

"So let me make sure I've got this straight. From your conversations with 'several contacts' who must remain nameless, you're ninety per cent sure that the Security Service had been keeping Granby and Backlash under investigation for some time – not because of Granby's addiction to child pornography, but because they suspected that Backlash was building an extremist far-right movement with links to the prison service, and possibly the police. As part of their surveillance operation, they planted an undercover agent in the Backlash network. Your theory is that MI5 panicked once it looked like the Backlash operation was about to be exposed by our evidence, as they feared that their agent would be in danger if they didn't get him out in time. Somebody in the Service then got the idea that Marion could unwittingly identify this person, so they had a motive to eliminate her. You also believe that there are inconsistencies in the autopsy report. Unfortunately, you can't share how you got this information with me, as you don't want to put me at risk."

Emily paused and looked quizzically at her friend and lover, who said, "You summed that up very well. You should be a lawyer."

"For God's sake, Julie, this isn't funny. Have you any idea how far-fetched this sounds without any evidence to back it up?"

"I didn't say I don't have evidence. I do. Admittedly, some of it is weak and certainly wouldn't stand up in court, but I'm not going to involve you in this, ever. This is something I have to pursue on my own."

They walked along for a couple of hundred yards in silence. As they approached a café, Julie said, "Let's have a coffee."

"Good idea. More stimulants; just what I need at the moment."

Emily bought them a cappuccino and pastry each and they sat at a table overlooking the canal. There was a definite bite to the breeze, softened by the warm summer sunshine. It should have been an idyllic scene, but they were both too unsettled to appreciate it.

"I appreciate your concern for my welfare, but can I push you a little on what exactly your next steps are going to be?" Emily asked.

"What do you mean?"

"Are you trying to find concrete evidence that MI5, or some proxy, killed Marion? And if so, and you find out exactly who's responsible, what are you intending to do about it?"

Julie sat looking out at the water as a narrowboat chugged past with the unmistakable beat of its single-cylinder engine. She looked at the middle-aged white couple on board taking up their ordained positions – him with his arm along the tiller at the stern; her reading a book on a cushion at the bow – and envied their apparent equanimity. *Though appearances can be deceptive*, she thought. *Maybe they're Russian agents. It seems anything's possible.* She'd known Emily would eventually ask her a question like this, but had kept putting off formulating an answer. Now she couldn't duck it any longer; it wouldn't be fair on Emily or Lily. Or Deepak, for that matter. "The honest answer to your question is 'Yes.' If I haven't got anywhere in a month's time, I'll give up. If I'm successful, I still haven't decided what I'll do. But please don't worry, Emily. I won't be attempting a citizen's arrest or any stupid direct confrontation, and I promise I'll keep you informed as things play out. If I do find out his or her identity, you'll be the first to know. I'll seek your advice before taking anything further."

Emily watched as the man on the narrowboat shouted at the woman she assumed to be his wife to "Put the bloody book down and get ready for the next lock." She felt a sickening sense of foreboding. If Julie really believed that digging around to find the name of the spook who'd killed Marion wouldn't put her health and well-being at serious risk, she was delusional. *Maybe she is*, she thought. *Maybe the shock of Marion's death has affected her mental state.* That thought threw Emily completely off balance, but she had to stay calm.

Julie continued. "One option, obviously, would be to go to the *Guardian* with everything I've got. Look how great they've been over the phone-hacking scandal – they've got Murdoch on the run."

Now Emily was really worried. "You can't compare the risk of exposing criminal journalists with that of going after MI5, for God's sake!"

"I'm not going after MI5, only the person or persons who did this. I'm doing this on my own, Emily, but I need to know that you'll be there for me. Can you handle that?"

"As long as being there for you doesn't mean identifying your body on a slab after it's been dragged out of a lake. I want you to promise me that if you do find out who killed Marion, you'll tell me before you take any further action. You've got to understand that this doesn't just affect you, Julie."

Julie walked around to Emily and held her in her arms. "Of course I'll tell you. I realise I've been sounding very selfish, and I'm sorry, forgive me. I need you on hand to hold up a mirror to my wilder ideas. I'll take things a step at a time, I promise. Anyway, I can't put my life on hold completely; I've got a mortgage to pay and a boss whose understanding I'm stretching to the limit."

Emily embraced her reassuringly. But deep down she knew that her relationship with Julie wouldn't ever be the same again. Up to now, she'd felt that there wasn't anything that either of them wouldn't tell the other. Sadly, that closeness had gone, and she realised that there would always be secrets from now on.

For the rest of the weekend there was an unstated agreement between them not to allow that realisation to intrude, for Lily's sake as much as theirs. In fact, the three of them had the happiest two days they could remember for a long time. The weather was exceptional for the north-west – the days were warm and the light evenings seemed to go on forever – and the four of them – Daisy came over and stayed on Saturday – had a hilarious time playing Stop the Bus late into the evening. In bed that night, Julie assuaged Emily's anxieties about their sex life. But her concerns about Julie's increasingly obsessional behaviour couldn't be swept away so easily.

The following morning, Emily encouraged Lily to go into the village with Julie for a coffee. She knew that they would be seeing less of each other in the coming weeks, and wanted her daughter to make the most of this time. Julie had become an important part of Lily's life, and Emily was sad that she wouldn't be around so much.

As Julie left she promised to keep in daily contact and tentatively made a date to stay over in two weeks' time.

"This is only for a few weeks, Emily. Please don't worry about me; I'm not going to take any risks. My life with you and Lily means too much to me for me to do that."

20

MANCHESTER AND SCOTLAND

"So we're just going to roll over like a bunch of women and disband, are we? What a pathetic bunch of revolutionaries we are, beaten by a couple of middle-class lawyers."

Colin thought better of pointing out the contradiction in Dave's last two sentences. The mood in the room wasn't conducive to such sophistry.

"It's not that simple, Dave. If we're going to fight back against this we've got to know what we're up against. I've heard that the police raided that paedo Granby's house because they had someone on the inside providing information, which means those two were just a sideshow."

"Oh, so sorry, Darren, I'd forgotten you've got a direct line into police operations. Who are you fucking kidding? The only thing we know for sure is that those two were determined to bring us down."

"And how do you explain that when we attacked her house, the police just happened to be on hand to catch Ron and Andy red-handed? Seems to me they were getting information about our plans in advance. Or do you think that they just happened to be driving past, into a cul-de-sac, at the very moment of the attack? Bit unlikely, don't you think?"

Colin could see this rapidly degenerating into a 'mine's bigger than yours' contest that would go on forever without anything concrete being agreed. This was exactly why he'd held back from joining Fathers 4 Justice or the men's rights movement before: too much talking, constant challenges to the leadership, factions splintering and reforming. *For a group of men who hate women, they seem to spend a hell of a lot of time talking about them.* He'd thought Backlash was different, and they might have been as long as Granby was in charge, but now that he'd gone the regional groups were starting to fall apart or get busted by the police. Darren was right, of course: there had to have been an informant. But where did that knowledge get them? Nowhere.

Colin had more cause to be angry than most of his 'comrades'. Because of some CCTV footage near Granby's house in Cromer Street, he'd had a visit from the police – and not your usual woodentops, either – asking him some searching questions: what was his visit about, and what was discussed? He'd had sufficient foresight to prepare a story about trying to get funding for a pilot project for state-school kids who showed an aptitude for maths, but they were unconvinced. He hadn't been charged, but would remain under investigation. Unfortunately, that fact had been leaked to the press, resulting in a piece on page three of the *Manchester Evening News* headlined 'Manchester maths teacher helping police with inquiries into Backlash investigation'. He suspected Roy Milton was behind the leak, as payback for Colin informing the head about his affair with Shirley Hazlitt. There'd been a very unpleasant scene in the car park after work that had lost Roy all chance of promotion.

As a result of the story in the press, Colin had been summoned to the head's office and informed that he was to be suspended on full pay for as long as the police investigation continued. "Given the nature of the charges against Granby and your connection with him, the governors wish to send a clear signal to parents that you won't be allowed in the school until you're exonerated." Informally, she'd added that whatever the outcome of the investigation, he should assume that he was unlikely to ever teach in her school again, and suggested that it might be wise to begin establishing himself as a private maths tutor for middle-class kids whose parents were prepared to game the exam system.

So Colin didn't particularly care about whether there'd been an informant inside Backlash or not. But he couldn't calm the anger he felt towards Emily Fowler and Julie Taylor. If justice had been done in that case, instead of Fowler walking away scot-free from attempted murder, then he wouldn't have had anything to do with Backlash, or Granby, or this bunch of losers who were still droning on. He needed to make the bitches suffer; the desire for revenge was driving him crazy. First, he had to cut his ties with Backlash. From now on, he would be a one-man operation. No one would be able to finger him for Fowler and Taylor's unfortunate accidents this time. They'd occur at a time and place of his choosing.

"Colin, are you with us? What do you think?"

Colin looked around the room at the eight men assembled there; he felt varying degrees of contempt for every one of them, but took care not to show it. "As some of you know, I've been going through a difficult time recently, and with much regret, this will be my last meeting. I've met some good comrades here, and we were getting somewhere until Granby was exposed as a disgusting paedo. But I'm rowing back from active service for the foreseeable future, and will carry on the struggle in an individual capacity. I wish you all the very best for the future."

He wasn't surprised when no one asked him to change his mind or pushed him on his reasons for leaving, as he knew he'd never really been accepted within the group. A few called out, "See you around, Colin," but he knew the chances of that were zero.

At home that evening, he resumed his online research on Julie Taylor and Emily Fowler.

Ben Trafford woke to the sound of torrential rain from another westerly storm drumming on his bedroom window. Since taking up residence here four weeks ago, he could count the number of dry days on one hand. As he lay in bed, putting off the moment when he'd have to throw back the blankets, he reflected on the events of the past few weeks.

There hadn't been a huge choice of locations when his head of section had called him in and told him that he needed to go off-grid for at least six months. A pain-in-the-arse investigative journalist had been ringing his contacts in the Service to try and uncover the identity of the person MI5 had placed undercover in Backlash. It would have been obvious to any journalist with a brain that the hard evidence against Granby came either from an informer or an undercover agent.

Journalists weren't Ben's biggest problem, though. There were some very angry members of the House of Lords and London gentlemen's clubs who wanted him taken out. Granby had been the tip of the iceberg; investigations into a number of individuals who'd supported and funded Backlash were proceeding at an uncomfortable pace, and it was clear to Ben that not all of their hurriedly assembled firewalls were going to hold up. Some of those people knew people who did very bad things if the money was right, and the intel from the Service was that a contract on his life had been taken out. From his time in Special Forces he knew the calibre of ex-SAS men who'd been seduced by the money to be made by joining private security outfits working for the Americans in Iraq. It was a small step from there to becoming a self-employed assassin. So changes to his identity, appearance and address had been prioritised. As soon as his new name and identity documents had been produced (driving licence, credit cards, utility bills), and his beard grown, hair dyed and coloured contact lenses prescribed, he'd packed a large rucksack, collected his tickets from the courier and taken the 11pm sleeper (double-berth room, single occupancy) from Kings Cross to Glasgow. He was still coming to terms with his change of appearance, and as the sleeper carriage attendant had studied his ticket, then shown him to his compartment, the face reflected in the mirror took him aback.

"You look like you've been around, sir."

He'd noted her badge, her deep brown eyes, her sallow skin and her Glaswegian accent with the edge taken off. *Who knows?* he'd thought. "Here and there."

"Are you staying in Oban, sir, or heading off to the Islands?"

"I'm catching the ferry to… What time does the bar open?"

"Not for half an hour, sir. But I could bring you something now, if you want."

"I'll have a Laphroaig, please – a double, no ice, with a glass of water, thank you, Alison."

"I'll be back in five minutes, sir, and please call me Allie."

"And please call me… James, Allie."

She'd smiled and left, returning a minute later with his drink. *Did she notice my hesitation? You've got to do better than that, mate. An attractive bit of skirt and you almost slip at the first hurdle.*

At half past midnight, he'd gone along the corridor to the toilet, passing Allie in the train manager's booth. She'd smiled broadly at him, and on his way back asked him if there was anything he wanted. Afterwards, when a furious Allie had left his compartment in tears, he'd be prepared to swear on oath that she'd consented. She'd returned with his Laphroaig, then gone into his compartment willingly when he'd said he couldn't find the light switch. *I mean, she knew what was going on, right?* She'd reluctantly accepted a drink when he'd suggested it – "Go on, just a little one. Please?" – then given him a half-hearted shove when he'd tried to kiss her.

But when he'd put his hand between her legs, she'd switched, shouted, "Stop that now!" and called the other train manager on her radio.

"What did you do that for, you bitch? Nothing happened – get out."

"That was sexual assault, you bastard. Men like you make me sick. Get help before you wreck some woman's life."

The train had been due into Glasgow at 7.40, but he'd been woken at the stipulated 6.40 by a different attendant banging on his compartment door, even though they were running half an hour late. Allie wasn't around as he left the train. Other passengers hurried on around him. In spite of the late arrival, he'd had forty minutes to catch his connection to Oban, where he was due to connect with the 3pm ferry to Lochboisdale, South Uist, and from there by taxi to his home for the next six months in Balivanich on Benbecula. His ferry crossing, with clear, gradually darkening skies and a calm sea, had little prepared him for the weather to come on the Outer Hebrides. He'd carried out a cursory check around both decks and then sat on the upper deck, port side, and watched the sunset over Castlebay around 6pm.

That train journey was the last uninterrupted night's sleep he'd had since arriving on Benbecula. Most nights he'd been woken by dreams referencing the rape and murder of Marion Davies. He was haunted by the knowledge that his increasingly psychopathic behaviour towards women was now out of control. He'd become the kind of man he used to loathe – treating women as objects to be used solely for men's gratification. He despised men like Granby – born into privilege, pretending to respect the salt-of-the-earth British working man, but using all means necessary to make sure they stayed in their place and didn't threaten the established class hierarchy. As for working women – in fact, all women – Granby held them in contempt. Going undercover, you didn't get to pick the people you were embedded with. Even so, Ben hadn't liked the sound of Backlash during his initial 'deep cover' briefing. It was clear that Granby was using the men's rights agenda to recruit a network of dissatisfied, violent misogynists, but with a much wider objective than simply reversing 'the so-called equality legislation of the past thirty years'. Granby's big idea – to use the men's rights movement to build a neo-fascist party embedded within sections of the police, prison service and army – was just beginning to show results. When they finally realised what was going on, MI5 immediately moved Backlash from 'under observation' to 'actively engage'.

Once Granby had put the word out at his club, getting the job of his assistant and problem solver had been remarkably easy. An ex-MI5 club member 'happened' to bump into Granby and recommend a good chap he'd served with in Afghanistan, and the deal was done. Ben disliked Granby, but orders are orders. Initially, he hadn't been asked to watch the porn movies, or Granby's hook-ups with escorts, and felt he was managing his deception well. So well that Granby insisted he join him for the sex sessions. It was a disastrous test for someone with post-traumatic stress disorder; a legacy from Afghanistan. Ben's last relationship had ended abruptly when his partner left him because of his increasing desire for violent sex. He knew he urgently needed treatment for a condition that was fast deteriorating, but he couldn't reveal that to the Service; he would be transferred to a desk job the second they knew. For Granby, those sessions weren't really about sex; Ben soon realised that sex played a supporting role at best. He was a sadist who got intense pleasure from hurting and humiliating women; the greater the pain and humiliation, the more turned on he became. He only stopped when carrying on risked causing serious injury or worse, and Ben had found it increasingly difficult to separate playing his undercover role from active participation in the sadism.

The session with Marion Davies was the worst. He'd tried to send her a warning signal at the start, but she was either too scared or too high to pick it up. Afterwards, he'd felt sickened by the person he'd become and swore to himself that he'd find an excuse to absent himself in future. Luckily, he'd only had to do that once before Backlash was busted. At that point, the Service had immediately pulled him out. But the suits were concerned that he'd been seen with Davies and Granby on CCTV, and there was a possibility that she would give evidence against Granby at his trial. The risk to Ben's cover was considered too great, and he was instructed to eliminate her. It was the worst assassination he'd ever carried out; she'd put up fierce resistance. He knew he needed to leave active duties for good, but the Service had persuaded him to go off-grid for six months with a new identity instead.

Putting aside thoughts of his uncertain future, he got up, showered and then put on a cotton shirt, sweater, hiking trousers and waterproof jacket. He fancied a walk to the bakery on the outskirts of the village to buy home-made bread and oatcakes, stopping on the way back to get a few provisions at the general store. As he was leaving, he unlocked a drawer in the bedside chest, moved his underwear aside, lifted the false bottom he'd installed when he moved in, took out his Glock pistol and slipped it into the pocket sewn into the inside of his jacket. He'd had to hand in his Service-issue firearm, of course, but like almost every Special Forces soldier he'd acquired a trophy firearm in the course of his operations. There were no bars in the village, which suited him; going into a local bar would only invite unwanted questions. If he wanted a drink, he could walk the three miles to the bar in the Isle of Benbecula House Hotel. Should anyone engage him in conversation about anything more serious than the weather, and they hadn't yet, he'd tell them he was taking a few months' solitude to write a revisionist history of the Crimean War between Britain, Turkey, and France and Russia. A subject he'd always been interested in.

The rain had eased enough for the Monach Islands to be clearly visible to the west. Carry on in a westerly direction and there was no landfall until Newfoundland. The airport was operating again; a twin-engine Bombardier climbed into the clouds. The Service had arranged for landings at the airport to be monitored for any unusual arrivals. If there were any, Ben would receive an immediate message to be on his guard. But you can never be too careful, so he never left the cottage without the Glock. He had to assume that at some point they'd work out where he was, and from then it was just a matter of time before one of the passengers getting off the ferry or the plane had orders to kill him. He accepted that stoically; it was the business he was in.

21

POOLING RESOURCES

"Hello."

"Can I speak to Nigel Hatfield, please?"

"Speaking."

"My name is Julie Taylor. I represented Emily Fowler in the recent trial of her husband, Robert Mason, for murder and attempted murder. He was convicted about fifteen months ago. You may remember the trial?"

"I certainly do. I followed it closely."

"Then you presumably know that Sir Geoffrey Granby was charged by the CPS last month with possession of child pornography and directing a campaign of violence against women. Much of the evidence that led to those charges was unearthed by Emily Fowler, a police officer and me."

"I am aware of most of what you've just told me, although not your role in it. So why are you ringing me?"

"I know you've been reporting on a particular aspect of the trial, and it's probably better that I explain in person rather than over the phone. Do you have any time free in the next two days? I'm happy to come to London."

There was silence for several seconds, then Nigel said, "I understand why you don't want to speak on the phone, but I can't afford to waste time on a wild goose chase. On a scale of one to ten, what's your assessment of how interested I'll be in what you've got to say?"

"Honestly? I will be amazed if it's not a solid nine."

"All right, I'll trust you. Can you meet me at twelve this Friday, in the Pizza Express on Euston Road? It's between Euston Station and St Pancras International; convenient for you."

"That's good for me, thank you. I'll see you then."

Since her meeting with Anthony in the car park, Julie had been fitting together the pieces of the jigsaw that was the circumstances surrounding Marion's death, based on what he'd told her. Assuming Marion had been murdered – which, given Anthony's autopsy findings, seemed incontrovertible – then who had done did it? Given the speed at which Granby and his co-conspirators had been arrested and the local groups folded up, the police and Security Service must have had more information to go on than was contained in the relatively slim folders Emily had provided to the police. So, assuming that Anthony was correct that an undercover agent had been embedded in Backlash, giving MI5 chapter and verse on names, cells and structures, that man's evidence would be crucial at Granby's trial. It would obviously be given in camera, but if MI5 had good reason to believe that Marion had met this man and could identify him, then it was possible that they could have arranged her death to protect him. That didn't mean that the agent himself had killed her, but he was Julie's best lead to find out who had. And she did have the CCTV image of the three of them – Granby, Marion and a third, younger man – going into Granby's house on the occasion when Marion was assaulted. Emily was certain that the man who'd tailed her back from Macclesfield had been the same one who'd entered Granby's house with Marion. Could he be MI5's undercover agent? Marion had called him

Ben, and Emily had heard him give his name to the police as Ben Trafford.

The final piece of the jigsaw had inadvertently been provided yesterday during a phone conversation with Emily. Half-listening to her partner's latest news about Lily, Julie had realised with a shock that Emily had changed the subject.

"…don't know if you've read that this *Guardian* journalist is really ruffling feathers with his story that MI5 had someone working undercover in Backlash for nearly a year, and asking questions about whether this spook took part in illegal activities to maintain his cover, such as child pornography and—"

"Where can I find the name of this journalist?"

"Just go to the *Guardian* website and look up 'Backlash'."

Judging by a glance around the biggest Pizza Express she'd ever seen, Julie assumed she'd arrived first. But as she made her way to a relatively empty corner, she noticed a casually dressed man in his early forties looking at her, and recognised him from his picture on Wikipedia.

"Hi, Nigel, it's good to meet you. Thank you for agreeing to this meeting at such short notice."

He got up and held out his hand. She mentally changed 'casual' to 'borderline scruffy'. "Good to meet you too, Julie. Shall we order before we get into the serious stuff?"

"Good idea. I'm going to have a glass of Pinot and a capricciosa pizza."

They exchanged small talk about working in London and Manchester, the state of print journalism, and forthcoming plans by the coalition government to undermine legal aid, until their food arrived.

"You have my word that I'm not recording our conversation. Here's my phone. Please check my bag if you wish."

Nigel reciprocated, then Julie began.

"I suspect that we've both done some research on each other in the past couple of days, so hopefully I'll not be wide of the mark if I assume that you're currently investigating whether an MI5 operative embedded in Backlash was complicit in any illegal activities?"

"For the sake of speeding things along, let's assume that's close enough."

"I believe I know his identity. I also believe that he will be a key witness should Granby go to trial."

Julie studied Nigel's face. Journalists learned not to react or give their feelings away, but she clearly saw a tic at the corner of his mouth.

"You'll have to give me rather more than your belief to convince me that this meeting isn't a 'one' rather than a 'nine', Julie."

"I wouldn't expect otherwise." Step by step, Julie then laid out the strands of the story that she, Emily and 'a police officer' had uncovered to reach their conclusion about the identity of the MI5 agent. She started with their luck in stumbling upon the Cromer Street address; a London-based escort called Marion; CCTV pictures putting Marion, Granby and a mystery man together at Granby's address; Emily's evidence that the man who had followed her in Granby's car was called Ben Trafford (a name corroborated independently by Marion); Marion's evidence that Trafford was Granby's brutal right-hand man; and evidence from an anonymous source that Marion hadn't committed suicide, but had been brutally murdered. "What I *don't* have," she concluded, "is direct evidence that this man was MI5's Backlash informer. However, that's where you come in, as my hunch is that you may have contacts who could confirm whether the man in our CCTV image is on the government payroll."

Nigel had tried but failed to maintain his 'Am I supposed to be impressed?' face as Julie told her story. He clearly was. "For a lawyer, you make a passable investigative journalist, Julie. I'm assuming that you're not about to give me our suspect's picture without wanting something in return. Before you tell me what that is, though, I'd like to know what's behind your continuing interest in this? I mean, from what you've said, the three of you have achieved what you set out to do: break up Backlash and put Granby out of action."

Until this moment she hadn't decided how to answer this question, which she'd guessed he'd ask her. There was a risk that he might regard her as ruled by her emotions, and therefore not want her as an accomplice. But she had a good feeling about him, and on the spur of the moment decided to tell him the truth. Or, at least, the partial truth. "I thought you might ask that. About eighteen months ago, Marion and I were in a relationship for six months. Nothing serious – we were very different people. When I discovered what she did for a living, I ended it. We briefly got back in touch before she died, and I was moved by the desperate circumstances she'd been suffering in the preceding six months. I was so shocked when she died that I decided I had to uncover the truth, whatever it took. As to what I want in exchange for the man's picture, that's simple. I want your word that once I show you the picture, we're in a partnership until the culprit is uncovered or we admit failure. Everything I know I share with you, and vice versa. After that, the story is yours."

"You must know I can't agree to that, Julie. Even assuming I can trust you – which I admit I'm minded to – I can't risk going into a partnership. You'd slow me down and possibly compromise my investigation."

"I'm not going to haggle, Nigel. That's the deal. If you accept, you gain a vital lead; otherwise, I'll carry on with my investigation, which, given that I'm not a professional, may inadvertently make waves that are unhelpful for you. If I don't hear from you by the end of tomorrow, I'll assume your answer remains 'No.'"

22

A SHOCKING ADMISSION

"I've missed you, Emily. It seems much longer than two weeks since we walked along the canal. I'm sorry I had to cancel last weekend, but I was chasing a possible connection between Marion's death and MI5's infiltration of Backlash."

Looking around Julie's lounge, Emily was remembering the first time she'd been in this room. The two of them had been about to go to the Christmas party at Julie's firm; later that night, they'd slept together for the first time. She noticed that the pictures above the fireplace of Julie's family, and Claire and Julie skiing, had been joined by two new ones. One was of Emily and Julie outside a café in Lyme Park. She was astonished to realise that the other was of Marion smiling broadly at the camera. Trying to recover a semblance of composure, she said, "No need to apologise; it worked out well in the end. Lily and I spent the time getting stuff she needs for the school summer camp. God, you should see the list of equipment they want them to bring. Not like school camps when I was young. So, what have you unearthed?"

"Well, there has been a development. I made contact with the journalist who's been trying to establish if MI5 planted an agent inside Backlash and, if so, whether that individual was complicit in any of the crimes the police are now investigating. He was intrigued enough to meet, and when we did I told him all I know, except for the name of my source. I then offered him a deal: I would give him a copy of the picture of Ben Trafford, if he agreed to share any information he uncovered about Trafford with me. At first he declined, but he got back to me within twenty-four hours and agreed. I assume he'd been checking with his contacts in the Security Service how much information they could provide on Trafford from one picture. No news as yet."

Emily had been listening with increasing concern, and now she tried unsuccessfully to keep any hint of that from her voice as she responded. "And what happens if Nigel Hatfield comes up with the real identity and possible whereabouts of Ben Trafford, if that's even his real name? Do you dash off in pursuit of a trained killer, track him down, interrogate him, get him to confess and then bring him in? Have you thought this through further than the next ten minutes? You're really scaring me, Julie, and I'm starting to wonder just how involved you really were with Marion. Leave this to the journalist – it's his job, and presumably he has experience in confronting armed psychopaths like Trafford." Her voice had been rising as she spoke. She could see that Julie was angry.

"Your response confirms that I was right to have doubts about telling you any of this. I don't know what we'll decide to do if Nigel unearths any information about this bastard, but it's unlikely I'll be sharing any of it with you. And since you asked about my involvement with Marion, I suppose I should admit that I wasn't honest with you about that last time we were together in her flat. We realised we had deeper feelings for each other than I'd previously admitted to. Yet I then knowingly put her life at risk so that you and I could give the police additional information on

Backlash which the Security Service already had anyway – our amateurish sleuthing made little difference. So yes, I'm determined to get justice for a lovely woman who had lost her way, and I hoped my partner would be there for me and understand that."

Emily had grown sadder, but calmer. As she heard the harshness behind Julie's words, she slowly realised that their relationship was coming to an end. "I'm sorry I'm not more understanding about hearing that you'd been far more emotionally involved with your ex than you let on. It makes me wonder what else you've been keeping from me."

"In that case, I might as well confess that I've been seeing other women on Tinder for a few months."

The shock of those words hit Emily like a slap to the face. Not only had Julie lied to her about her feelings for Marion, but she been having sex with other women. Her eyes moistened. "It's fucking unbelievable that you're just casually disclosing something so hurtful like this, Julie. If you're trying to upset me, then job done. I don't feel I know you anymore. When we start to gratuitously hurt each other, I think it's time we call a halt, don't you?"

"I know I should have told you all this earlier. It was spiteful and cruel to tell you like that just now. I'm sorry."

"It doesn't seem to have crossed your mind that your plans for tracking this psychopath down pose a real threat to Lily and me. Our names are linked on a number of men's rights websites, and we'll be regarded as fair game by any unhinged extremist. We're over, Julie. Please take care of yourself over the next few weeks."

Emily hadn't been to Deepak's flat since their premature celebration seven weeks ago, following the news that Granby had been charged.

"I'd never tire of these views. It's amazing; the Manchester skyline seems to have grown since I was last here."

Deepak raised his glass. "Cheers. So, what's this latest news from Julie you wanted my advice on?"

"I never imagined that she'd take her quest to unearth Marion's killer so seriously, but she's become obsessed. A few days ago she met the investigative journalist who's been asking questions about the involvement of MI5 in Backlash, and they've made a deal. In exchange for the CCTV picture of Trafford outside Cromer Street, he's agreed to share his information and work with her in the future. He's now given the picture to a former Special Branch source to establish whether he is a spook or not, and where he could be. When I asked what the plan was if they found out, she simply said that she had to do everything she could to expose Marion's killer. It's not only mad, it's selfish. My name and yours too, to some extent, are linked to her whether we like it or not. She's putting Lily and me at risk, but she won't listen."

"Fucking hell. I see why you're worried, but if she won't listen to you, she obviously won't take any notice of me."

"I wasn't going to ask you to talk to her. I agree that it would only annoy her and probably make the situation worse. I wanted your advice on whether I should let the police know what Julie and this journalist are planning so they can keep an eye on them and step in before she does anything crazy."

Deepak's immediate thought, which he instantly felt guilty about, was, *How can I extricate myself from the never-ending drama that surrounds this pair? A better man wouldn't have this reaction.* But Emily was right; Julie's latest crusade could end up putting a number of lives in danger, including his own. If Trafford was an MI5 agent who'd been embedded in Backlash for months, then the Service would have made sure that he disappeared for a while to protect his identity. If they got wind that an irritating journalist and an avenging lawyer were trying to find him – however unlikely they were to succeed – they wouldn't hesitate to protect their man. "The problem with informing the police is that they won't simply 'keep an eye on them', like Dixon of Dock Green. They will immediately pass the information on to MI5, who could take extreme measures to stop them. I suspect that they're keeping tabs on this journalist anyway, and your intervention may well cause them to come down harder than they might otherwise. My advice, for what it's worth, is to do nothing."

"I know you're right. I guess I just needed to hear someone I trust say it. Thank you."

"You're welcome. I'm sorry if Julie's obsession is damaging your relationship. I sensed that it might be."

"Thanks, I appreciate that. I'm afraid that our relationship is over, as I can't see how we can come back from this. But how about you? Have you faced any awkward questions since Granby was charged, such as how we came by our information?"

"It's strange, because I've been expecting something like that even if it was just an 'informal' off-the-record chat with the chief superintendent. But there's been nothing, apart from my boss congratulating me on the role I may have played in exposing potential police involvement in Backlash. My guess is that the spooks have taken over the case and the police are treading carefully. How about you – any unforeseen consequences?"

"None so far. It's coming up to two years since Robert tried to kill me, and two nights ago I was lying awake thinking how much Lily's life and mine changed forever on that afternoon. Then I realised just how much we've adapted to that new normal and got on with it; with a lot of help from our friends, of course – especially you, Deepak. You took some big risks, and I doubt I'd have kept it together without you. God knows what would have happened if you hadn't been there when those fascist bastards tried to torch the house. They're still around, of course, and that keeps me awake at night sometimes. Even if Granby and the rest of them are found guilty and given long sentences, there'll always be misogynists out there wanting to hurt women."

"Thank you, Emily. Burglarising Stroud's house was a bit nuts, but it got the adrenaline going and I had the best backup possible."

They both smiled warmly at the memory.

"Take care, and please call me whenever you need to talk," Deepak said.

"I will. Thanks for being such a good friend."

23

'JAMES'

'James' had got into a morning routine – against all tradecraft advice, he knew – of walking to the westerly point of Benbecula, following the coastal path south for a couple of miles, cutting inland before heading north, then skirting the airport perimeter and returning home. Not every day, but frequently enough for it to be against the rules. On his way through the village he'd sometimes stop at the general store and get a *Times* or a *Telegraph*. He could get the online versions – wi-fi signal was surprisingly good – but they sometimes missed out some of the niche stories from the print editions. Today he bought both, folded them into his backpack and walked back to the cottage through the sea mist that had suddenly descended.

He went through his daily forty-minute workout, made coffee and scrambled eggs, and sat down to read the papers. He'd always enjoyed the *Telegraph*. Its function as the Tory Party's house journal was tiresome, but there was some serious journalism that reflected his views on human rights (a get-out clause for bad guys), a woman's role (overrated, apart from childbearing and nurturing) and the impossibility of equality (there'd always be those at the top, the weak at the bottom and the rest of us fighting among ourselves). Today it was a short piece on page six of the *Times* that caught his eye. Summarising a story from a well-known left-wing journalist in yesterday's *Guardian* titled 'Possible involvement of MI5 in website group's illegal activities', it examined the question of the culpability of agents embedded in criminal groups for crimes committed by those groups. Specifically, how could the agent embedded in Backlash have gained evidence of the attacks on women and possession of child pornography without being complicit in those activities to some extent?

He poured himself a double malt – a pre-lunchtime drink had become a habit recently – and looked out towards the sea. The mist had cleared as quickly as it had arrived. The article wasn't a complete surprise – he'd heard the rumour that a journalist had been sniffing around before he went off-grid – but it jolted him out of his comfort zone. It was only a phishing piece, of course, designed to shake the tree and see if anything or anyone interesting fell out. *Presumably the journalist's got a traitorous and disaffected contact in the Service and he's hoping he or she might overhear loose talk about me. Very unlikely, but never say never. Actually, he's done me a favour; there's a risk that I'm getting complacent. Time to take the Glock and have some target practice in the usual place. I might just be able to handle a* Guardian *journalist after a dozen firefights with the Taliban.*

He had been getting more complacent than he realised. As he'd walked past the airfield, he'd paid little attention to a group of two men and a woman standing at the entrance fifty metres away. If he had, he might have seen that one of them was holding a video camera and a microphone.

"Hi, Nigel, it's Julie. Your piece in the *Guardian* was brilliant; I'm amazed that you got it past the lawyers! What are you hoping will happen now?"

"Thank you. You're spot on about the lawyers. If you think that piece is good, you should have read it before I had to change it.

They're very spooked – excuse the pun – by anything that crosses the line from a supposition to an inference. In the end, I think I got the strongest piece possible. I've already been attacked online by a number of right-wing commentators for daring to even question whether a member of our Security Service, bravely putting his life on the line, should ever be held accountable. But that stuff just goes with the territory – I'm a big boy now.

"To answer your question, I'll just wait and see. The best-case scenario is that my contact in the Service – let's just say he's disaffected with the unaccountable culture that's emerging – will overhear or read something and get in touch. If I get a good feeling, we'll arrange to meet. That's the riskiest part, because the Service could be setting me up. If I trust them, I'll see if they can identify Trafford as the agent. If they do, then it's decision time: do I out him, or try to contact him?"

"Remember our agreement, Nigel. Where you go, I go."

"Of course."

As the start of a new school year drew closer, Colin's low mood threatened to slip into depression. As much as he loved to moan about the school, the head teacher, his colleagues and, of course, the pupils, it had been his life for the past twelve years. Feeling superior to and contemptuous of those he worked alongside, with their pathetically insincere and unctuous commitment to 'the kids', provided a purpose to his days. And he would really miss the crestfallen look on a pupil's face when he pointed out some simple error in a maths calculation. The head had spoken to him a couple of times in the past about his inappropriate use of sarcasm with pupils. He'd duly apologised, kept his head down for a while and then carried on.

But now she was seizing her chance to get rid of him. He was, in theory, still employed, albeit suspended on full pay pending the conclusion of Granby's trial. The head would have to go through due process with a board of governors' hearing to sack Colin. But his trade union had advised him that there was enough evidence from his online comments about women, and his protests outside Fowler's office (which had come to the governors' attention as a result of the publicity about Backlash), to dismiss him on the charge of 'bringing the school into disrepute'. They were advising him to settle for a pay-off and a reasonable reference. As a woman and a feminist, the union rep had made it clear where her sympathies lay.

His numerous applications for teaching posts in private cramming schools specialising in getting pupils through the public-school entrance exam had received no replies. Since he'd left the Manchester Backlash group and been suspended from his job, he'd had little contact with his fellow human beings, apart from those who served him in the newsagent, supermarket and petrol station. His one foray into paying for sex had only deepened his mood. He'd finally steeled himself to go online and arrange a home visit from 'Sally', chosen because her website appeared the least intimidating of the many he'd looked at. Sally was friendly, a bit older and less attractive than she appeared in her video, yet patient and understanding. But the act itself, once she'd managed to arouse him to a functioning state, had left him feeling more wretched than ever.

He'd joined another online men's rights group, but it didn't have the harder edge of Backlash. Reading yet another story of a wronged father denied access to his children quickly bored him. He spent most days following the latest news about Backlash-related arrests and dreaming up ways to inflict pain and misery on Emily Fowler. Finding a way to take revenge on Fowler without getting caught was proving problematic; he had to be realistic about what he could attempt on his own. Posting misogynistic hate material on the web was always there as an option, but he strongly suspected that Fowler was either inured to such crap by now, or had taken herself off social media platforms that allowed hate speech. Her daughter, however, was far less cautious, judging by her Facebook posts. She was Colin's route in.

24
—

BREAKTHROUGHS
AND SETBACKS

Eight days after his piece appeared in the *Guardian*, Nigel received a coded WhatsApp message from Tom, as he wished to be known, indicating the date and time they should meet. Should Tom come up with something useful on Ben Trafford, Nigel had no intention of involving Julie on anything other than a strictly need-to-know basis. He also suspected that she knew that, and would be checking on him as best she could, given that she still had to devote some time to earning a living. But it would be foolish to try to cut her out altogether. Julie and the other two had clearly done some impressive detective work, given the amount of information they'd assembled on Backlash under the radar of the police and Security Service. Apparently, the officer in charge of MI5's undercover operation to expose Backlash's infiltration of the police and prison services had been apoplectic when he was informed of the quality of intelligence that two lawyers and a detective inspector had put together. He was dissuaded from prosecuting them under the

Official Secrets Act only when it was pointed out that they hadn't actually broken it, and that the resulting publicity would make the Service look ridiculous.

Tom's message indicated that Nigel should wait at the aviary in Clissold Park, Hackney, at 3pm in two days from now. If he couldn't make it then he would have to wait for Tom to propose another date and time, which might be several weeks away given the level of risk involved. So he took it, even though he had to miss Spurs at home to Manchester United.

Two days later, watching a pair of parakeets on a perch preening each other, he heard a female voice behind him. "I've never liked the idea of caging birds. Having the ability to fly, but never being able to use it, feels particularly cruel. But an ornithologist told me that a bird doesn't mind, as long as it's with a mate. If the mate dies, the other will pine to death soon after."

Nigel was so taken aback to hear a woman's voice that he had to compose himself before turning round. Not entirely successfully, as Tom looked at him and said, "I see you weren't expecting a woman, Nigel. Can I remind you that the most famous recent MI5 whistle-blowers were both women?"

"Point taken, my apologies." She was in her mid-thirties, and smartly dressed in an underplayed way. He didn't underestimate the risk she was taking. "Shall we take a walk? Up to the ponds would be nice; there are still some cygnets about. What should I call you?"

"Tom will be fine."

The park looked lovely in the warm August sun. It was the middle of the week and most visitors were sunbathing rather than exercising or walking. Even so, they kept their voices down.

"Did my piece in the *Guardian* rattle any cages?"

"What do you think? People were talking about little else around the water coolers. It's a funny environment; normally everyone is desperate not to let anything slip, but when something like this hits the papers, it seems to release us all from our oath of secrecy. In summary, our man's penetration of this revolting organisation was a fairly open secret in the Service, though not at my level, until your article loosened tongues. He was ex-Special Forces, not someone to be messed with; clinically ruthless even by his peers' standards apparently."

"Do you have a name for him? Even a fake one?"

"A couple of people were indiscreet enough to mention who they thought he might be – code name only, obviously – so I looked him up on our internal rogues' gallery out of interest."

"If I show you a picture, would you confirm whether it's the same man?"

"If I do, you have to swear that there won't be the slightest hint or implication that his identity has been confirmed by a source inside the Service. All hell would break loose and everyone's life would be turned upside down."

"You have my solemn promise, Tom." Nigel felt a rush of anticipation as he took Trafford's picture from his wallet and discreetly passed it over.

"It certainly looks like the same guy. So now you know what our agent looks like, but what can you achieve with that information? He's gone to ground, apparently on the orders of the head of the Service. And no, I don't know where he is, obviously, and wouldn't tell you if I did."

"I understand, of course. Could you give me an idea of where the suits might send him?"

"No one calls them that any more. It won't be London. My guess is that they'd go for somewhere remote but with a large enough community for him to avoid standing out. Doesn't narrow it down too much, I know. Good luck, and be careful."

"You too. And thank you. I understand the risk you've taken, and I'll never reveal my source."

Colin's attempts to befriend Lily on Facebook under the assumed identity of a sixteen-year-old called David Ramsey were an abject failure. Lily had reported his messages as suspicious to Facebook and then blocked him. Having no children, and never having established a normal, friendly relationship with any pupil under the age of sixteen, he was clueless about the use of social media among thirteen-year-old girls. What's more, now that he'd been suspended, he couldn't ask anyone at school.

With a surfeit of time on his hands, he eventually came up with another approach. He would orchestrate a subtle campaign of lies about Fowler's personal life, spreading doubt about her character among her colleagues and friends. His new plan was to place fake stories about her on social media sites that specialised in gossip and disinformation. But he had to be canny about it. Too personal at the beginning, and the stories would be written off as 'Backlash II'. His first story had to be relatively innocuous, and not linked to Fowler specifically – something along the lines of 'Human rights lawyers are making our soldiers' lives hell'. From there he could expand into the denial of human rights to fathers following divorce and the role in that of particular lawyers, giving Emily Fowler as an example. The next story would name her solicitor, highlighting the role she'd played in sending Fowler's husband to prison and breaking up her marriage before seducing her.

The plan was a good one; all he had to do now was research the most promising sites to spread the message.

As the train gathered speed, Emily watched the hills around Penrith slip away, deep in thought. She hadn't seen Julie for over three weeks, since the day she'd dropped her three bombshells: her true feelings for Marion, her obsession with unmasking the person who'd killed her and her succession of one-night stands. Without the latter, Emily might have tried to save their relationship, but she knew she'd never come to terms with that level of deceit. She now accepted that their relationship was over, which made her very sad. Julie had been there for her from the beginning, just as she'd begun to feel overwhelmed by a sense of hopelessness in the face of relentless abuse. She'd fallen in love with a woman for the first time in her life, and it had been liberating, until a month ago. She'd cried herself to sleep for the first few nights, but Julie had made it clear that there were other priorities in her life. Emily needed to get on with her own life and focus on her daughter.

Back in January, soon after she and Julie had got together, Emily had promised Lily that she would take her and a friend to the Edinburgh Fringe as a treat before she started Year 9 in September. Lily had joined the school drama club the previous October largely to meet a wider circle of friends, but had soon realised that she loved performing. When she heard about the Fringe from others in the club, she'd pestered Emily to take her. There had been a full-scale teenage meltdown three months ago when Lily realised that she would have to disappoint either Tamsin, her oldest friend, or Daisy, her newest, when Emily refused to take all three of them. "Two I can cope with; three is a recipe for tears. One will always feel left out." The crisis was only averted when Daisy told Lily, in passing, that her family would be renting a villa in the Marche in Italy for the whole of August, solving the problem.

Glancing away from the window to look at the two girls engrossed in their phones as the Trans Pennine Express made its relaxed progress towards Waverley Station, Emily looked again at the empty seat beside her and thought of Julie, who should have been there. She hadn't cancelled the ticket. It was nice to have a spare seat next to her.

They got a taxi to their 'hotel' – actually an overpriced B&B just off Leith Walk, which was all Emily could afford at festival prices. She was in the only en-suite bedroom, and the girls were sharing a small twin. This evening they were planning to walk into the centre, see three performances, soak up the atmosphere along

Lawnmarket and grab a meal. Emily unpacked and switched on the TV. She wanted to catch the news headlines at six o'clock. There was a story about English students having to pay fees at Scottish universities while other EU students didn't, and another about the SNP's gains in the opinion polls. She took a half-bottle of wine from the minibar and poured a glass as the local news came on. About to switch it off, she paused as a piece to camera began about plans for the airport on the Outer Hebridean island of Benbecula. As an interview with a man she presumed to be the airport manager came to an end, the camera swung round to show viewers the gorgeous scenery. Emily continued to watch as she'd often thought of visiting the Outer Hebrides. In the foreground she saw a figure walking along the perimeter road towards the camera, oblivious to the filming taking place.

Later, she couldn't rationally articulate the physical shock that her body experienced in the moment she realised that she knew this man. She didn't recognise him at first – it wasn't until the middle of the night that it finally came to her – but buried inside her memory, she knew that she'd seen him somewhere. She continued to watch for several seconds as the man walked on and the camera stayed with the view. Her certainty that their paths had crossed was only partly based on his face, the lower half of which was bearded. It was as much to do with his gait, the way he held himself, the fluency of his movements.

Her thoughts were interrupted by Lily knocking on her door. "Are you ready, Mum? We want to go."

As the three of them walked along Leith Walk into the centre, Lily and Tamsin fizzing with excitement about the evening ahead and discussing which of the pre-booked shows they thought they'd like best, Emily kept turning over Benbecula Man's image in her mind, trying out different periods and contexts to unlock her memory.

As they approached Princes Street, Lily turned to her mother and sarcastically asked her if she was ready to join them now.

"You've been dragging along behind us the whole way, in a world of your own. We've come all this way to have fun, Mum, so please snap out of whatever mood you're in."

Tamsin glanced at Lily and then at Emily, waiting to see how she'd react.

Emily looked at her daughter, who appeared momentarily worried until she saw a smile forming at the corners of her mum's mouth. "You're absolutely right, Lily. Apologies to both of you; I saw someone I thought I recognised earlier on the telly in my room and I've been trying to remember who it was. What's our first performance?"

After taking a taxi back to the B&B at the end of the evening, she said goodnight to the girls, went to her room and poured out the remainder of the wine. The evening had been a great laugh; a real girls' night out, the first time she'd experienced anything quite like it with her daughter. Tamsin was a few months older than Lily, and that made a difference at their age. Not wishing to appear to be the younger one, Lily had raised her maturity level. *Amazing how they can do that*, Emily thought.

She hadn't thought about her mystery man all evening, and was too tired to start now. After hurriedly removing her make-up then scrubbing her teeth for ten seconds, she crashed into bed, switched off the bedside light and was asleep in two minutes.

She was driving fast along a winding mountain road in the Scottish Highlands. Lily's school had phoned her at work and told her to come and get her because she was sick. It didn't make sense because Lily's school wasn't in Scotland; it was in Macclesfield. Then she saw a car behind her, going crazily fast and getting much closer by the second. She sped up, but the driver behind was much faster, and swerved into her and pushed her off the road, through a fence and into a tree. As she got out of her car, miraculously unhurt, she saw the other driver walking towards her. She'd seen him before, she was certain of that. Twice before: once when she'd been chased by him in a Mondeo after she left Macclesfield Station, and the other time was only a few hours ago…

Emily woke up suddenly, heart racing, with no idea where she was. Realising that she'd had a nightmare, she slowly relaxed, switched on the bedside light and reran the dream. *It was him*, she thought. *The man I saw on TV was Ben Trafford, the one who followed my car months ago. The man who was working for Granby, whom Marion believed to be an MI5 agent, and who possibly killed Marion.* Still agitated, she went to the bathroom, splashed water on her face and looked at her reflection in the mirror. *God knows what he's doing there. Trying to lie low until Granby's case is over?* But she refused to dwell on it, and promised herself that she would concentrate on having a good time with the girls over the next three days.

"So, have you had any ideas?"

This was the first time that Julie had spoken to Nigel since he'd phoned her two weeks ago and confirmed that the man in the CCTV picture taken outside Granby's office was the agent who had infiltrated Backlash. On that occasion, they'd agreed that there was no need to contact each other until either had a new, practical suggestion for finding Ben Trafford. But she'd contacted him anyway, as she didn't trust him not to cut her out.

"None that we can use. We could leak the picture, either to the press or on social media, but there are several things seriously wrong with that. One, it's ethically wrong. We'd be deliberately putting Trafford's life at risk, because there are almost certainly some very nasty people whom Granby has paid to track him down and kill him. Two, Trafford is a potential witness in a high-profile trial, and we would be prosecuted for corrupting state's evidence. Three, we'd become targets for revenge attacks by his colleagues. Four, as soon as the photo went public, he'd immediately take steps to become more invisible, making him even more difficult to find."

"Can't you make contact with your source again and pump him for a bit more information?"

"That's not how these things work, Julie. You've got to trust me on this; if I lean on a contact too heavily, trust disappears and I've lost them for good."

"So that's it, then? We give up?"

Nigel sighed. "I could go back to my source and say that we would be very grateful to know if he hears any more rumours about our man, implying that there could be a financial reward. I need to think about that, and we'd have to come up with the dosh. How much are you good for?"

Julie's income had dropped substantially and she was only just breaking even each month. She had about twenty thousand pounds in various savings accounts, so, without giving the question much thought, said, "I could go up to a thousand, assuming you can match it."

"OK, if I do make contact again, I'll let you know the outcome. I'd better go; I've got a story to file in a couple of hours and it's two hundred words over. Take care, Julie."

"You too."

Julie felt despondent. Nothing seemed to be going right in her life since she'd decided to pursue Marion's killer at any cost. Was it time to give up, make her peace with Emily and begin to live her life? She pushed the idea aside. She knew this quest made no rational sense. Even if she and Nigel managed to somehow track Trafford down and persuade him to admit to his role in Marion's death – highly unlikely – MI5 would do everything to prevent that getting into the public domain. And if Nigel managed to find a newspaper to print the story without Trafford's collaboration, there was no way they would include the specific allegation about Marion's death, as she wasn't alive to give evidence. Deep down, Julie knew that this was about her as much as Marion. The only way she would be able to establish some equanimity and live at peace with herself was to know that she'd done everything possible to achieve justice for Marion.

25

LOUISE PROVIDES ASSISTANCE

"Lily, I asked you to put that letter about start-of-term arrangements somewhere safe, so it's no good asking me where it is. If you can't find it, you'll have to ask Daisy or Tamsin."

Emily spent the days since returning to Manchester helping Lily to sort out back-to-school arrangements and reading background papers on a new case. She'd decided not to do anything further regarding the sighting of Ben Trafford.

Then a friend at work forwarded her a selection of recent social media posts that had appeared on a website used by men's rights advocates. 'I thought you should see these. The site reaches a wider cohort than the usual nutjobs, and it's known for spreading conspiracy theories.'

Whose interests are the activist human rights lawyers, who've multiplied since the UK's 'Human Rights Act' came into force, actually serving? Not mine or those of working people like me, that's for sure. But if you're an asylum seeker (i.e. illegal immigrant), or a rich woman divorcing her husband, or a terrorist, then roll up!

Notice how the courts are applying the Human Rights Act in divorce cases lately? Thanks to a new breed of feminist lawyer, judges are bending over backwards to come down on the woman's side, and increasingly, men are losing out.

Yet another case recently of a woman walking free after attempting to murder her husband. Her lawyer successfully argued that the only way the wife could resist her husband's alleged abuse was to try and end his life. This is a wake-up call to all men who still think the justice system is fair to us.

Her friend's accompanying email had highlighted the diatribe's emphasis on 'activist' and 'feminist' human rights lawyers, and ended by asking, 'Are we seeing the start of a trend?'

Emily was in little doubt. She was ninety-five per cent sure about the direction in which these posts were going. They had all the hallmarks of enemy action, with an ominous twist. Compared to the online hate she'd already received, which had ultimately backfired as it ended up eliciting huge sympathy and support for her, this was more subtle. She'd sent an immediate reply:

Thanks so much for bringing this to my attention, Joan. Definitely looks like a new anti-feminist front opening up, so I'll monitor the site from now on.

Hope all's well with you.

Emily x

Three days later, her remaining doubts were swept away.

In a case similar to the one mentioned in my previous post, it appears that the solicitor defending the wife involved (who is also a lawyer) is now in a relationship with her! That gives a new meaning to lawyers sticking together. Emily Fowler and Julie Taylor, both from the Manchester area. Unprofessional behaviour, surely. Do their bosses know?

Who was behind the posts? They could be from a new group, but Emily thought not. It was far more likely that there would be a Manchester Backlash connection; possibly Stroud again. The online harassment she'd experienced ten months ago had taught her the importance of fighting back immediately. She knew now, although she hadn't then, that the police were able to hack into posts like this if they had good reason to do so. She could ask Deepak for advice about the protocol of taking that step. But he'd given her so much support over the past year, including risking his career for her when he'd burglarised Stroud's house. Plus she knew his feelings for her weren't just platonic, and she didn't want to take advantage of that. The only other person she could go to for advice about this was Louise. She hadn't been in touch with her for two months and it would be good to catch up.

Louise was intrigued and delighted when she saw Emily's name come up on her phone. They agreed to meet in a Northern Quarter bar she'd not been to before, and had just sat down with their wine when a man in a suit approached Louise and tapped her on the shoulder.

"Hi, Louise, how've you been? Long time."

Louise turned, a look of surprise on her face. "Oh, hi, Anthony. Yes, it has been. Work has been crazy lately; I've hardly got time for a social life these days."

Anthony looked at Emily and then back to Louise.

"Actually, Anthony, this is work."

Emily picked up the frisson between them. "It seems you two might have stuff to talk about, so why don't I leave you to it?"

"Sorry, Emily, that was rude of us. Let's do this some other time, Anthony."

"Sure. Good to meet you, Emily; have a nice evening."

As he walked off, Emily smiled and said, "I admit I'm intrigued, but you don't have to tell."

"Better not to go there. Let's just say there was a little misunderstanding about the parameters of our friendship. So, how can I help?"

Emily looked across the table at Louise, who met her gaze and smiled warmly. She wasn't sure how to read it, but it didn't matter. Her relationship with Julie had just ended, and she wasn't ready to start another one. She briefly went through the latest sequence of posts – how they'd built up to attacking her personally, the difference between them and the earlier, cruder posts, and her conclusion regarding where they might be coming from.

"So what's your question?"

"Do the police have the ability to hack into a site like this one and uncover the identity of the people behind the posts?"

Louise looked surprised. "Strictly speaking, the police can't do that unless we have clear evidence that a crime is being committed, as I'm sure you know. From what I know about you, you're not averse to pushing boundaries, so if we can satisfy ourselves that the person posting these claims has committed a crime, then we can investigate their identity. Given the history of online abuse that you've suffered, I think I can make a case to my boss that we need to investigate and stop this before it develops into something nastier."

"That would be great, Louise, thank you, but please don't push it if you think your boss could be awkward."

"Don't worry about my boss; she'll probably make a sarcastic comment about the importance of keeping my personal life and work life separate, then agree to the investigation."

Emily felt slightly unsettled. She wasn't sure what was happening between them, and moved the conversation on. "So, what was going on between you and… Anthony?"

"An impressive swerve there, Emily." Louise paused. "OK. Anthony's a pathologist. That's how we met: through work, after a particularly grisly murder. I liked him; he seemed like a good bloke – sensitive, funny, laid-back, particularly compared to my male colleagues in the force. We met occasionally for a coffee and a catch-up. I enjoyed having a friendship with a straight man – most of the men I know socially are gay. He knew that I was a lesbian, I knew he was straight and sexuality was never an issue in our friendship – at least, I didn't think it was. Then one evening, after we'd been out for a beer or two near my flat, he walked home with me. As we were saying goodbye, giving each other our usual casual hug, he kissed me full on the mouth. Tentative use of the tongue! I had no doubt that this wasn't a platonic kiss, and I was shocked. I turned on him, really angry, and said something like, 'What the fuck was that?! Is this Turn a Lesbian Straight Week? You realise you've just fucked up a great friendship; how can I trust you now?' And I hadn't seen him since then, until tonight."

"That explains the chill in the air. What's the matter with men – so stupid that they screw up a friendship because they can't resist going in for a quick snog? So you're none the wiser about why he did that?"

"Actually, he emailed me the next day, mortified, full of remorse and with a bizarre explanation of his behaviour. I could tell you if you're interested?"

"Am I interested? You're joking, right?"

"Just checking. About a week before this happened, he'd arranged a date with a woman who'd got in touch through his online dating page. Then, at the start of the date, she explained that her real reason for meeting was to ask him about her ex's unexplained death, as Anthony had conducted the autopsy. He told her that it was really shitty to deceive someone like that and walked out. But then he had second thoughts. There was, apparently, something dodgy about this autopsy – he never told me what – and he thought this woman deserved an explanation. As I said, he's basically a good bloke. So later that evening he contacted her and suggested that they meet in a car park near Hayfield. According to Anthony, the woman got very emotional when he told her the truth about her ex's death, and so he consoled her. That led to kissing, which led to roving hands, until she stopped it. Somewhat incredibly, this incident put the idea in his head to try it on with me, 'as I've always fancied you, so I had to find out'!" Louise paused, concerned. "Are you OK?"

"I'm sorry, Louise, I'll explain. Do you remember when this was? Or the name of Anthony's date?"

"Yes, I think so. It must have happened around the end of July, and I think the date's name was Julie."

Emily caught her breath, then said softly, "Oh, Julie, how did you get so lost? I've let you down. I'm sorry, Louise, but Anthony's date was—"

"Your partner, Julie. I've just realised." Louise reached over and took Emily's hand.

"It's a surprise, that's all. I'm fine. We split up a month ago. It was a good story, just not the ending I expected!" Emily laughed.

As a waitress walked past, Louise asked her for a brandy, keeping Emily's hand in hers until the drink arrived. "Drink this, it really will help; it's not just in the movies."

"Thanks, Louise. The date matches the occasion when Julie told me that she'd got hard information, from a source she wouldn't reveal, that her ex, Marion – at least, I thought she was an ex – had been murdered by the Security Service. After Granby and his accomplices were charged, Julie became obsessed with finding out whether Marion was murdered, and by whom. I started to get really worried about her state of mind – was she becoming delusional? I mean, how was she going to track down this person, and if she did, what did she intend to do?

"She then met with this investigative journalist, who's got a source in MI5 who might be able to find out if the undercover agent in Backlash was Ben Trafford, the guy you stopped when he was following me. And now you've just told me that Julie's source was the pathologist who carried out Marion's autopsy, whom Julie ended up meeting in a public car park.

"Sorry, this isn't fair on you, but it's been a shock realising that I don't really know the woman I was going out with for eight months."

Louise let go of her hand. She really liked Emily, but was determined not to push things. *Probably a first for me*, she thought. "Can I drive you home? My treat; you deserve it. If you give me your postcode, I'll put it into the satnav and you can sit back and relax."

As they walked the short distance to the Piccadilly multi-storey car park, Louise assured Emily that she would talk to her boss tomorrow and persuade her to put resources into identifying the person (or persons) responsible for the latest posts. Emily was exhausted, and relieved to see Louise getting into a comfortable-looking saloon car. She hadn't fancied squeezing into the sporty little two-seater she'd imagined Louise would own.

"Not the sort of wheels I thought you'd be driving, Louise, which suits me tonight. This is very good of you, thank you."

She was asleep before they left the car park and didn't wake up until Louise pulled up outside Emily's house. As Louise undid her seat belt and gently shook her awake, Emily saw the living-room curtain being pulled back slightly. Half awake, she said, "Do you mind if I don't invite you in? I don't want Lily to get the impression that this is anything more than a friend giving me a lift home."

"Which is exactly what it is, isn't it?" Louise said. "Try and get a good night's sleep. I'll ring you tomorrow and let you know what the boss says."

Emily leaned across, kissed her on the cheek, thanked her again and got out. As Louise drove out of the close, Emily found it funny that her car sounded like the one Steve McQueen drove in *Bullitt*. It was one of Robert's favourite films.

Louise felt unsettled, even reckless, as she drove home. The knowledge that Emily and Julie were no longer together had got her adrenaline flowing. On a whim, she went the long way back to her flat in Manchester, through Macclesfield and Alderley Edge. On a long stretch of deserted dual carriageway she put her foot to the floor and kept it there until the four-and-a-half-litre V8 engine had taken the car past 135 miles per hour; twenty miles per hour short of the MG's top speed.

26

ROBERT REFORMS

"Come in."

Three weeks had gone by since Robert had made his request to see Deputy Governor Colin Derby to discuss a personal matter, which was quick, apparently. He knew he'd have to tell a convincing story if Derby was going to help him, so he'd put himself in the position of a parent trying to persuade him, as a head teacher, not to exclude his son. *Present the case firmly, compassionately, but not argumentatively.* He would almost always end up excluding the pupil if the parent got stroppy. On a good day, he could laugh at the irony of his move from secondary-school head to prisoner. But only on a good day.

"Good afternoon, Mason. I'm sorry it's taken a while to fix this up. Please, tell me what you want."

Robert took a breath and began his well-rehearsed request. "I expect you know that it's been difficult adjusting to the huge changes in my life and circumstances. It's taken me a year to come to terms with the dramatic change in my status, and no longer being a respected figure in society. I'm at the other end of the spectrum, and I know which end I like best.

"Now I face the prospect of losing contact with my daughter, Lily. Consumed by anger, I allowed myself to become the figurehead for a horrible hate campaign against my wife, which has led to Lily ceasing contact with me. I heard about the 'Justice for Mason' group here in the prison and did little to discourage it, which I sincerely regret now. But losing Lily has focused me on the future. With parole, I might be free in another twelve years or so. Lily will still be only twenty-six, me fifty-eight; easily young enough to play a role in her life. But for that to happen, I need to repair the damage I've done during her previous visits.

"I'm going to write to Lily and ask her to visit me, on the understanding that I'll never lose my temper ever again. I'm determined to rebuild the trust that we had. So I'm asking if you would be prepared to write a letter to my wife and daughter in support of my request."

Derby had been glancing at the file which lay open in front of him as he listened carefully to the case Robert was making. He looked up, thought for a moment, and said, "Normally, when I make a decision on a special request from a prisoner, I draw heavily on his record. In your case, Mason, that poses a problem. On the one hand, you've been convicted of two very serious crimes, and I understand that one of our officers, since dismissed, was passing you notes about the activities of this outside group, which you failed to report. Apart from that, though, your behaviour has been exemplary and you're running sessions in the library teaching other prisoners to read. This isn't a fair question, but let me ask you, as a former head teacher, what would you do in a case like this?"

You bastard, Robert thought. *Damned either way.* "It would depend on how sincere I believed the pupil was about the difference that my letter would make to their achieving a successful outcome."

Derby smiled at him. "I can see that you were probably a decent head teacher, Mason. I will consider your request and give you an answer tomorrow. Please see yourself out."

The following morning, Robert received a note from Derby.

Give your letter to me before you send it, and I will write a short letter in support.

He hadn't been this happy since he'd got the news that Emily had been assaulted.

Louise was as good as her word; she texted Emily at 11.30 the following morning.

Hope you're feeling better this morning. I spoke to the boss and she's agreed to allocate resources to investigate the posts. Don't be a stranger – I'm here if you need a friend to talk to. Love, Louise.

The message lifted Emily's mood, but only so far. The revelations about Julie the previous evening hadn't really changed anything; Emily had already accepted that her relationship with Julie was over. But she was still uncomfortable with the way their last conversation had ended, and wanted to finish things on a less bitter note.

She had another decision to make before she made the call. Should she tell Julie that she knew where Ben Trafford might be? She decided to ask how she and Nigel were getting on with their search, and then play it by ear.

"Hi, Julie, how are you?"

"Emily, this is a surprise. I'm sorry about being so insensitive last time we spoke. I think you were about to go to Edinburgh with Lily and Tamsin. How did that go?"

That reminded Emily of the decision she would have to make before the call was over. "It was amazing! The girls loved it, although some of the acts should have had a content warning. I was uncomfortable at the thought of explaining some of the dialogue to them afterwards, but they'd got it all, and then some. They're only thirteen, for God's sake! Anyway, we had a great time, and now it's back to work for me and school for Lily.

"I called to let you know that there's a new online smear campaign against us, in case you hadn't seen it. I've gone to the police to try and get it stopped, and saw DS Crisp, that detective who helped stop Trafford when he was following me months ago."

"I remember. You made a point of telling me that she'd asked if you wanted her number."

"I wasn't trying to make a point, but yes, that's her. She was really helpful, and her boss has agreed to allocate time to hacking the site and tracing the culprit. Hopefully we can nip this in the bud. I'll let you know if there are more developments. How's your quest to find Trafford going?"

"No new leads so far. Nigel's gone back to his source and offered him money if he can find out anything more, and we're waiting to hear from him. I know what you think, Emily, but please don't lecture me again about the futility of this. Just accept that it's something I have to do until every possible lead has been investigated."

Emily bristled. *Christ, a bit of lecturing is nothing compared to your behaviour*, she thought. And then the question just came out, before her brain had sanctioned it. "Why did you have to sleep with all those other women, Julie? You must have known we wouldn't survive that level of deceit."

"There you go again, asking me a question when you don't really want to know the answer. The truth is that I was missing the thrilling, no-complications sex I got on Tinder dates before we met. Let's face it, that wasn't our normal experience, which tended to be comforting, vanilla sex. When I fell in love with you and realised we might begin a relationship, I honestly thought I wouldn't miss it. But I did, a lot. The first time, I told myself it would be a one-off and no harm would be done as long as you didn't know. I was wrong again, clearly. I'm sorry that I hurt you, Emily."

"You did. I can't help but think that if Marion hadn't died and we were still a couple, you'd still be having sex with other women behind my back. What kind of relationship is that? Where's the respect? I feel sick just thinking about it."

"OK, let's not exaggerate. You've got the moral high ground and I know you like it up there, so I think I'll leave you to it and get on with 'my quest', as you patronisingly call it."

As she listened to Julie's hurtful barbs, Emily became increasingly angry. *How dare she try and equate her months of deceit with me taking the moral high ground?* In a controlled, flat voice she said, "Good luck with your quest, Julie. Sorry if you think I was patronising you; a part of me respects your determination." She paused. "If you're really set on this, surely you're more likely to find your man somewhere remote, rather than in a big city with loads of CCTV. If I were you, I'd be concentrating my efforts on more remote places, like the Outer Hebrides, for instance."

"Oh, so now you're the expert on where MI5 operatives who've blown their cover are likely to hide?"

"Call it women's intuition."

There was a pause, then Julie said, "Please give Lily my love. I miss her." Then she put the phone down.

Emily spent the rest of the day trying to distract herself from the emotional fallout from their conversation. She went for a run along the Middlewood Way, made a long-overdue attempt to get the weeds in the garden under control, and cooked a vegetarian lasagne for her and Lily – one of her favourites.

It didn't work, but at least she felt she'd achieved something constructive by the time Lily came home from school. Instead of her usual friendly but brief greeting – 'Hi, Mum, what's for tea? Can we eat soon? I'm starving' – Lily walked into the kitchen and said, "Would you be upset if I wrote to Dad again? I don't mean next week, but at some time in the future? I've been thinking that I don't want to cut him out of my life forever, so I should give him one more chance. If he still can't have a normal conversation without erupting into a rage about you, then I'll accept it's over. What do you think?"

Emily had been half-expecting this. "I think it's a good idea. He'll always be your father and he loves you very much. He could be out on parole before you're thirty, and if you haven't kept in touch it will be very difficult to start afresh then. Let me know when you plan to write; I could help you."

"You're such a brilliant mum. Thank you. Are you OK? You look upset."

"Sorry, I didn't think you'd notice. Julie and I had another argument this morning; the worst one yet. We'd already agreed that we want very different things in our lives at the moment and ended our relationship. I knew it was coming, but I'm sad."

Lily gave her a huge hug. "You can always tell me when you're feeling low. I'm a big girl now. What time is tea?"

Two hours after her phone call with Emily, Julie remained angry with herself. Yes, she'd been resenting Emily's patronising attitude towards her determination to reveal Marion's killer for weeks, but they'd ended their relationship. So why wasn't she feeling the sense of release that she'd felt before in these situations? Probably because she'd said such horrible things to Emily about their sex life.

But there was something else. That final remark Emily had made about concentrating her search somewhere like the Outer Hebrides. Julie knew her well enough to know that she didn't make throwaway remarks about things like that. It would have come from a process of reasoning, deduction or induction, at the very least. Maybe she was getting carried away, but Julie had an idea. She pressed Nigel's number on her phone and waited.

"Hi, Julie."

"Hi, Nigel. Has the offer of two grand brought forth any further information?"

"I'm afraid not. To be honest with you, this would be a great scoop for me if I could track him down, but it's proving to be such a distraction that I'm hardly working on anything else. My bank balance is turning a deeper shade of red by the day; I think I'm going to have to draw a line soon, much as it'll grieve me to do so."

"Don't give up yet, please. I've had a lead. I'm not able to reveal my source, just like you, but before we give up, can you ask your source if he can confirm that the Service has a safe house in the Outer Hebrides? That's it: one simple question for two grand."

"OK, I won't ask how you came by this information, but can you swear to me that the source is reliable, and not some bloke in a pub you had a drink with?"

"I'm a lesbian, Nigel; I rarely have drinks with blokes in pubs. I can confirm that my source is totally reliable."

"I'll leave my guy a message this afternoon. Let's hope your source is kosher. I'll get back to you as soon as I hear anything."

It took a couple of days for Louise's request to reach the top of the cybercrime team's inbox; once they'd begun, it took them less than two hours to find the author of the posts targeting Emily and Julie. When her phone rang, Louise was deep into a cold murder case file her boss had given her, looking for connections to the recent drowning of a well-known Manchester property developer.

"DS Crisp?"

"Yes?"

"We've found your online pest. He's called Colin Stroud; lives on Hart Road. I'll send over the evidence and you can take it from there. For what it's worth, I don't think this will merit more than a formal warning, so your friend shouldn't get her hopes up."

Louise noted the sniggering way that he'd said 'friend', but chose to ignore it. "Thanks for that, Jim. I'll look out for your email." She could see that it would be difficult to get the CPS to prosecute. Emily and Julie were named in the final post, so the decision would probably rest on whether the language used posed a credible threat, directly or indirectly, to them personally. It was certainly harassment of sorts, but the bar for proceeding with a charge in cases like this had been raised recently.

After work, she called Emily to discuss the options.

"So you're saying that it's probably less than fifty-fifty that the CPS will take this further?"

"That's my assessment, I'm afraid."

"Well, from my experience of dealing with the CPS, if it's less than fifty-fifty then it's probably not worth our time trying to push it. But I want to let the bastard know that the police are on to him, to frighten him off. Any ideas?"

"I'll see if there's anything in his history that might give us leverage. Don't worry, we'll find a way to scare off this pathetic little man."

"Thanks, Louise, I know you're going way beyond your remit with this. Can I cook you a meal in return? What are you doing tomorrow evening, or the next one?"

"That's a lovely idea. I'm always up for having a meal cooked for me; I'm so bad at making proper meals for myself. The day after is better; I'm seeing a friend tomorrow. What time?"

"Come around seven. Is there anything you don't eat?"

Robert was finding writing the letter to Lily harder than he'd thought. He had to be contrite, obviously, and sincere, which he was. He'd written few letters to his daughter in the past and she would've grown up a lot since his last proper conversation with her. He had to pitch the language right. Most importantly, he knew that Emily would read the letter too, and influence Lily's decision about replying to him. She was too smart to try to ban their daughter from seeing him, but he needed to convince Lily that a third visit wouldn't turn into a repeat of the last two. He handed in his final draft to the deputy governor's office five days after their meeting.

Dear Lily,

I've thought about you every day since your last visit. I'm very ashamed of the way I behaved on that day, and I want to apologise to you and your mum for the things I said. It's taken me a long time, but I've now come to terms with the fact that I'm going to be here for many years. Some days are worse than others; I think that on the days you visited my frustration with my situation came to a head and got the better of me. But that's no excuse.

It breaks my heart to think that your last memory of me is of an angry man shouting at you and saying hurtful things about your mum. I know she's been through a lot, and we'll probably never be friends again. But I'm genuinely sorry for what I did to her that day, and for the horrible names I called her when you visited.

So I'm writing to ask you to please consider visiting me again. It's a big ask, I know, after the way I behaved, but I want a chance to remind you of the dad I used to be, and can be again. I promise there won't be any repeat of the last two visits. I may be out on parole by the time you're twenty-six, and I want to be a part of your life again, but that won't happen if I leave things as they are.

Please think about my request, Lily. I miss you very much and would love to hear about your life.

Love, Dad xx

Colin Derby replied five days later.

I've written a brief letter in support of your request and posted both letters today. Good luck.

27

THE DAYS GET SHORTER

"Come in, I'm really glad you could make it. It's such a lovely evening, I thought we could take our wine outside before the sun goes down. I can't believe it's September; the weather's going crazy."

"Sounds wonderful; lead on." Louise followed Emily through the lounge, into the kitchen-diner and out to the garden. She suddenly realised that she was walking through a crime scene from just over two years ago. *Emily nearly died here*, she thought, *and nearly killed her husband into the bargain. Yet she's chosen to stay and bring up her daughter. The woman's amazing.* "Cheers – here's to Indian summers, and more of them."

"Cheers. I went for seven o'clock as I was hoping for some sun, but I realise that's probably too early for you on a weekday. You look lovely – I assume you haven't come straight from work?"

Louise smiled to herself at the thought of her earlier preparations: leaving the office early and going home for a shower, an underarm tidy-up and a change of outfit. She'd gone for something dressier than she'd normally wear to a friend's for dinner; an emerald-green wrap dress from Topshop, black tights, her hair loose. "Too right I haven't! I wouldn't inflict the police-station scent on you." In a casual, disinterested tone, she added, "I meant to ask you when I rang earlier – did you and Julie sort things out?"

Emily didn't answer immediately, so Louise continued, "Sorry, that's none of my business; I shouldn't have asked."

"Don't be silly. After our evening out two weeks ago, I don't think there are many secrets I can't share with you. Julie told me she'd been dating women on Tinder during our relationship, we had a big row, things were said that shouldn't have been and we've split up. It's sad, but I'd seen it coming for a few weeks and we've got different priorities in our lives now. Actually, I'd like to ask your opinion about something, but it's personal."

Louise had stopped concentrating after 'we've split up', so had to refocus on Emily's last words. "Sure, go ahead. This is lovely wine, by the way."

"Something Julie said at the height of our row has got to me. She hinted that because I'm bisexual, our sex life was always going to be a bit vanilla. I'd always thought that part of our relationship was good until she became fixated on Marion, so that hurt. Do you think that she was just being nasty in the heat of the moment, or is that a common view? Please be honest."

Louise was laughing gently, not in a mocking way. "God, Emily, you don't beat around the bush, do you? Honestly, I think she reached for the thing she knew would hurt you most. There are some lesbians who regard bisexual women as frauds, wanting to have their cake and eat it, but they're too fanatical for me. I've slept with several bisexual women and I certainly wouldn't agree. I need another drink after that." *Let's go upstairs now and I'll give you a second opinion*, flashed through her mind, though she left it unsaid.

"Thanks for being honest. I'm going to sort out the dinner; I'll call you when it's ready."

Louise smiled at Emily's use of the word 'dinner' – she'd kept her southern vocabulary – and watched her walk into the house. *You can't possibly make a move on someone you really like whose first sexual relationship with a woman has just ended unhappily. You're not staying over, Crisp, so go easy on the wine.*

"OK, Louise, it's ready."

The evening was everything Louise had been hoping for. Just once, as Emily's hand brushed her shoulder as she got up to serve dessert and their eyes met, she wondered if she'd keep to the commitment she'd made in the garden. But she did, and they talked, laughed and flirted their way through Louise's regret that she couldn't have children, being a woman detective in a man's world, Emily's divorce and Lily getting back in touch with her dad. Being with Emily had felt right from the first time they'd met. After they'd discussed the next steps for putting the frighteners on Stroud, Louise steeled herself and said, "I've had such a great evening, Emily, thank you. I've got an early start tomorrow so I should make a move. I'll ring you in a couple of days when I've fleshed out the details of our plans for Stroud."

"You've drunk too much to drive, Louise; you can stay over. There's a sofa bed in the lounge, and I get up early so I can make breakfast."

"That's a tempting offer, but I've got to be in Rochdale at eight tomorrow morning and the M60 is awful at the moment. Besides, I think I'd get a few comments if I turned up in this dress!"

"But what if you're stopped?"

"As soon as I show my warrant card to the copper, I'll be sent on my way. Unless an officer is involved in a fatal crash, no one ever gets done for a traffic offence. But I will drive safely, don't worry."

"Text me when you get home, please."

They gave each other a hug and a brief kiss at the front door, then Louise drove out of the close.

Ten miles away, Julie was saying goodbye to Zoe, the PE teacher date, when her phone rang.

Hi, Julie, I have some interesting news from you-know-who. We need a discussion, and it's probably wise to meet in person. Can we meet in Manchester tomorrow, near Piccadilly Station?

Julie shivered as she read Nigel's text. She replied immediately:

Sounds interesting. Let me know what time your train gets in, I'll meet you on the concourse.

She easily spotted his gangly figure among the crowds coming through the gate for the 10.05 from Euston.

"I can't wait to hear your news. There's a coffee shop around the corner that has booths."

The place was empty save for a couple seated near the window at the front. They ordered an Americano and a latte and sat in a booth towards the back.

"According to my informant, there are two MI5 safe houses in the Outer Hebrides: one on Lewis, which is the largest island, and the other on Benbecula, which is the smallest. He doesn't know their exact locations – that's above his pay grade – but he believes that the one on Benbecula is near the small airport, and the one on Lewis is in Stornoway, the main town. Of course, this proves nothing by itself. It all depends on the accuracy of the original intelligence, and as I don't know your source, only you can judge that. There must be scores of safe houses dotted around the UK."

Julie felt exhilarated. If she was right, and Emily had been deliberately giving her a lead regarding Trafford's whereabouts, then what had looked unattainable a week ago now seemed possible. But how could she check that Emily hadn't merely said the first thing that came into her head? "I will go back to my source and double-check. But assuming that it's sound information, what are our options?"

"Having got this far, I think we've narrowed them down to one, which is to go to Benbecula and Stornoway and try to find our man. If you're convinced that this is based on hard evidence and not a hunch after speaking to your source again, then I think we should get to the Outer Hebrides as soon as possible."

They continued talking for about an hour about the journey to the Outer Hebrides, where they'd stay, how they'd approach Trafford if they saw him. They agreed that they needed at least a week to have a realistic chance of finding him, and that their earliest window for the trip was in five days' time.

"Julie? Gosh, I wasn't expecting to hear from you again." Emily squinted at her phone. Why was Julie ringing at 7.30am on a Friday morning?

"Sorry, have I woken you up? I thought you'd be up getting Lily ready for school."

"She does that herself now; she's thirteen going on sixteen, remember?" Emily found it difficult to keep the irritation out of her voice. Why was Julie ringing her out of the blue, carrying on as if they hadn't had a massive row?

"Yes, of course she is. I've not been able to get your remark at the end of our last conversation out of my mind – the one about the Outer Hebrides – and I wanted to ask you if there was a reason you said that?"

"'Conversation'? That's an interesting choice of word to describe a full-blown row during which you told me how crap our sex life was. That really hurt, Julie." Emily decided to be the grown-up and fill the silence from the other end. "There was nothing behind my remark about the Hebrides. How have you been?"

Julie felt chastened, but not enough to apologise, and she wasn't in the mood for a casual chat. "I'm OK, thanks. I just wondered why those particular islands popped into your head?"

"Probably because Lily and I had recently been in Edinburgh for the Fringe, and while we were there I saw a short piece on TV about the Inner and Outer Hebrides. I'm thinking of going there for a holiday in the spring. I've had some success tracking down the person behind that latest round of hate posts. You'll never guess who—"

"Sorry, Emily, I didn't really phone for a chat, so if there wasn't anything else behind your remark, I'll say goodbye. Take care."

And she was gone, leaving Emily fuming. *How does a relationship go wrong so fast?* she thought. *I don't recognise the person she's become. There was no way I was going to tell her I've seen Trafford; we may dislike each other at the moment, but I don't want to see her killed by some psychopath from the Security Service.*

After Louise had texted her last night as promised, she'd taken two paracetamol and gone to bed. But she was still drowsy after the early call, so she got back into bed and reflected on what exactly had been going on between her and Louise last night.

Julie stared at her phone, pissed off and frustrated.

Her story about the Hebrides was too rehearsed. She isn't giving me the whole truth.

28

STROUD MEETS HIS MATCH; LILY MEETS HER DAD

"Mum, can I talk to you for a minute?"

"Of course you can. What do you want to talk about, lovely?"

"You remember I asked you a couple of weeks ago if you'd be OK with me writing to Dad?"

"I do. Would you like me to help you with the letter?"

"I'd like you to read it before I send it, please. The thing is, Dad's just written and asked me to visit him, and I'd like to write back soon and tell him that's fine. His letter came yesterday, but I couldn't show you as you were still in bed and I had to leave for school. I wasn't trying to keep it from you."

Emily knew she shouldn't feel annoyed with Robert; he had every right to ask to see his daughter. And it was understandable that Lily wanted to reconnect with him, too. *He's paying his debt to society, and society has decided that he shouldn't be punished on top of that. Which is a principle I support – through gritted teeth in his case – but I know the bastard was somehow involved in the Backlash* campaign against me, which is still going on through that pathetic *Stroud creature, so I'm entitled to be annoyed.* "I know you weren't, Lily – I trust you; I hope you know that. Can I see his letter, or would you like to keep it private?"

"Sure, I wanted to show you. Here you are."

Emily took the envelope and saw that there were two letters inside.

"The other one is a note from the deputy governor supporting Dad's request; you don't need to read that one."

Smart move, Robert, thought Emily as she opened his letter. She was aware of Lily's gaze upon her as she read:

> *It's taken me a long time, but I've finally come to terms with the fact that I'm going to be here for many years.*

What took you so long?

> *I know your mum's been through a lot, and we'll probably never be friends again. But I'm genuinely sorry for what I did to her that day, and for the horrible names I called her when you visited.*

Another nice move, Robert, pretending that you give a shit about what you've put me through.

> *I want a chance to remind you of the dad I used to be, and can be again… I may be out on parole by the time you're twenty-six, and I want to be a part of your life again.*

Remember all the good times, Lily? I can't be that bad, can I? Emily handed the letter back, smiling at her daughter's expectant face. "Thank you for showing me. Once you've done a first draft, I'd love to look at it."

"Thanks, Mum. Love you."

"I love you too."

Julie was watching the local evening news on BBC *North West Tonight*, waiting to catch tomorrow's weather forecast. It looked like the mini heatwave was ending. The owner of a bed and breakfast in Blackpool was being interviewed about the growing number of hen parties in the town, and their increasingly wild behaviour. "I mean, us girls knew how to have a good time in our day, but we didn't go round waving giant penises at people. Some of the inflatables they wave in your face are disgusting." The camera zoomed out to show couples walking along the Golden Mile, and Julie smiled to herself, hoping for their sake that none of them were in Blackpool for an extramarital fling. *Several million people now know your secret, guys!*

She went back to half-heartedly reviewing the file on one of the two cases she was currently working on – a couple in their sixties divorcing after thirty years of marriage, following the husband's announcement that he was gay and intended to move in with his boyfriend. It should be a simple divorce as their children had all grown up, but the wife was devastated and two of the children were encouraging her to insist on a punitive settlement.

She thought back to the scene of the Golden Mile, and a light bulb went on. *That could be it! Emily said that she watched a programme about the Outer Hebrides when she was in Edinburgh. If it was live from Benbecula, and Trafford is staying there, she could have seen him in the background. She knows his face well – she's seen him close up.* Yes, it was far-fetched, but not impossible. And let's face it, any explanation as to how Emily knew Trafford's location was likely to be pretty extraordinary.

She checked the dates Emily had been at the Fringe, and began to search through local news items on iPlayer from Stornoway and Benbecula. She nearly missed him but, about to give up on an interview with the exceedingly boring manager of Benbecula Airport, kept watching as the camera panned round and zoomed out. Clearly in view, walking along the road in the middle ground, was a figure who bore more than a passing resemblance to Trafford. Julie couldn't be sure – she'd only seen him once on that CCTV footage, after all. But when she put everything together – Emily's hint, the existence of an MI5 safe house on Benbecula, this figure's resemblance to Trafford and the fact that he was walking past the airport, near the safe house – she'd certainly got enough to take the train to Scotland.

"Fucking hell, yes!" she screamed, then picked up her phone and called Nigel.

Emily was sitting by the window in Waterstones' café, looking at the afternoon shoppers ambling along Deansgate. Louise was running late, and Emily realised that the anticipation of seeing her was making her apprehensive. Her feelings for Louise had grown beyond friendship – she found her attractive, no question – and she was pretty sure Louise felt the same way. But they were being cautious about making the next move. *And why not? There's no need to rush this. If it happens, Louise will only be the second woman I've slept with.*

They'd agreed to meet to fine-tune their plans to bring Colin Stroud's online activities to an end, before surprising him at home this afternoon. Even though he'd been suspended from work, Stroud was still a member of staff at his school and an employee of the local authority. His union were aiming to cut a deal that would enable him to leave with a good reference, so he still had a lot to lose. Between them, they'd researched the names and addresses of every member of the governing body, the head teacher, and the director of education. Louise had printed a summary of the evidence from the hacked posts that proved Stroud's culpability, to be delivered to all of the above should he fail to cooperate.

Emily came out of her contemplation to see Louise walking towards her in a well-cut navy trouser suit, blue eyes smiling, attracting glances from other diners.

"It's all right for some, with nothing better to do than watch the world go by at three in the afternoon. Some of us started at six and have just come off the morning shift."

As Emily got up and kissed Louise on the cheek, she caught the natural smell of her skin and the scent of her shampoo. "Oh yes, I'm a woman of leisure these days. Well, for two days a week, anyway. Thank you for helping me to shut this man up, Louise."

"It's my pleasure, believe me."

Once they'd ordered coffee and cake, Louise showed Emily the documents she'd printed off and outlined the plan for the afternoon. "Let me take the lead; your role is to give him a huge shock and throw him off guard. I'll outline the investigation that took place following your complaint, the evidence trail that's led to him and finally the offer he can't refuse. If he agrees to delete his history and never post anything that could be taken as a reference to you ever again, then our evidence won't be disclosed to the great and the good. Every month for the next two years, I shall check that he's complying."

"Are you sure about this, Louise? This could have serious repercussions for you if he calls our bluff and lodges a complaint."

"I'm very confident he won't, given what he's got to lose. Shall we go?"

As they walked up to Stroud's front door, Emily thought about the time when Deepak had walked up this same path prior to burglarising the house. *Amazing, the risks he took for me.* Louise took out her warrant card and rang the bell. Standing next to each other, they looked at each other and laughed.

"He's coming, just behave," Louise rasped.

She was interrupted by the latch turning, then the door opened. Stroud looked a mess. Unshaven, unkempt, wearing a cardigan with food stains down the front. Emily almost felt sorry for him, until he recognised her and snarled, "What the hell are you doing, coming to my house? This is harassment. Leave now, before I call the police."

That was the perfect introduction for Louise to hold up her warrant card and say, in a calm, measured tone, "Sorry to bother you, Mr Stroud, but I'm Detective Sergeant Crisp. Ms Fowler I believe you know. I'm here to ask you questions about the abusive and illegal online posts that you've made, threatening her safety. May we come inside?"

Stroud's bravado was evaporating before their eyes, his gaze darting from Louise to Emily. "Have you got a warrant?"

"No, Mr Stroud, I haven't. But I'm not interested in searching your house. I need to ask you questions about certain posts you've made, and explain the consequences for you if you don't stop immediately."

"I don't know what you're talking about."

Louise took out a printed page showing his latest post, and held it up to him. His face crumpled. "This is what I'm talking about, Mr Stroud. We can have this conversation on your doorstep, or inside. What's it to be?"

"You'd better come in." He showed them into the front room, which smelled of a thick film of dust, stale food and ingrained filth. They both decided to remain standing.

As Louise went through the papers in her folder, explaining the evidence, it was clear that Stroud was going to cave quickly. As she was explaining that copies would be sent to his head teacher, governing body and the director of education unless he agreed in writing to cease his activities, he broke down.

"No, you can't do that. I'll be finished; I'll never get another job."

Emily couldn't help herself. "But you were quite happy to inflict that on me and my daughter, weren't you? You have no idea how much pain you caused a thirteen-year-old child."

"Thank you, Ms Fowler. Do you understand the hurt you've caused, Mr Stroud? Will you agree to stop this illegal harassment completely?"

"Yes, I swear. Just show me where I sign."

Outside, the two women grinned at each other.

"Thank you so much, Louise, you were brilliant. I think I owe you another meal."

"Absolutely not; it's my turn to have you round to my place. But please feel free to spend generously on the wine."

"That's a deal. There's still so much I'd like to know about you: your family; who you've loved; what makes you happy, mad or sad…"

"As long as I get to ask some questions as well. Can you make this Saturday?"

As the train taking Julie and Nigel to Glasgow was passing through Milton Keynes, Emily was dropping Lily outside Robert's prison. She was just providing a taxi service; once she'd accompanied Lily as far as the visitors' reception, she'd find a nearby café and nurse a coffee until Lily texted that the visit was over. She knew the wait would be stressful; during Lily's previous visits, Robert had flown into a rage, and Lily had returned terribly upset. Emily realised, selfishly, that this could be to her advantage, but she knew that Lily wouldn't feel completely secure until she believed that her dad loved her unreservedly and no longer hated her mother. *Good luck with the second of those two*, she thought.

"The prison officer will take you through from here, Lily. You've got your list of things that you want to say to him, so be firm about sticking to that. I hope he won't get angry like last time, but if you sense that it might be happening, you can ask him to agree to pause for a minute."

"Thanks, Mum, you've been great. I've got a better feeling this time; I think it will be fine."

Emily found a basic but sanitary coffee shop close to the prison in Pendlebury, ordered a cappuccino and opened the *Guardian*. She'd brought the paper with her to read about the shocking murders of two women police officers in Manchester, apparently lured into an ambush and executed. Louise hadn't been involved, thank goodness, but Emily had immediately thought about her when she'd heard about it.

When she'd fallen in love with Julie, she'd assumed it would be for keeps. She'd met Louise just as she and Julie had started to unravel, and she was finding it difficult to separate those facts from each other. She worried that the feelings she was developing for Louise might be partly a rebound response, and that would be so unfair on Louise. She spent the rest of her time at the coffee shop trying to figure out, honestly, what she felt.

Her thoughts were interrupted by the ping of a text message from her daughter.

Can you pick me up at the visitors' reception, please? I'm glad I saw Dad. There were no arguments, so I agreed to see him again.
Lily xx

Emily waited until they got home before gently quizzing her daughter about her meeting with Robert.

"I had a surprise when I walked into the visiting room; he seemed older than I remembered. He looked a bit…"

"Scruffy?"

"Yes. He hadn't shaved, which I didn't think was a very nice way to greet me. Anyway, he was very sweet – wanted to know what I'm doing at school, what I did over the summer, if I'm still friends with Daisy. I told him you took us to the Fringe and what a great time we had, and he didn't make any nasty comments about you, just asked me about performing onstage."

Emily allowed her own thoughts to intrude as she listened to her daughter go over the details of her conversation with Robert. Not taking care of his appearance was obviously a deliberate move to tug at his daughter's heartstrings, and it appeared to have worked.

But Emily felt surprisingly sanguine about the reconnection between her daughter and her ex-husband. It was going to happen sooner or later, and if it was what Lily wanted, then Emily could be the big one and accept it.

She realised that Lily had moved the conversation on.

"So I said I'd have to talk to you about it, but he asked if I could visit him more regularly from now on, like once a month? Is that OK, Mum?"

"If that's what you'd like, then as long as he doesn't go back to saying nasty things about me, it's cool."

"*You* can't say 'cool', Mum. It's not cool."

29

DIFFERENT JOURNEYS

"Tickets, please."

At the sound of the guard's soft Glaswegian accent, Nigel and Julie rummaged for their tickets and handed them over. As Julie looked up, she held the gaze of the olive-skinned young woman with deep brown eyes for a fraction too long.

"Thank you, sir, madam. Are you travelling on from Oban?"

"Yes, but we're not a couple. It's just a coincidence that we're in these seats."

"Then have safe, separate journeys onwards. I'm in the train manager's booth in coach five if you want anything."

Julie smiled as the guard handed back her ticket. The stroke of her finger against Julie's palm was unmistakable. "Thank you, Alison."

"Aren't you taking the cloak-and-dagger stuff a little too seriously, Julie?"

Nigel was clearly taking the piss, but Julie ignored him and said, "I just think there's no harm in being careful about our mission."

The wariness between them had been there since they'd boarded the train at Euston; Julie told herself to make more of an effort, otherwise it might go on for the rest of the trip. They settled back into their books – *Behind the Scenes at the Museum* for her, *The Poisonwood Bible* for him.

After they left Preston, Julie got up. "I'm going to stretch my legs." She walked towards coach five, swaying with the train, wondering what she thought she was doing. *What if I misread the signals? She probably lives in Glasgow, so how would it work?*

Alison was sitting in her tiny compartment on the left. When she saw her, she picked up her radio, locked the door, then set off down the gangway to the first-class carriage. It was only a quarter full, so they could sit facing each other in the two single seats on the left-hand side.

"I've got to prepare for the next station in five minutes, so we don't have much time. I live in Glasgow but regularly stop overnight in Manchester if I'm rostered for an early train the following morning. I wondered if you'd like to meet up for a drink next time I'm there?"

Julie felt Alison's foot against the back of her leg and laughed. "I'd like that. And if you fancy it, we could get the tram back to my place for a nightcap."

"That sounds nice. It would be good to explore… Manchester."

Julie got her phone out. "What's your number?" She added Alison's number to her contacts, then sent her a message.

See you at Piccadilly, under the clock.

Alison smiled, then said, "So what is it you do when you're not venturing up to the Islands with your non-companion back there?"

"All right, so we are travelling together, but we're not *together*. I'm a solicitor."

"Interesting. I started a law degree but had to drop out – family stuff – so we'll have lots to talk about. I'd better get back to work, but you can stay here for a while if you like. See you soon, I hope."

On the way back to her seat, feeling oddly elated, Julie heard Alison announcing the next station. Her voice sounded different; half an octave higher. "Our next stop is Lancaster. The train will be pulling into Lancaster Station in approximately eight minutes. Please make sure you take all your belongings with you when you leave the train."

Julie sat back in her seat, nodded to Nigel and relaxed, feeling happy. *Something to look forward to when all this is over,* she thought. Then she had an idea, and checked that the picture of Trafford was in her bag. It was a long shot, but she had nothing to lose by showing Alison his picture as they left the train.

Alison was standing at the carriage door as they got off.

"Can you carry on, Nigel; I just want to ask the guard something. I won't be a minute."

"OK, but don't be long; we can't miss our connection to Oban."

Julie got out the picture and showed it to Alison, pointing to Trafford. "I can't explain why I'm asking, but do you recall seeing this man on a train to Glasgow in the past month or so?"

"You do understand how many people I must have seen in that time? But I'll have a go." Alison studied the picture for several seconds, then swore. "He looks like the bastard who assaulted me on the sleeper train to Glasgow a couple of months ago. His general appearance fits: build, height and the features I can make out. He had a beard and longer hair, but it could be him. He tried it on, then assaulted me when I pushed him away. He seemed to get off on it. Funnily enough, he was going on to Oban and catching the ferry too."

The dates matched; the journey matched.

They made the 3.24 to Oban in good time, and once they were settled in their seats, Nigel turned to Julie and said, "Are you going to tell me what was going on as we left the train? You seemed to be showing the guard something?"

"I was showing her Trafford's picture, just on the off chance that he caught a train to the Hebrides. She remembered him immediately. She had a horrible experience with him on the sleeper train to Glasgow about two months ago; he groped her, then assaulted her when she pushed him off. He was going to Oban too. She was pretty sure it was the beginning of July on a Monday. That fits with the date Granby was arrested; MI5 would have wanted him out of circulation soon after that."

"So we know that our man, if it's him, has been on Benbecula for nearly two months. Combining that knowledge with his image, we've significantly narrowed our chances of tracking him down. Congratulations, Julie; allow me to buy you a drink when the bar opens."

Lily hadn't said much more about her visit to Robert three days ago, and Emily had decided not to push her. Her daughter seemed happy and relaxed, which was good enough for her. Over the past few months, it had become clear to Emily that the breakdown in communication between father and daughter had unsettled Lily more than she'd let on. On balance, she knew that it would be better for her own relationship with her daughter if Lily and her dad were in regular contact. She'd have to tell her soon that Robert had lost his appeal against his sentence; Emily had been given a heads-up yesterday by an acquaintance in the firm handling the case. While she'd never been in any real doubt about the outcome, her daughter still brought it up and Emily knew that she'd be upset. Her relationship with Lily these days was strong enough to handle any fallout directed her way. She expected Robert to take it badly, and to find a way to have a go at her. *So be it*, she thought, *as long as he doesn't take out his anger on Lily.*

The break-up with Julie had been painful and left her feeling undermined. Julie's serial deceits, which she didn't seem to think were a big deal, had gnawed away at Emily's confidence, and the things Julie had said at the end, and her obsession with Marion's murderer, had made the gap between them unbridgeable. Emily was pondering this as she drove to Fallowfield on a Saturday evening. Coincidentally, Lily had arranged a sleepover at Tamsin's tonight, but Emily had ruled out staying the night with Louise, still confused about where their friendship was leading. Louise was smart, sensitive, warm and interesting, and there'd been an immediate connection between them. But they lived in different worlds; Louise was in her mid-thirties, with no children and no past relationships that had lasted longer than a few months. Emily didn't just want a fling that fizzled out after a month or two; it would be good to have sex again, but what then? *I don't want Lily to think that her mum is going to have a succession of girlfriends, but if I raise that issue with Louise it could ruin the evening*, she thought. Her uncertainty had led to a wardrobe crisis. Louise had dressed smartly when she'd come to Emily's for a meal, but Emily had guessed that that was what Louise had thought she would like, rather than her own choice. In the end, she'd gone for jeans and a close-fitting cream cashmere top with a low V-neck.

She pressed the buzzer labelled 'L. Crisp', pushed the door on Louise's command and walked up to the second floor, two bottles of wine clinking in her cool bag.

Louise was standing at the door to her flat, smiling broadly. "Welcome to my cosy little abode."

They gave each other a quick embrace as Emily stepped over the threshold, indecision precluding anything more intimate.

"Pouilly-Fumé, nice and chilled."

"Thank you! Let's go through to the lounge; I'll get you a drink."

Emily followed her into the lounge-diner, pleased that Louise had also dressed down, and took in her surroundings as Louise poured the wine. Simple and uncluttered, but with a number of flourishes reflecting Louise's taste: a large Turkish rug, art deco sideboard and sofa. Emily relaxed, and found herself thinking that this would be a pleasant place to spend some time in.

"I've made a variation on ratatouille by not slavishly following a Jamie Oliver recipe. I hope it's OK." Louise paused, handed Emily a glass and said, "I want to propose a toast. To my wonderful new friend, and to us, whatever 'us' turns out to be in the future."

"To us. And to the coolest police sergeant I've ever met. And I've met a few. The ratatouille smells wonderful. Full marks to you and Jamie."

Over the course of the evening, Louise revealed far more than before about herself. After she'd come out and been thrown out by her parents, she stayed with her aunt, got the A Levels she needed to do criminology at Manchester University, had a wildly promiscuous three years at Manchester, got a first, travelled around Europe, India and South America with an older lover for a year, tried a number of jobs when she came back but couldn't settle down in a career or a relationship, joined the police on the graduate entry programme at twenty-seven and been sexually assaulted by a male trainee and ostracised by her colleagues (including some women) when she'd made a complaint, then graduated from the programme with the second-highest score. She'd since reconciled with her mum and hadn't had a serious relationship in three years.

"How old was your travelling companion?"

"She turned thirty-one during the year we were travelling."

"So nine years older. Do you go for older women, then?"

"I go for gorgeous older women, as a rule, but I made an exception in your case." Laughter. "Tell me honestly – didn't women ever come on to you before you met Julie?"

Emily blushed. "If they did, I didn't notice."

Louise went quiet for a moment, then said, "So, what do you want 'us' to be in the future?"

Emily refilled her glass and topped up Louise's. She'd decided she had to give her the honest answer she deserved and not avoid the question. "I've been thinking a lot about us and where we're going over the past two weeks, including on my way here. Unless I've completely misread the signals, there's something more than just friendship developing between us. There is for me, certainly. But I'm confused. Julie and I were a serious item and I thought we'd be together for a long time. She'd become good friends with Lily, and that was important to me. Yet look what happened to us."

Louise was looking at her with a slightly anxious expression. But Emily carried on, talking frankly about her concerns regarding their different lifestyles, stages of life, situations, and the possible impact on Lily.

"I need time to know beyond doubt that my feelings for you have nothing to do with the break-up with Julie. That damaged my confidence, which has gradually been recovering since we've got closer. You also need to be sure that you want to take on someone on the wrong side of forty who has a teenage daughter. I know that no relationship can come with a lifetime guarantee, but it's important you understand that I don't want a two-month fling."

Louise pulled Emily closer. "Thank you for being so honest. I'm sorry if I've been pushing things, because you clearly need time to get over the pain of the break-up with Julie. As an aside, I reckon I'm pretty good at connecting with teenagers. And I can wait for as long as it takes, because I'm crazy about you."

"I'm crazy about you, too."

They carried on talking over coffee, grapes and cheese until one in the morning, when an idea formed in Emily's head. As they hugged and kissed each other goodbye on the doorstep, she said, "How do you fancy meeting again in two weeks, if you're not working over that weekend? I'll arrange a treat, on me."

"But I specifically reserved a room with two single beds."

"I'm sorry, madam, but I'm afraid my colleague failed to make a note of that, and the twin room has already been taken by another couple."

"That's why I specified single beds: we're *not* a couple, but we couldn't afford two separate rooms, so you'll have to give us a second room – for no extra charge, of course."

"That's impossible; we're fully booked. We can put a folding bed in your room. I'm sorry; it's the best we can do."

"It isn't. You can put the folding bed in, *and* give us a good bottle of white wine with our meal this evening."

"Actually, make that a red as well. I don't drink white wine – what's the point?"

The receptionist went for the line of least resistance and reluctantly agreed.

Julie and Nigel had had to make an enforced overnight stay in Oban, as the daily ferry to Benbecula left early in the morning. Confirming their table for two at eight o'clock, they went out for a walk around the port. Rather than discuss their plans for the next week, which they'd already gone over at length, they agreed to talk about anything else for this evening.

Nigel told Julie that he'd been a journalist since joining the *Sheffield Telegraph* as a junior reporter after leaving school at eighteen. Several newspapers later, he landed a job as a staffer on the *Guardian*. Initially he'd loved it, but he'd soon realised that it was investigative assignments that really excited him, and unfortunately the *Guardian* had enough full-time investigative journalists on its staff. So he'd gone freelance on the understanding that the paper would look favourably on his stories, which had worked well until recently, when he'd hit a dry patch – hence his desperation to break this story. He'd married in haste at thirty when his girlfriend of nine months became pregnant; the marriage had lasted longer than anyone thought possible, but finally collapsed after eight years due to Nigel spending long periods away from home, chasing stories all over Europe. At forty-three he'd never stinted on maintenance for his son, but financially things had never been tighter. He didn't have a regular partner, but occasionally hooked up with a woman he'd gone out with in his twenties, who was in a similar situation. As he finished his story, he looked expectantly at Julie.

"I came out in 1996, in my mid-twenties. Hardly a pioneer, but it was before civil partnerships were introduced and if you weren't living in London or Manchester – my first job after graduating was with a solicitors' practice in Buxton – then it felt ground breaking. I'd dated a few men at university. One, Brian, I really liked. We had loads in common – politics, sense of humour, films, the usual 'lonely hearts' list – and our friends had us down as a cert to be the first in the group to be married. But as we walked around campus I'd find myself looking at and lusting after women, wondering why I never had those feelings for Brian. Sex was something I just participated in. I don't find men's bodies revolting; I'm just not sexually attracted to them.

"I eventually came out to Brian. He was devastated, which I thought was a bit over the top, but he understood. He was my last boyfriend. By then I'd left university and was working as a junior solicitor. I started dating women immediately and of course fell instantly in and out of love with all of them. I left the Buxton job for a much bigger practice in Manchester, specialising in cases of domestic violence and sexual assault. About nine years ago I met Claire, and in 2005 we formed one of the first civil partnerships in Manchester. She was the love of my life, but she was five years younger than me and suddenly decided she wanted children. I wasn't prepared to take on such a life-changing responsibility at thirty-nine, so we broke up. I then became a Tinderholic, having a wonderful time with lots of gorgeous women. When I saw Emily's case, I knew I had to take it on. But life doesn't always turn out the way you expect it to; as you know, I fell for Emily, then threw myself into supporting her throughout the Backlash attacks. Sadly, we've now split up."

"I didn't know that. I'm sorry."

"Once Granby was arrested and the police began to break up the Backlash cells, she wanted to move on, but I couldn't, because of Marion. I have to find out what happened to her, but Emily became increasingly exasperated with my 'quest', as she called it. If I'm honest, I've probably never got over Claire completely. Also, I didn't think through the implications of starting a relationship with a woman who'd been happily living with a man for seventeen years. We were probably doomed, anyway. Are you hungry? I'm starving – shall we go back for dinner?"

Ben was feeling restless. It was the beginning of October, the nights were quickly drawing in and lasted longer than the days. Depressing, but it did mean he'd be less conspicuous. Not that he worried too much about that now that he was the owner of a bushy beard and hair growing over his ears.

His book on the Crimean War was making slow progress, if any. He hadn't had the luggage space to bring much reference material with him, and while there was a library on Benbecula, its resources were limited. If he joined, the librarian was happy to order books from Oban library for him, even asking on one occasion if he'd like to go for a drink, but he knew that the smaller the trail he left, the better. He hadn't ordered materials online for the same reason. He could, and did, research information on his browser, but that was slow going. The world would just have to wait a bit longer for his magnum opus.

He'd initiated a once-a-week around-the-island walk, which he could yomp in under seven hours. The tough walking was on the east side, where the soft, peaty terrain was criss-crossed with countless inlets and streams, making progress slow. A body left in one of the more remote inlets might remain undiscovered for weeks in the winter. At the end of each walk he'd developed the habit of calling in at the Isle of Benbecula House Hotel, breaking another rule. Apart from a 'What can I get you?' from Farquhar, the landlord, he was usually left to enjoy his pint by himself.

This week's walk proved an exception. The weather had been filthy; a gale-force north-westerly carrying driving rain that had penetrated his waterproof gear within two hours. Even though he'd cut short the walk, he was soaked through by the time he got to the hotel. He'd expected to be the only customer, and was surprised to see that there were three others in the bar. *Sheltering from the storm, of course.* He took his Guinness and haggis to a table away from the bar, then began scrolling through his phone after removing it from its waterproof pouch. This was aimed at warding off unwelcome attention from friendly locals, as he'd checked his phone before he left that morning.

He heard a car door slam outside, before an overweight middle-aged man holding a coat over his head burst through the door. Ben recognised him as a taxi driver he'd seen parked up in Balivanich, waiting for a fare. The man ordered a pint and a pie, brought them over and sat at the table next to Ben's.

"You got caught in it, I see."

"I certainly did."

"Haven't I seen you in Balivanich a couple of times?"

"Possibly; I sometimes go to the bakery."

"I take a lot of my fares there. Trade like that keeps me going through the winter, now that the tourists have almost stopped. Mind you, eight came off the Oban ferry yesterday, including a couple I've never seen before. I took them to Balivanich."

"What makes you think they were tourists?"

"Apart from my experience picking up hundreds of them every year for the past fifteen years, you mean? They told me they were here for a couple of weeks' walking and birdwatching."

Ben needed to know more, but he also knew he had to be careful not to arouse interest by asking too many questions. "Not exactly a romantic getaway, then?"

"I wouldn't think so. They were both around forty and quite business-like with each other, especially her."

Ben sensed that he'd gone as far as he could, but then the taxi driver said, "I did overhear her asking him if he'd told the paper that he was here. Maybe he's a journalist doing a piece about the wildlife."

"Oh, really? I'd be interested in talking to him about that. I don't suppose you noticed where they went when you dropped them off?"

"Afraid not. They asked to be dropped by the general store, not their accommodation."

"No worries; I may see him around. Thanks, anyway."

After Ben got home, he showered, dressed in dry clothes and sent a message on the secure phone asking for a picture of the *Guardian* journalist. Then he went online and checked current availability for short-term rentals in or near Balivanich.

30

ARRIVALS

Julie and Nigel's Airbnb cottage was a pleasant surprise. It was set back on a turning off the main road south from the village, a short walk to the dunes and the Irish Sea, and ten minutes from the village stores. They'd asked the driver to drop them there deliberately; if Trafford was living in Balivanich, they didn't want a local taxi driver to know where they were staying, and it meant they could stock up with a few extra provisions. It helped that they'd agreed to travel light; they had everything for their trip packed into a forty-litre rucksack each, and it was dark by the time they walked through the village to the cottage.

Much of the housing looked like it had been built in the past twenty years: single- or two-storey terraces of boxy cottages, painted off-white and arranged in small estates off the main road. In addition to the mini-market, they passed a bakery, a garage and a primary school. The population had to be less than a thousand, probably nearer five hundred, and the landscape was surprisingly flat. Not what they'd imagined. After following the owner's directions along the main road south for about five minutes, they took a right turn and in three hundred metres arrived at their home for the next week. Unlike almost all of the housing they'd seen so far, this was a modernised crofter's cottage, probably about two hundred years old. Inside it was clean, functional and well equipped, though little of the original character remained. Warm, though, as the owner had put the heating on in advance. Two bedrooms and a bathroom upstairs, with the living room, kitchen, utility room and toilet on the ground floor. They dumped their rucksacks on the beds and started on the evening meal. They'd agreed to cook it together on the first evening – she'd do the starter, he'd cook a beef stroganoff.

Sitting at the table an hour later, Nigel raised his glass of red. "Here's to you, Julie. I want to admit that I underestimated you from the start, and apologise for my unconscious sexism. Without your somewhat unorthodox methods of retrieving information, we wouldn't be remotely close to where we are now. Cheers. And thank you."

About fucking time, she thought. *Though I'm not too sure about the 'unconscious' bit.* But in the interests of continuing the close working relationship they'd built up over the past month, she bit her tongue and said, "Thank you for that, Nigel, I appreciate it. We've got very different reasons for pursuing this guy, but I feel there's real trust between us. I'm here for you as well as me, and I feel it's the same for you. I know we'll support each other."

"I second that. As a journalist, I'm not used to working with anyone else, so this has been a revelation for me. Here's to us." Nigel hoped he'd sounded convincing, as there was no way that he saw this as a cooperative venture. He was here to get a meeting with Trafford and an admission that he'd infiltrated Backlash and committed illegal acts while undercover. He'd work hand in glove with Julie until they tracked Trafford down – if they did. After that, he'd use every trick he'd learned in twenty years as a hack to put himself in front of her. He wasn't even sure how she intended to get Trafford to admit he'd killed Marion. Why would he?

They spent the rest of the evening discussing their plans for tomorrow, which they'd agreed to review at the end of each day. They would work independently, in plain sight, under their respective cover stories: he was an amateur ornithologist hoping to grab memorable pictures of migratory birds massing as they set off for Africa; she dabbled in watercolours and hoped to paint the spectacular sunsets that occurred at this time of year. And all of the time, they would be looking around for Trafford. If one of them saw him, they'd attempt to follow him back to his house without being seen. They agreed that neither of them should approach him without other people around – it was too risky. Their routine would be governed by the weather. Luckily, dry spells were forecast in between the regular rain showers.

Emily had followed through on her promise. In the bar on the twenty-third floor of the Manchester Hilton, Louise took another sip of her mojito, turned her gaze from the view over the city towards Emily, and said, "This is fantastic, Emily. When you say 'a surprise treat', you don't mess about, do you?"

Emily grinned back at her. Two weeks ago, when she'd promised to arrange a treat for their next date, she didn't have anything particular in mind. The following morning, thinking about their conversation the previous evening – 'I'm crazy about you', 'I'm crazy about you too' – she'd thought, *If that's the case, there's no point in hedging your bets. Go for it and fix a night to remember.*

"After our last evening together, I wanted to dazzle you a bit. Plus I've never been here before. I hope you're hungry."

They moved on to the Podium restaurant in the same hotel. They'd just ordered when Louise leaned across the table, lowered her voice and said, "Don't turn round, but there are four guys from the force on a table behind you. Three of them are OK, but I've had a run-in with the fourth one in the past. He's a homophobic prick and has been glancing over here. Just ignore him if he starts anything; I'm not going to spoil the evening by responding. This is such a wonderful surprise, Emily, thank you. If I didn't know better, I'd think you were trying to seduce me."

Emily laughed, thinking, *If only you knew*, and said, "As if."

Halfway through their main course – over-presented but delicious – they heard a man's voice, louder than was appropriate for the setting. "They're obviously paying detective sergeants too much these days, if they can afford to eat here. What do you think, lads?"

Louise looked at Emily and said, "Ignore it."

"Mind you, she's probably not paying, looking at the posh totty she's dining with. Not paying in cash, at least."

Laughter.

Emily turned to look at the group, got her phone out of her bag, took the heckler's picture and turned back to Louise, who was looking furious and mortified in equal measure. "What is it about women that some men find so threatening? I'm never going to get it."

"Sorry, love, am I disturbing you eating out with your 'friend'? Never mind, I bet you'll be enjoying more eating out later, won't you?"

More laughter.

"Sorry, Louise, but I haven't spent the past year fighting misogynistic abuse like this from pigs like him to sit here and do nothing."

Louise smiled. *This I've got to see*, she thought.

Emily got up and walked over to the men's table, heart racing. She didn't have a speech in her head, but knew the words would come. She stood in front of them and looked straight at the culprit.

The smirk on his face was fading, but he hadn't given up yet. "Sorry, darling, have I interrupted your meal with my gay colleague over there? I didn't mean to upset you. Go back to your seat, there's a love."

By now, other diners were looking in their direction and the room had gone oddly quiet. Emily was horribly aware of how exposed she was. *Forget everyone else; just imagine you're in court and focus on this idiot in front of you,* she thought. In her courtroom voice, she said, "I've spent the past nine months working with the police to uncover the names of officers connected to a revolting group of men who hate women. You may have heard of the operation; it culminated in the arrest of Geoffrey Granby, the group's leader, three months ago, and the suspension of several officers. We're uncovering more names all the time. Does that ring a bell? Can you guess where I'm going with this?"

The loudmouthed man's face had gone very pale, and the rest of the group were squirming.

"The deputy commander of the Greater Manchester Police asked me to join a panel advising him on ways to stamp out sexual harassment in his force. You can be sure that he'll hear about your little show this evening, gentlemen, names included. Enjoy the rest of your meal."

One of the other three men at the table called out, "It was only Derek, not us. He's an idiot."

"But you just sat there and said nothing, didn't you? Until blokes understand that as long as people say nothing while misogynists like your mate spew out their poison, it'll never stop."

As Emily turned away, a woman at a nearby table applauded, followed by another, then another. As she sat down, a young woman approached with a menu in her hand.

"You're Emily Fowler, aren't you? I think you're amazing; I followed your case all last year. Can you sign my menu, please?"

Emily signed, embarrassed. The four men were now receiving abuse from diners at several tables, and quickly got up and left. The manager came over to Emily and Louise's table, carrying two glasses of champagne.

"I must apologise for the behaviour of those men, and would like to offer you this meal on the house and two glasses of champagne to make up for the disturbance to your evening."

"Thank you, that's very much appreciated."

Ever since Emily had sat down, Louise had been staring at her with a look of amazement and admiration. She lifted her glass. "To my amazing friend. Cheers! It wasn't just what you did; it was the way you did it. The look on his face! Is it true – are you really on some panel advising the deputy commander?"

"Of course, though I probably implied that it carries more clout than it actually does. I understand if you don't want me to raise this with your boss, given that you might have to work with those creeps."

"You must be joking; I insist you take it up with him."

Half an hour later, Louise said, "Thank you, Emily. This has been such a brilliant evening, I don't want it to finish."

"Who says it's finished? Come on."

After Louise had downed the last of her champagne, they collected their coats and went to the lifts. As she entered the lift, Emily shielded the buttons from Louise and pressed number eighteen. They descended five floors, then stopped, and Emily got out and held the door.

"Are we getting out here?"

"Well, I am, so I think you probably should as well."

"Where are we?"

"Let's see. Here, it's got a number on it that corresponds to one of these doors, I believe." Emily handed Louise a card with a room key inside.

Louise looked at Emily, wide-eyed, mouth open. "I don't believe this! You've got us a room in the Hilton?!" She looked at the number, ran down the corridor, stopped at the door, waited for Emily, opened it, walked in and shrieked. "Are you kidding me?" Then her huge grin softened, and she said, "There might be one problem. I haven't got any stuff, or a change of clothes…"

Emily picked up a small case next to the bed. "I may have missed a couple of things, but I think all the essentials are there."

"How did you…?"

"It was a combination of grabbing a few things from your flat when I used the en-suite bathroom, and buying stuff like tights, cleanser, eye make-up and so on. If there's anything else you need, you can use mine."

"I don't know what to say, Emily. I'm blown away. The whole evening… I've never had anything like it. And when you got up and challenged those guys, seeing you standing there, confronting them – my God, it was such a turn-on. It's OK, I'm not making any assumptions; we'll take our time."

"Louise, do you think I'd take you out to dinner and book a room at the Hilton if I just wanted to sleep? What a wasted opportunity that would be. Why don't you check the case and slip into something more comfortable while I go to the bathroom?"

Louise unpacked the case and undressed while Emily brushed her teeth and took her clothes off. She was pleased with herself for bringing this off, and so happy to see Louise's reaction. Glancing in the mirror, she opened the door and stepped into the bedroom.

Louise was in bed, under the covers. As Emily walked towards her, heart racing, Louise pulled the sheets back. "Emily Fowler, come here. I'm taking you into custody."

Ben knew that he must now work on the assumption that a journalist and his accomplice – probably a photographer – had tracked him to Benbecula. According to the taxi driver, they could have been there for up to two days, but as they hadn't yet come knocking, he could also assume that they didn't know where he lived. His first priority was to find out where they were staying. First rule of his trade: *Find the enemy before they find you.* Online he'd found six possible places for rent in or around Balivanich, and identified them on his map. Four were newer terraced houses in the estates in the middle of the village, and two were older cottages on the outskirts. His plan was to observe three tonight, and three tomorrow. He decided to begin with three of the more modern houses, his theory being that if a civilian was putting himself in harm's way by trying to track down an MI5 officer, he would want to be surrounded by as many neighbours as possible. Of course, that also meant that Ben would stand a greater chance of being seen.

Two of the houses backed onto open moorland, so he'd decided to approach them across the fields to the rear at 8pm. At that time, there was a good chance he'd see the occupants moving about inside or putting rubbish out. Setting off across the field, he crouched down and ran the final twenty metres to a low fence at the back of the first house. If anyone saw him, he'd say that he'd lost a small pair of binoculars this afternoon and gone back to search for them. Crouching next to the fence, dressed from head to toe in black, a passer-by would be very lucky to spot him. Using a night-vision scope he could see into every room that didn't have curtains drawn, and after ten minutes he'd seen enough: two adults, around thirty, with a young child and a baby. He crossed the next house off his list immediately; there were several students sitting around a brazier on the patio, smoking joints and drinking vodka. *I wish I could join them*, he thought.

The last house of the evening could only be observed from the road at the front, which was a cul-de-sac. Ben had collected some promotional flyers from the general store to provide cover as a leaflet distributor. As he passed the house on his way to the end of the close it seemed deserted, so he carried on, turned round and started to walk back, putting leaflets through a couple of doors on the way. Reaching the target house, he walked up the path to the front door and peered into the front room. It was obviously occupied, and he was about to look through the letter box when he heard voices. Following the sound, he saw a young couple, all over each other, walking into the close. He put a leaflet through the door and walked away from the house towards them. He nodded in their direction, just as the woman said, "Did you just come from our house?"

He held up the sheaf of leaflets, as if by way of explanation, and walked up the path to another house for appearances' sake. As he left the close, he turned to see the couple letting themselves in. *Another one crossed off*, he thought.

Back in his cottage, shepherd's pie leftovers from yesterday warming in the oven and a double Laphroaig to hand, he worked out the safest route for tomorrow evening's observations. If his database of available accommodation was correct, it had to be one of the remaining three cottages.

At the end of their first unsuccessful day attempting to spot the elusive Mr Trafford, Nigel and Julie sat catching up in their comfy little lounge, peat burning surprisingly well on the multi-fuel stove. Julie seemed deflated; this didn't surprise Nigel, who knew she'd had an overly optimistic idea of how easy this would be. But even he had to admit to being disappointed.

"I obviously didn't think we'd bump into him on our first walk down the main street, but I soon realised that the problem with my 'amateur painter' cover story is that all the places that make any sense for a painter to set up are isolated. I hardly saw anyone all day, except when I went into the village to get rolls from the bakery, and then I probably drew attention to myself by constantly looking around for anyone resembling Trafford."

"Unless we got lucky on the first day, this was always going to be a frustrating period. If I was him, a super-fit action man cooped up in the back of beyond, I would be desperate to maintain a certain level of fitness. The obvious time to do that is early in the morning, so I'm going to get up at dawn tomorrow, dressed in my twitcher paraphernalia, and patrol the dunes from here to the airport. I'll then swing back around in a loop through the town."

Julie decided to ignore the mansplaining lecture about how 'this was always going to be a frustrating period'. "That makes sense. My artist guise just doesn't work, though. The weather makes it unsustainable – someone striding out with an easel and a box of paints when it's either about to rain or actually raining looks fucking ridiculous. I've decided to keep things simple and go for walks around the village and the surrounding area in the morning, afternoon and evening. Hopefully I'll be seen by a different group of residents each time and won't arouse suspicion. Here's to better luck tomorrow."

"And to you, Julie."

"Try not to wake me in the morning, please. I'm not at my best before eight o'clock."

Julie was woken just before seven as Nigel banged the door on his way out. Cursing him, she decided to make herself a cup of tea and go back to bed. She was more pessimistic than at any time during the past two weeks, when each day had seemed to offer new hope that she'd finally confront Trafford. That hope had now received a reality check.

Out of the blue, she thought of Emily. Their last conversation a month ago had been awful, when she'd rung to ask Emily why she'd mentioned the Outer Hebrides in their previous conversation. Of course Emily had seen Trafford in the BBC Scotland clip about Benbecula; she'd denied it at the time, quite possibly because she feared for Julie's safety if she confronted him. Or maybe because Julie had said such hurtful things about their sex life, which she'd never apologised for. She'd felt like a complete shit after that call, but couldn't bring herself to apologise because she was angry with Emily for not understanding how important it was for her to find out who killed Marion.

She decided to text Emily with an update.

Hi, Emily, I don't think we've gone this long without contacting each other since we met. I miss you. A lot has happened in the past few weeks. Nigel Hatfield and I are in the Outer Hebrides, on the trail of Ben Trafford. Your slip of the tongue got me researching it, and we've also had independent confirmation that he's here. No sign yet, though. I hope we can still be friends after I've laid this to rest. Love, Julie x

It was still only 7.30; she pressed 'Send'. Writing the message had brought a pang of regret, and now Julie was thinking about everything they'd been through together and the happiness they'd once shared. *I might as well get up and make myself some porridge,* she thought.

31

HUNTER AND HUNTED

Emily's phone had been on silent all night, so she didn't hear Julie's text message arrive. At that moment she was enjoying breakfast with Louise in their bedroom on the eighteenth floor, thinking about what had happened between them a few hours ago. Slowly exploring each other, delighting in the smell, taste and feel of their increasingly sweaty bodies as they merged and uncoupled. The prolonged anticipation, then exquisite release, at the end. *Carpe diem.*

Louise looked at Emily. She didn't need to ask what she was thinking. Last night had been different to her other 'first times'. *I'm falling in love with you, Emily, and there's nothing I can do about it,* she thought. "This has been amazing," she said. "Everything – the surprise, the hotel, you facing down those twats in the restaurant. Then last night..."

Emily came out of her reverie and smiled. "It was pretty good, wasn't it?"

Louise leaned over and kissed her, sliding her hand along her thigh. "What time do we have to check out?"

"Not for two hours."

"I can't get enough of you."

"Hmm. Well, I'm here for the taking."

Trafford had got up at dawn for an early morning run along the dunes. If Nigel had left five minutes later, he would have passed him, but all he saw was a well-built man in a tracksuit with the hood up, running at a medium pace about five hundred metres ahead. After trying to track him for five minutes, Nigel gave up, lungs bursting, coughing up phlegm. *The guy's clearly fit*, he thought.

Ben wanted to think through his next moves and check that they made sense. Running helped him to do that. Assuming he managed to track down his pursuers this evening, he'd decided to surprise them in their cottage at the crack of dawn the following morning. People were always least well defended when roused from sleep, and he wanted to make the most of that advantage. He would take the gun with him, just to make sure they complied with his reasonable requests: sit two metres apart, hands on heads, while he went through their ID to see who he was dealing with. If, as he assumed, they were both journalists, he'd outline the only deal he was prepared to offer them; take it or leave it. If they decided to leave it, he knew what he had to do.

On the spur of the moment, he decided to extend his run: past the three houses he'd checked out yesterday, then skirt the airport, over the causeway, turn around, return via the outskirts of the village and loop back to the cottage. It was on his return leg, distracted by thinking about how much he'd demand for information about Backlash, that he saw – too late – a woman walking along a side road that intersected with his. She was definitely not a local. There was less than thirty metres between them as he passed the end of her road. At least he had his hoodie pulled up over his head, but he had to assume that she'd clocked him. He kept running, picking up his pace enough to ensure that she couldn't follow him for long. It didn't change anything; by midday tomorrow, this would be decided one way or another, assuming he identified their cottage this evening.

Julie had been traipsing round the village for half an hour on her first walk, a light but penetrating rain beginning to soak into her poor choice of coat, and feeling increasingly despondent, when she suddenly saw a man running along the main road ahead of her. He was wearing a hoodie and his beard made positive identification impossible, but he could be Trafford. He had the right build, and looked to be around the same height and age. Frustratingly, she couldn't run after him; if he saw her, he'd realise immediately what was going on. Luckily, she had a signal and Nigel picked up on the third ring.

"Nigel, I've just seen a man running south along the A865 who looks like he could be Trafford. If you're anywhere near that area, watch out for him."

"Great, well done. I'm not that far away, so I'll run over there now. Speak later."

Scrolling through her messages, she noticed that her text to Emily hadn't been picked up yet.

Emily had only just remembered to message Lily and check that her sleepover at Tamsin's had gone well. As she and Louise stepped out of the lift into the lobby, she turned her phone on, heard a ping but ignored it as they were about to say goodbye. Louise had to get home and start work on two crime reports that were due in on Monday; they'd agreed to see each other next Friday.

"It's been brilliant, Emily. Difficult to top this, but I promise I'll work on it! I'll see you on Friday."

"I've had a wonderful time, Louise; it's just great being with you. Have a good week, and thanks for taking my extra case back."

They kissed briefly, though not unobtrusively, and said their goodbyes. Emily checked her phone and, intrigued, opened Julie's message.

Hi, Emily, I don't think we've gone this long without contacting each other since we met. I miss you. A lot has happened in the past few weeks. Nigel Hatfield and I are in the Outer Hebrides, on the trail of Ben Trafford. Your slip of the tongue got me researching it, and we've also had independent confirmation that he's here. No sign yet, though. I hope we can still be friends after I've laid this to rest. Love, Julie x

Emily felt touched, and initially not as alarmed by the risks they were taking as she'd been when Julie had first told her about her plan to confront Trafford. That was inevitable, as the connection between them had waned over the past few weeks. But anxiety about her friend's safety quickly resurfaced, and she texted back immediately.

Thanks for updating me. Please remember what he's capable of and don't take any unnecessary risks. If you find him, think carefully about how and where you confront him. This guy likes to hurt women. Let me know when you're back in Manchester, and we can arrange to meet up. Emily x

Her thoughts were interrupted by another text from Louise.

I can't wait till Friday. xx

"On a scale of one to ten, how sure are you?"

"As I said, build, height and age all fit our man. To that I would add a high level of fitness and upmarket outdoor running gear that you don't see many locals wearing. I'd give it a solid eight."

Nigel and Julie were back at the cottage. They'd agreed to meet there the minute he'd texted her to say that he hadn't seen Trafford.

"Assuming we can agree that it's very likely Trafford is living in or around Balivanich, and probably clocked you as a stranger in town, what do we do?"

Julie wondered fleetingly why Nigel was asking her rather than making a proposal himself. But she'd been thinking about this all morning and had come up with a slightly crazy idea. "It's clear that we didn't think through the problem we've created for ourselves. Trafford has the edge in this game of hide-and-seek. All he has to do is stay out of sight – something he's very good at, I would imagine – while we chase around trying to catch a glimpse of him. If he sees one of us first, he can quickly go to ground. Unless we find out where he's living, we could be here for weeks before we confront him, which neither of us can afford. And even if that did happen, he could simply choose to run off rather than wait around to hear what we've got to say."

"It sounds like you may have come up with a solution?"

"We turn the situation on its head, by provoking him to find us rather than the other way round. We make it riskier for him to stay hidden away compared to meeting us and finding out what we want. And we do that by going public about what we're doing here, taking his picture round the shops and garages, and asking people in the street if they've seen him. We might get lucky – someone might know where he's staying – but I think it's more likely that in a small community like this, word will get round and he'll hear that we've been asking questions. His safe house will become not so safe if he thinks the locals are talking about him, and he will search for us. He'll assume we're staying in a holiday rental, and it won't take him long – there are only six available. Obviously, it's risky – we know what this man is capable of. But then we're at risk anyway. What do you think?"

"Just when I think I've got used to your adrenaline junkie side, you go one higher. You're right, it is crazy, but I can't fault your logic. Let's do it. I can go into the post office tomorrow and make copies of the CCTV picture. They won't be great quality, but as you say, the aim is to start the rumour."

"Why not go now? It should still be open."

"You're right – again. I'll get the copies, then take a walk around the island to the Isle of Benbecula House Hotel. I've been wanting to check it out since we arrived, and I can show the picture to the barmen while I'm about it."

"You won't mind if I stay here, will you? I fancy sitting in front of the fire with my book. But try to get back before dark; I'll make us something to eat this evening."

Lily was still at Tamsin's when Emily got home from the Hilton, so she changed into a sweater and jeans and walked round to meet her. She texted to let her know she was coming, waited five minutes, then set off in the sunshine. Her daughter wouldn't appreciate her turning up unannounced. She couldn't remember feeling this good about herself and her life since… when? The early weeks of her relationship with Julie had been glorious, but they'd taken place when the verbal and physical attacks on Emily (and Lily) were at their height. *Maybe our relationship would never have lasted. It was born out of such a nerve-racking period in my life. Our feelings for each other weren't based in reality,* she thought. *Once that context changed, the cracks began to show.* The last time she could remember feeling remotely like this was after she and Robert moved into their first house together in Brixton. It was a wreck, and they'd spent the whole summer renovating it.

"Hi, Mum! You look happy; what's happened?"

Emily came out of her reverie to see her daughter bouncing towards her. "Hi, you. Nothing's happened, but yes, I do feel good. How was everything at Tamsin's?"

"Yeah, it was cool. You look different, somehow. I can't explain it – you're sort of chilled but glowing."

Emily smiled. *Some things you can't share with your thirteen-year-old daughter.* "Thank you, that's lovely to hear. Have you had any lunch?"

One of the things on Emily's to-do list for the weekend was to get back in touch with Deepak. She'd been feeling guilty that they'd not been in contact since August, when he'd sounded horrified to hear about Julie's plans for tracking down Marion's killer. She remembered thinking at the time that he must surely regret getting involved in the whole Backlash affair. Burglarising Stroud's house – were they mad? It could have ended his career.

He didn't pick up, so she left a message, then confirmed with a text. She'd love to see him and catch up.

As there was no moonlight tonight and no street lights near the isolated cottages Ben was observing, he could set off soon after dusk. As he walked up the lane to the first cottage, alert for the slightest incongruous sound, he doubted that this could be the one. No lights on, no smoke from the chimney, and even with the little light remaining in the sky, he could see that the cottage was in a shabby state. Somehow he didn't think that a London journalist – he now knew he was called Hatfield – would be staying somewhere this basic. He lay down by the low wall at the front and remained perfectly still for several minutes, listening. Only then did he roll over the top of the wall, into the turfed area at the front, and run, crouching, up to the side of the cottage. Most of the ground-floor windows had the curtains drawn, but one look through the unobstructed kitchen window confirmed his first impression. The beam of his torch failed to pick out a single sign of recent habitation, and he left immediately.

The next cottage was a ten-minute walk away through the village, or twenty via the coast, which he took in preference. He'd now eliminated four out of the six possible homes that Hatfield and his companion might be renting. The chance that this was the one, and therefore the risk of being seen, were high. As he left the foreshore and began to walk up the lane leading to the cottage, he could see that it looked promising from two hundred metres away. Well cared for, wood smoke from the chimney and several lights on, judging by the windows. He half-ran in a stooped position the last fifty metres to the cottage wall, before adopting the same routine as before: lying prone on the peaty ground, listening. After two minutes, just as he started to get up to roll over the wall, he heard the faint sound of footsteps approaching and flattened his body against the earth. They were coming from the opposite direction, from the village, and he had to move fast. Keeping flat, he crawled backwards until he reached the corner of the perimeter wall, manoeuvred his body through a right angle and crawled four metres against the wall at the side of the house. Thirty seconds later, he heard the front gate clang shut against the latch.

He waited until he heard a key turning in the lock before risking a glance through a narrow gap in the wall. The tall man pushing the door open was the man in the picture he'd been sent. After a few seconds he heard voices – presumably Hatfield and his companion – calm to begin with, then rising quickly in volume and pitch as they began to argue. Ben couldn't make out what it was about, so cautiously moved round to a window whose curtains hadn't been closed fully, placing each footstep carefully. He pulled the balaclava down over his face and cautiously peered through the gap in the curtains. The woman was clearly annoyed with Hatfield about something, but he couldn't hear what she was saying. It didn't matter; he savoured the moment as he watched the two of them, outwitted and out of their depth.

He took one last look at the layout of the room, then made his way to the wall at the side of the house. As he started to climb over, he dislodged a large stone, which clattered to the ground. Hearing the cottage door opening, he knew that his best chance of escaping unseen was to head to the rear of the cottage, which backed onto a field. He ran up to the wall behind the building and launched himself over, landing on lumpy ground that reeked of cow shit. He was lying among a herd of cows, and they had calves with them. Years ago, during his SAS training in the Brecon Beacons, another squaddie had tried to run through a similar herd and been badly trampled as the cows mobbed him. Army career over. So Ben lay there while the idiot Hatfield walked around the cottage, shouting, "Is anyone there?" *Civilians – what are they like?* he thought.

When he was sure that Hatfield had gone back inside, he climbed over the side wall, walked back home, threw his clothes in the washing machine and took a shower. Then he poured himself a treble.

Sunday afternoon, and Emily had just finished reading through the background papers for a client's divorce. Predictably, perhaps, she was picking up more than her fair share of Pearson, Shallice and Grant's divorce work these days, but she didn't mind. Quite the reverse. She was about to run a bath when her phone rang, and was going to ignore it until she saw that it was Deepak.

"Hi, Deepak, how are you? I'm so glad you rang. I realised yesterday that it's over a month since we last saw each other, and I want to do something about that."

"It was lovely to get your message. I'm good. I seem to have escaped any censure from the powers that be for our little off-the-cards escapade, probably because it meant that the Security Service couldn't ignore the role of the police in the follow-up. Not only have I escaped censure, I'm being encouraged to apply for promotion. Palvinder has started uni and is loving it, and the two of us are getting on fine. I'm even tolerating my ex-wife's new partner these days, so life's good."

They talked for an hour, re-establishing the connection they'd had from the moment they met, when Deepak was assigned to the 'body in the reservoir' case in April 2010. Two and a half years ago!

That body was Sue Goodall, murdered by Emily's husband, Robert Mason.

"How is Julie? I heard a rumour from a colleague of yours that you two weren't together anymore. Please tell me that she isn't still trying to find out who killed Marion? The last time I saw her, when we were celebrating in my flat after Granby was charged, she was becoming fixated on that to the point of paranoia."

"I'm afraid her obsession got worse, and came between us in the end. We split up a couple of months ago. Believe it or not, she's teamed up with the journalist who's been pursuing the story about MI5's infiltration of Backlash, and now claims that they've discovered Ben Trafford hiding on Benbecula in the Outer Hebrides. She's convinced that he's responsible for Marion's death, and is determined to confront him."

The alarm evident in Deepak's next words shocked her. "If you're in touch with Julie, you must try and persuade her to back off. Because the police are working on the Backlash investigation alongside MI5, I hear things. Apparently, Trafford's mental state had been worrying his bosses for some time and they were on the point of pulling him out when our little investigation forced their hand. They realised that the PTSD he suffered after Afghanistan had recurred, and there were frequent outbursts of anger and loss of control – sometimes directed towards women."

Emily felt a chill. "Thank you, Deepak. Now I'm really worried; I need to warn Julie as soon as possible. I'm sorry, but I think I should end our call and phone her. She probably won't want to hear what I've got to say, but I've got to try. I'll be in touch again soon to fix a time and place to meet."

"I'll hold you to that. Bye, Emily. Take care."

"You too."

There was no answer from Julie's phone, so Emily sent a text. She had to get the tone right, otherwise Julie would simply dismiss it as another of her finger-wagging lectures.

Hi, Julie, I've just spoken to Deepak. It was a social catch-up call, and he asked about you. When I told him where you are and that you and Nigel are hoping to confront Trafford, he became alarmed. From his contact with MI5 he understands that they were on the point of pulling Trafford out due to a recurrence of his PTSD. He's become unpredictably violent towards men and women. I'm asking you again to think carefully about how you confront this man. Love, Emily x

She pondered over the wording, then thought, *Fuck it – she won't take any notice of what I say anyway,* and sent it.

32

DEPARTURES

Ben had got up at dawn and walked the longer route to his pursuers' cottage, so it was daylight by the time he approached the front door. A last check of the Glock in his inside pocket, then he knocked hard. A light came on in the kitchen, followed by movement inside and a bolt being slid back. The door opened to reveal an astonished Nigel Hatfield in a tartan dressing gown at least one size too small for him.

"I hear you're looking for me," said Ben as he pushed through the door, grasping Hatfield's shoulder and forcing him further inside. Closing the door behind him, he instructed Hatfield to sit at the small kitchen table. When he demurred, Ben put his thumb into a pressure point at the side of Hatfield's neck and, in excruciating pain, he complied.

At the sound of a door opening, Ben turned.

"Who was that at the..." Julie froze as she beheld the scene in front of her. She wasn't fully awake, and stood staring at Ben for several seconds until he said, "You too – sit at the kitchen table."

"Just tell me, did you kill Marion Davies?"

"You don't get to ask me questions. You've completely fucked up my plans by blundering around the village, and I'm not in the mood to be pissed around by either of you."

"I'm not doing what you say until you answer that question."

Ben took the silenced Glock out of his coat, and aimed it. "Yes, you will. Stop this ridiculous performance and sit down, or I'll shoot you in the thigh and you'll walk with a limp for the rest of your life."

Julie thought for a second about telling him to go fuck himself, then remembered what this man had done, and would no doubt do again if he was cornered. She sat down.

Ben told them to cross their hands behind their backs and then secured their wrists tightly with cable ties. "Why have you followed me here, and what do you want? Let's begin with you, Mr 'How Can I Drag This Country Down' Hatfield."

Nigel decided that this wasn't the time to debate whether 'Every democracy needs a free press to hold its institutions to account', so he spelt it out, his heart feeling as if it was beating its way out of his chest. "I believe that, in a justifiable operation to expose Backlash and the extent of its police officer membership, MI5 planted you inside the organisation. In the course of that operation, serious illegal acts were committed. The Secret Service can't be above the law. I want you to go on record and admit that those acts took place."

"Is that all? So how do I benefit, financially, from betraying my Service and my country?"

"My paper would only be able to pay a small sum to recompense you for your time and inconvenience, I'm afraid."

"Don't tell me – my reward is clearing my conscience. I can't believe you went to all this effort, believing you stood a chance of getting me to betray my Service with an offer like that. And what about you, motormouth? Are you just along for the ride, if you'll excuse my double entendre?"

Julie felt sick. Not so much from fear, but from revulsion at being in his presence. "Marion Davies was my friend and lover. I know that you and Granby were responsible for sadistically raping and abusing her. The three of you were caught on CCTV going into Granby's house. Did you kill her as well?"

But Ben's attention was elsewhere. He was looking at a message on his phone that had arrived just as Julie had begun to speak.

Two hostiles reported arriving at Benbecula Airport yesterday evening. Assume they have knowledge of your whereabouts, acquired through torture. The SBS will extract you from Cula Bay beach at 09.30 hours this morning.

"I'm afraid that life is what happens when you're busy making other plans, love. I've got to leave you. Here, cut yourselves free." Ben slid a kitchen knife along the floor at the very moment he heard the faint sound of a stone falling from a wall outside.

He went to the back door, unlocked it quietly and knelt down behind a chair as two men, dressed entirely in black combat fatigues, burst through the front door levelling machine pistols. It was much darker inside the cottage and they shot at the first target in view. Two bullets passed through Julie's body as she was reaching for the knife, one emulsifying the right ventricle in her heart before exiting under her right shoulder. She was dead before she hit the floor.

Trafford put two dum dum bullets into the head of the first assassin, which became a formless blancmange. The second sprayed his weapon in Ben's direction, missing with all but one bullet which hit him in the shoulder, but not before he'd shot the other man in the upper arm. Ducking low, Ben ran out of the door and vaulted the back wall, landing next to the ruminating herd, who immediately began to stand up, agitated. He ran around behind them as a shot rang out, then turned. Number Two was heading for the wall, straight towards him... and the cows. Cresting the wall, the assassin screamed as Ben put a bullet in his thigh, then fell into the middle of the herd. His body would be found that evening, unrecognisable after the cows had finished making sure he posed no threat to their calves.

The pain in Ben's shoulder was intense but bearable, though he quickly realised that he was losing too much blood to make it to the beach. He tore apart the lining of his jacket, stuffed the wadding into the hole in his shoulder and taped it in place with a length of gaffer tape from the roll in his pocket. He sent a response to the earlier message:

Hostiles engaged at remote location; one dead, one presumed dead. One civilian dead, another missing. Assume you're sending cleaning detail for the safe house; they will also need to check on location of firefight for incriminating evidence.

He got to the shore with fifteen minutes to spare. His wound was fucking painful, but not leaking too badly, and he was now feeling the post-adrenal exhilaration. *So be careful.* He'd seen no one, nor heard any police sirens, so he assumed nothing had been reported yet. It had been close; closer than he'd come to dying in a long time. There was no way he'd have been able to take down the two of them if he hadn't been warned; if the message had arrived thirty seconds later, he wouldn't be sitting here on the beach, thinking. They'd obviously gone to his cottage early this morning, hoping to surprise him while he was sleeping. Presumably they'd seen him leave and followed him to the journalist's place, which had allowed enough time to elapse for him to get the warning. Going to the rental house early this morning had saved his life.

He watched as the RIB approached the shore, two men in the front poised to jump out. As soon as they landed on the sand, one ran up to Ben. "Are you OK? We're here to clean up the safe house. We also need to know the location of your firefight with the hostiles, and if there's a remaining threat."

Ben gave them precise directions to the journalist's house. "There were two of them. They were pros but careless, otherwise I wouldn't be here. One is dead in the house. The other I shot in the arm; he followed me outside, then got trampled by a herd of cows. Assumed dead, but be careful. You'll find everything in the safe house easily enough; there's nothing hidden, it'll all fit into my rucksack. Help yourselves to the Laphroaig."

"Take your time, gents, there's no rush," said the NCO from the boat.

Ben wished them good luck and ran to the RIB, ignoring the NCO's sarcasm. Five minutes later, he was bouncing around on the floor of the boat while a member of the Special Boat Squadron applied a more effective dressing to his wound.

"Did you get the hostiles?"

"One dead, the other probable. It was a joint effort between me and the cows."

His stand-in paramedic ignored the obvious question. "Any other casualties?"

The boat hit a large wave, took off and landed in the subsequent trough with an unyielding slap.

"Christ, that hurts – haven't you got any morphine?"

"Nah, morphine's for the SAS. Any other casualties?"

"One civilian, a woman, certainly dead. The other civilian will be if I ever see him again, the fucking prick."

"Sounds like they messed up."

Ben looked at him. Was he being ironic? Probably not; he guessed that the SBS guy's sense of humour was an irony-free zone. "Well, not from my point of view. But that's one way of looking at it, I suppose."

Nigel had thrown himself onto the floor, grabbed the knife and started to cut his bonds. Lying under the table, in shock, he was desperate to get away from the traumatic scene around him. Julie had been projected backwards by the force of two bullets and ended up lying beside him, blood draining from the gaping wound in her back and pooling on the floor. One of the assassins – he assumed they'd come to kill him, but why? – had fallen in the middle of the room, his faceless head, brain partially exposed, turned towards Nigel.

After the second assassin had chased Trafford out of the door, Nigel had heard a shot – or was it two? – then a cry, and then nothing, save for the bellowing of the cows outside. The pool of Julie's blood had almost reached him, which made the decision to move easier. If the other assassin had survived, and came back to check that there were no witnesses, Nigel would be a sitting duck anyway. Rolling away from Julie – the smell of blood and gunpowder was overpowering – he levered himself into a standing position. That simple manoeuvre seemed to take all his strength, but he had to find out what had happened outside.

As he stepped through the back door, terrified, he was confronted by the sight of around a dozen cows on the other side of the stone wall, agitated, bellowing and jostling. There were no human beings to be seen, so he went round to the front of the house and checked the lane. Again, no sign of anyone. *Maybe we're too far away from the neighbours for them to have heard anything*, he thought.

He took several deep breaths, trying to think rationally about his next move. The place was a multiple crime scene. Hostage-taking, attempted murder and at least two killings, one clearly murder. As a citizen who believed in making the right moral choice, he should contact the police immediately and remain in situ. But as a man who'd just survived a murder attempt and didn't know if there was a third (or fourth!) assassin on the loose, and as a journalist with an incredible story to file, he had to get away now. Once the police were involved – and God knows MI5 would want to close this down – he wouldn't be allowed to leave the island, possibly for days. He could be accused of leaving a crime scene, but it was a risk worth taking. He looked at his watch, smeared in Julie's blood. His last image of her swam into view, but he refused to go there. He couldn't believe it was still only 8.15. If he packed fast and took a taxi, he could make the twelve o'clock ferry, take the first train to Glasgow and maybe even catch the last train to London. Then he would phone the police, hopefully before the bodies were discovered.

He hurried upstairs, evacuated his bowels, dressed, combed the room and threw his belongings into his rucksack. He repeated the sweep downstairs in the lounge and kitchen, careful not to move anything as he stepped over the blood, bone fragments and brain matter. The pool of blood around Julie seemed to have stopped spreading; he'd never seen someone who'd died from a gunshot close up before. She was lying on her side with her face towards him, eyes closed and mouth stretched in a tight grimace. He stood there for several seconds, paying his respects, in spite of the need to leave the scene immediately. He'd only spent four days with this reckless, driven, passionate woman, yet he'd already developed a huge respect and fondness for her. Only ten minutes ago she'd been her feisty self, arguing with a man holding a gun! He couldn't take it in.

As he turned to go, he noticed that the cows seemed calmer, so he went out back to check. They'd moved away from the wall, and when he looked into the field there seemed to be a pile of clothes half buried in the mud and shit, about ten feet from the wall. He was about to go back inside when he spotted a short metal tube beside the clothes, then a hand holding the tube, which then resolved itself into a gun. The type of gun the assassins had used. Realising what the clothes contained, Nigel vomited over the wall, hurried back inside and closed the back door.

He walked into the village – he didn't want a driver coming to the cottage – and caught a taxi from the rank to the ferry terminal, relieved that the driver wasn't the one who'd brought him and Julie here three days ago. He was in no mood to answer questions. It was only when he was on the ferry with a large brandy in front of him that the horrific savagery of the scene when the two men burst into the cottage finally broke through his defences. He started to shake uncontrollably, put his head in his hands and sobbed unashamedly.

He just managed to get a reclining seat on the sleeper train back to London, and spent most of the journey sleeping or trying to work out who the fuck the two men could have been working for. His initial theory was that they'd been after him, as they'd arrived at his and Julie's cottage. But he'd seen Trafford receive a text and immediately pull out his weapon, then throw them a knife to cut their ties. Someone had warned him that he'd been tracked down; he was prepared. Nigel had to admit that it was impressive how cool Trafford had remained under fire, killing one of the attackers and wounding the other. Whatever had happened with the cows, it wasn't a good way to die.

So who wanted Trafford dead that badly? Perhaps rogue elements associated with Backlash, furious that his duplicity and the evidence he'd provided had scuppered their deluded plans to build a far-right terrorist group around a hatred of women?

Images of Julie's tragic, violent death haunted Nigel in his sleep. Her quest for 'the truth', which she'd never discovered, had killed her. When he finally got home at 7am, too exhausted to make the call to the police, he went to bed and slept until mid-afternoon.

As soon as MI5 heard that associates of Sir Geoffrey Granby (some of whom had dined with Service members at their club in the past) had put out a lucrative contract to kill Ben Trafford, it was just a matter of time before someone talked. But it had taken too long, and when the intelligence finally came in, the operation to kill Trafford was under way. The nearest SBS team had been helicoptered into Benbecula Airport with orders to pick him up from Cula Bay beach at 9.30 that morning, accompanied by two agents with instructions to clean up any trace of Trafford's presence.

Inevitably, Trafford's quick heads-up on the beach for the clean-up squad had omitted some details in the rush to get him off the island. As soon as they entered the cottage, the two men realised that the task required rather more cleaning up than they were equipped for. A search of the upstairs bedrooms revealed the identity of the dead woman. Clearly someone else had been staying there too; probably a man, judging by some of the toiletries. Trafford appeared to have left no incriminating trace; they searched the dead man's clothing, took his prints (there was no point taking his picture) and had a quick look around the garden. They couldn't see any cows up next to the back wall, so they left and set off quickly to the safe house. At the junction with the main road, a couple of locals gave them a hard stare, then quickly looked away.

Can't wait to see you on Friday evening. You'll be glad to know it's not ratatouille – sea bream baked with garlic and oregano. The food of love! So much to talk about. Love, Louise xx

I loved your ratatouille – among other things! Love, Emily xx

Louise had decided to invite Emily round to her flat for "a meal, a drink, a chat and who knows what else" instead of going out. She hadn't stopped thinking about her since they'd said goodbye outside the hotel, and they'd been sending each other increasingly passionate text messages. The previous weekend at the Hilton had been amazing, but if she and Emily were heading where Louise hoped they were – growing into a serious relationship – then she wanted to spend time together in surroundings where they could have that conversation, which would be impossible in all of the venues she knew on a Friday evening in Manchester. This was the time to be open with each other about their values, hopes and fears.

Emily had been reflecting on her relationship with Julie and the warning signs they'd both ignored; partly because of the maelstrom around them, and partly because Julie had made herself indispensable when Emily was at her lowest ebb. She knew Louise wanted to talk about them and their future this Friday, which she and Julie should have done at the start of their relationship.

So, after dinner, they stayed up late talking openly about children (Louise wasn't likely to have a successful pregnancy), Louise's doubts about spending the next twenty years on a career path in the police and compromising who she was, Emily's sexuality ("I can't say I'm going to stop fancying men." "I wouldn't believe you if you did."), and her anxieties about not being a good enough mother.

Emily admitted to concerns about jumping too quickly into another relationship. "I know 'on the rebound' is a cliché, but that doesn't mean there's no truth in it. But I'm sure that my feelings for you aren't about needing to replace her. It feels good when we're together; I desire you and I want to be with you. What's happening between us is real, Louise, but it's been so fast that I'll need time. Time for evenings like this, getting to know everything about each other. You must say if you're not prepared to wait. I mean that."

Aware of the increase in her heart rate, Louise said, "Listen, I've made enough mistakes like that in the past and I totally understand. I don't want to be a confusion in your life; please tell me if there's a danger of that happening. I'm falling for you too, but we'll take time to see if we're going to be the next Thelma and Louise."

"I didn't think they were lesbians."

"They were in love. You need to watch the final scene again."

"But they died driving off a cliff."

"No relationship is without its ups and downs."

The following morning, Emily got up early and made herself a coffee. Louise surprised her as she came in quietly and wrapped her arms around Emily from behind.

"Good morning. You look very peaceful; what are you thinking about?"

"Our conversation about *Thelma & Louise* last night."

"Which one of us is Thelma?"

"You, of course! In spite of your name, you're the younger and sexier one."

Louise kissed Emily on the back of her neck, slipping her hand inside her dressing gown, under her breast and around her nipple. "You're a very sexy woman."

Emily had just got her stuff together and was about to head back to pick up Lily and get on with a divorce case when her phone rang. It was Deepak.

"Hi, Deepak."

"Have you managed to contact Julie yet?" He sounded tense.

"No, I'm afraid she hasn't responded to my messages. Why? You sound worried."

"You know I get regular intel about the follow-up to Granby's arrest. I've just seen a report about an incident on Benbecula. I'm sorry, Emily, but it doesn't sound good. At some point yesterday, police on the island reported finding the bodies of two men and a woman at a cottage. All three had been shot dead. That's all the information I've got at present, but when we last spoke I think you said that Julie and the journalist were staying on that island, trying to trace Trafford. I thought I should tell you, and I'm sorry if that was the wrong call. Obviously, we don't yet know the identity of the victims, but they don't get many incidents like that in the Outer Hebrides, as you can imagine."

He paused. All he could hear was the sound of Emily's breathing.

"Emily? Are you OK? I'm so sorry, but I thought you'd rather hear it from me."

"You did the right thing, thank you, Deepak. I can't speak any more now, but please let me know as soon as you hear anything else. Thank you again."

Emily sat down, trembling, ashen-faced. The news she'd dreaded, but half-expected ever since Julie had announced her intention to chase Trafford up to the Hebrides, had almost certainly come. She wouldn't give up hope until confirmation was received, but she knew, really.

Louise walked back into the kitchen and gave a start. "God, Emily, what's happened? Who was that on the phone?"

Emily struggled to get her words out. "That was Deepak. He's seen a report from Police Scotland of a shooting in the Outer Hebrides where Julie and the journalist have been looking for Trafford. Bodies of a woman and two men with gunshot wounds have been recovered from a cottage. He's going to let me know when he gets more news, but I'm sure it's Julie, Louise. I begged her not to go, but she was determined to confront this maniac."

Louise drew up a chair next to Emily, put her arms around her and held her tight. She broke down and began to sob.

"Why did she do it, Louise? I tried, but I couldn't get through to her. I should have done more."

"I'm so sorry, my love, I know how much she meant to you. Stay here for as long as you want – is there anything I can do?"

"Thank you, I will stay for a while before I pick up Lily. Would you mind ringing her and saying that I'm going to be an hour later than we agreed, and is that OK with Daisy's mum?"

"I'll do that now. Can I get you anything?"

"A cup of tea would be lovely, thanks." Emily paused, then blurted out, "Fucking hell, Julie, why? All those Tinder dates you could have had, all those places you'd have visited, all those moments watching your nieces grow up, if only you hadn't gone after this psycho." She paused a moment. "I'm sorry; ranting won't bring her back."

"Rant as long as you want. If you don't want to be on your own tonight, I could come over and stay with you, if you like?"

"That's a lovely offer, but I'll be OK. It's probably better if I'm there for Lily tonight."

In the lounge that evening, after she'd taken Lily home, cooked them an omelette and talked with her daughter about a nasty time one of her friends was going through on Facebook, Emily made herself a large gin and tonic and went over the memories she'd shared with Julie over the past eighteen months. Then she did it again, until the tears rolled down her face and she could start to mourn her friend. Tomorrow morning she'd ring Lily's school and explain that there'd been an unexpected death of a family friend and Lily wouldn't be coming in. Then she'd sit down with her daughter and, as gently and honestly as possible, explain that Julie had been killed by men who placed no value on human life; one of the most important things that defines us as human beings, in its observance, and in the breach of that observance.

Nigel woke with a start and looked at his watch. It was nearly thirty hours since he'd left the island; thirty hours in which he should have reported the two – or was it three? – murders he'd witnessed. He'd got away with a number of minor legal transgressions in the past twenty years by playing the 'censoring the free press', 'public's right to know' and 'Big Brother state interference' cards, but he knew he was fucked on this one. Leaving the scene of a double (triple?) killing and not reporting it to the police for a day and a half, he'd be fortunate to get a non-custodial sentence.

But putting it off would only make things worse, so he shaved, showered, put on his least creased shirt, trousers and jacket, and took the Tube to Hammersmith Police Station. After standing in a queue for thirty minutes, he walked up to the front desk with an apparent confidence and announced, "I'd like to report two, maybe three, murders," which got the attention of the constable on duty and the woman behind Nigel in the queue.

Mid-morning on the day after he phoned Emily, Deepak received an update from his MI5 contact about the 'Hit in the Hebrides', as the press would soon be calling it.

> *The dead woman's name was Julie Taylor, a solicitor living in the Manchester area. Inquiries into why she was there are ongoing. Police were keen to identify the second occupant of the cottage, which was resolved at 5pm yesterday when a man walked into Hammersmith Police Station and admitted that he'd been there. He's currently helping police with their inquiries, and his name has been withheld for his own safety. Two other bodies were found at the scene. For reasons that cannot be disclosed, it's believed that both men were there to kill one or both occupants of the house. One was found shot dead inside the cottage; the other in a nearby field, trampled by cows – a more common occurrence than many would believe. Until forensics can establish whether the same weapon was used against all three victims, police are keeping an open mind as to whether they're looking for one or more killers.*

A part of Deepak had still been hoping that the woman in the report wasn't Julie. He sat quietly at his desk for half an hour before ringing Emily.

"Hi, Emily, I'm afraid that I have received confirmation that the murder victim in the Hebrides is Julie. I'm so sorry."

"Thank you for ringing, Deepak, but I can spare you the next part. I was contacted by the police an hour ago; they asked if I knew Julie and then confirmed that she's dead. They'd found text messages on her phone that identified me as her ex-partner, and I have to go to Central Manchester Police Station tomorrow morning to give a statement."

"They'll no doubt ask if you have any idea who might have wanted to kill Julie, when you last saw her, what you were doing at the time of her death. Routine stuff."

"I assume I should tell them the whole story about what she was doing there?"

"Absolutely. If you're not doing anything afterwards, ring me when you've finished and we can meet up for a coffee and a debrief. I'm so sorry, Emily."

Ben's wound had damaged the muscles and joint in his shoulder more than had seemed likely initially. He'd spent several days and had several operations in a private hospital in Buckinghamshire, becoming more belligerent and offensive towards the medical staff as the days went by. On his last day in the hospital, Rachel, his long-suffering physiotherapist, finally snapped when, as she was taking him through his post-op exercises, he told her to, "Stop treating me like a little girl and get on with it, woman."

"I'm used to the occasional ungrateful prick like you, Sergeant Trafford, but when it comes to being an obnoxious arsehole you're in a league of your own. Have you ever stopped to consider the impact that your gratuitously vile behaviour has on those around you? We can't wait to see the back of you here, frankly."

Temper flaring, he went to grab her forearm and just held back in time, but not before she noticed. She glared at him.

"Try that again, and I'll damage your shoulder for life, then say it was an accident because I was fighting you off. Everyone here would believe me. You're too arrogant to heed any advice, but it's not your shoulder that really needs treatment. You're not mentally fit, Sergeant. In fact, you're very unwell in my opinion. Until you can be humble enough to admit that and seek treatment, your condition will only deteriorate. I'll write out the rest of your care plan. Goodbye."

Ben rose slowly out of the chair, wanting to apologise, but unable to get the words out; they stuck in his throat. She was both right and wrong. He accepted that he was ill, of course he did. But it wasn't a lack of humility that made him fight the suits in the Service who'd told him that he was no longer on active duty and insisted he undertake treatment for PTSD, but a determination to get through this on his own. Anything else would be a negation of the principle he'd lived by since his father had kicked him out of the family home when he was fourteen. From that moment, he'd understood that there was only one person he could rely on to solve his problems: himself.

His first appointment with the shrinks was at 2pm this afternoon. He'd play along with it in order to reassure them that he accepted that he needed treatment. That way, they'd hopefully keep surveillance of him to a minimum and he'd be able to track down the idiot journalist who'd nearly got him killed – and caused the death of the woman – then negotiate a deal for his story. If the journo wouldn't improve on his previous pitiful offer, Ben would persuade him to provide the name of one who would. And if he refused? The world wouldn't miss another journalist.

33

AFTERMATH

"So, did they give you a hard time?"

Deepak waited for Emily's response. She'd been subdued as she'd walked into their usual Italian café bar five minutes ago – not surprising, as she'd just left a police interview and learned only two days ago that her ex-lover and friend had been brutally murdered.

"Not really, no. They obviously knew more details about Julie's death than I did, and were reluctant to share anything but the headlines, which were brutally painful to hear. As you predicted, almost all of their questions were about what I knew about her trip to the Hebrides – why did she go there, what did she hope to achieve, did I know anyone who might want to kill her? I told them everything, including the hint I gave her on the phone about where I thought Trafford might be hiding. I'll never know if that played a role in her death. Was that information instrumental in her decision to go up there? If it was, then I have to live with the fact that she would probably be alive today, but for me."

Deepak quickly interrupted. "Julie was set on confronting Trafford sooner or later, and no one can be sure how that would have ended. Very badly, I suspect, so please don't torture yourself with 'what ifs'. Did they ask you where you were at the time of Julie's death?"

"They did. Luckily, I could tell them that I was in bed with a member of the Greater Manchester Police Force, who I'm sure will corroborate that. So, have you learned anything more about the murders or the murderers?"

Hiding the stab he'd felt on hearing of the nature of Emily's alibi, Deepak took a sip of his cappuccino, then said, "Analysis of the bullets taken from the deceased shows that the two intruders were shot by the same weapon: a Glock handgun which the police believe belongs to Trafford. Julie was killed instantly by a bullet from one of the semi-automatic guns the intruders used. According to Nigel Hatfield's account, Trafford was acting completely independently. He'd tracked Julie and Hatfield down to their cottage, forced his way in at gunpoint, tied them up and was questioning them just before the intruders burst in. Luckily he'd been tipped off by text and went into action-man mode, killed one and wounded the other. Hatfield got off the island and back to London as soon as possible. He's been charged with leaving a murder scene and released on bail."

"And what of Trafford? Are you allowed to tell me?"

"He was taken off the island less than thirty minutes after the shooting, almost certainly by the SAS or SBS. Whoever messaged him about the would-be assassins would have informed him of the time and place to meet. He was badly wounded in the shoulder and is currently being debriefed and treated in a private hospital somewhere. His superiors are seriously worried about his mental state and are determined that he won't go rogue again. You're not thinking of trying to track him down, I hope?"

Emily was shocked that Deepak could even consider that possibility. The three of them had worked together so closely to expose Backlash, right up until the end when Julie had become obsessed with finding Marion's killer. Emily knew that Deepak had regarded Julie as unpredictable, but he'd clearly had his doubts about her as well. "Of course I'm not! God, Deepak, I thought you knew I believed Julie's quest was unhinged, just as much as you did."

Deepak looked mortified. "Of course you did; I didn't mean it that way. I'm worried about you, that's all. It sounds very callous, but I was so proud of the role we all played in closing down Backlash that I resented Julie for carrying on and going it alone. Now I feel that we can get on with our lives. How has Lily taken Julie's death?"

"She's really upset. As much as this has been a massive shock for me, I'd already accepted that our relationship was over. But Lily is having to cope with losing a good friend on top of the shock. I asked her if she wanted to see a bereavement counsellor and she's thinking about it. But her resilience during these past two years has been inspiring. There were times – not many, to be fair – when the abuse threatened to overwhelm me, eat away at my sense of myself. But seeing Lily, at thirteen, dealing with much of the same shit that I was, that always snapped me out of it. Plus a little help from my friends, especially you. You've been amazing, Deepak – you know that, don't you?"

"Thank you. I'll graciously accept those kind words; they mean a lot. You mean a lot to me too, and I think you probably know that I don't just mean as a friend. I know it's not the same for you. But there, I've said it at last."

"I did realise that, Deepak. Just our luck that I discovered I was bisexual at the same time as we started to get to know each other."

"I'm sorry, Emily, but I can't relax. I promise it won't always be like this."

"I hope not, otherwise this relationship is going to be over before it's begun. Lily is completely OK with 'us'; she'll just need time to adjust. Of course the trauma of Julie's death is big for her at the moment, which means things will probably take longer. But

I know my daughter and I can see that she's comfortable with you being around. Maybe the fact that you're almost the same age is helping."

"Not funny. Remarks like that aren't helpful, just so you know."

Lily and Louise had met once before, but this was the first time the three of them had eaten together at Emily's house. More significantly for Louise's inhibitions at the moment, it was also the first time she'd slept with Emily when Lily was around.

"So is this the first time you've slept with someone when their son or daughter was in the house?"

"No, but those kids were three years old or younger, and that's completely different. I can't get over the fact that Lily is in her bedroom across the landing, fully aware that her mum and I are having sex."

"If only."

"Stop it, please, Emily. Enough."

"I'm sorry. But it's not a big deal for me or for Lily. I understand that it's a completely new situation for you, but the more you spend time with Lily, the more relaxed you'll be together and you'll stop worrying about what she thinks we're doing. I could list the things that the average thirteen-going-on-nineteen-year-old girl is obsessed with, and believe me, what her mum's doing with her girlfriend in bed doesn't make the top ten."

"Thank you for being patient. I'm being stupid, I know. But can we just hold each other tonight?"

"I think I can cope."

Not completely convinced by Emily's assurances, Louise nearly died in the morning when she left the bedroom to have a shower at the same moment Lily came out of her room.

"Hi, Louise, did you sleep OK? I remember Mum can snore sometimes, when we've shared a room in the past."

The relief that flowed through Louise washed away the tension. She felt like giving Lily a huge hug of gratitude, but restrained herself with a simple, "I slept really well, thanks. Mind you, I can usually sleep through anything, so your mum's snoring wouldn't bother me."

Lily pointed to the bathroom door. "Would you mind if I go in first? I'm running a bit late for school."

"Go for it. I'm on a later shift today, so I'm in no hurry."

"Thanks. See you again soon."

"Have a good day, Lily."

Ben had been cleared by the psychiatrist to continue as a member of MI5 in a non-active service role for a trial period of six months, provided he attended a programme of rehabilitation, took the medication, lived in secure Service accommodation and signed in every week with his superior officer. Almost nobody who knew him thought there was the slightest chance that he'd keep to the plan. At the end of the third week he walked off the base two hours after his scheduled meeting with his CO and made a three-hour journey to the flat of a fellow Special Forces veteran who'd agreed to put him up.

"You're welcome to stay as long as you like, mate. Sorry you've got to sofa-surf in the living room; this flat was all I could afford after that bitch threw me out and took out a restraining order. I've heard something about your last operation and how the bastards hung you out to dry afterwards. I don't want to know what you're doing; just don't bring it back here. Contributions to the food bill would be very welcome."

"I owe you one, Mark. They're still paying me, so let's say I start with a hundred for food this week, and see how that goes. I'm planning on being away for a few days next week – I'll tell you exactly when I know for sure. There's some business left over from that operation that I have to attend to."

Standing in the grounds of the crematorium with the late November sun warming her face, Emily looked out over the hills sloping down to the River Dart. She'd just left Julie's cremation ceremony, deep in thought. *'Life is what happens to us when we're busy making other plans.' Wasn't that John Lennon? Or did he get it from someone else? For Julie, it wasn't life, but death. One wrong decision, one wrong fork in the road taken, and our lives can be upended in a flash.*

She became aware of someone walking up beside her. It was Brenda, Julie's mother, looking strained and ten years older than she did in her picture on Julie's mantelpiece. "Thank you for coming, Emily, and for researching people who should be invited. I really needed your advice. Julie didn't leave a will – pretty extraordinary for a solicitor – and none of us had a clue about her close friends in Manchester. We're all still in shock, of course. John and I are burying our child, Jane's lost her big sister, the girls can't believe that they'll never see Auntie Julie again. We haven't told them any of the details, obviously, though the police are holding most of them back from us, anyway. All we know is that she was killed accidentally by a stray bullet meant for somebody else, and that it happened on an island in the Outer Hebrides, but the police clam up whenever we start to ask who and why."

Emily was tired. She'd arrived in Totnes yesterday evening after a five-and-a-half-hour train journey, then slept fitfully in her single room in the Seven Stars Hotel, overlooking the rowdy High Street. Totnes, a party town – who knew? Brenda had phoned her two weeks ago after Emily had sent Julie's parents a condolences card with her details 'in case you'd like to know anything about her last few months'. After they'd had a good cry together, she'd promised to send Brenda the names of Julie's close Manchester friends and colleagues who should be invited to the funeral. It was the right thing to do, but she'd regretted it as soon as she put the phone down. Should she contact Claire? Nigel? Deepak? And how could she get other contact numbers? Without Julie's phone, she'd had to go to her house (she still had the spare front-door keys) and look through her old address book. She hadn't been there for months, and as she'd walked into the hall an overwhelming sense of Julie's presence overcame her. She'd almost fainted, just managing to reach the stairs and sit down before she collapsed.

"Thank you, Brenda, it was the least I could do. I notice some of them couldn't make it, unfortunately." The family had wanted to bury Julie in a cemetery close to her parents' home just outside Totnes. Inevitably, the journey from Manchester had proved too much of a disincentive for a number of her colleagues and friends, including Deepak. Emily had brought flowers and a message on his behalf. Surprisingly, Nigel had initially said that he would come – the train from London was a much easier journey – but unsurprisingly he hadn't turned up. He'd messaged Emily to say that he was worried about his safety. Given the extraordinary events over the past months, she couldn't blame him.

She was about to leave for the gathering at Julie's parents' house when she noticed a young woman from a mixed ethnic background standing on the fringes of the main group of mourners. Intrigued, she walked over.

"Hello. I'm Emily, a good friend of Julie's. Did you know her well?"

"No, I hardly knew her. My name's Allie, and we met recently on a train from Manchester to Glasgow. It's a bit embarrassing, really. I'm a train manager on the West Coast Line, and as I was checking her ticket I noticed Julie was checking me out. We had a brief conversation, exchanged numbers and agreed to meet up the next time I stayed over in Manchester. Then a week ago I saw this story in *The Herald* about a lawyer from Manchester who'd been murdered in the Outer Hebrides. They printed a picture and I knew it was her. It was such a shock. I felt such a strong impulse to pay my respects and say goodbye, I managed to find out where the funeral was. So here I am. You knew her well, I guess. I'd love to know more about her."

Emily was laughing inside, thinking about Allie's story. It was so like Julie. "I'd love to tell you; she was an amazing force of nature. Let's sit over there and I'll tell you about the Julie Taylor I knew."

On the way back to Manchester later that evening, Emily decided she had to see Nigel Hatfield. She needed to know more about Julie's final days on Benbecula.

Three days later, relaxing with Louise on the sofa in her living room after they'd got back from watching *The Angels' Share* at the HOME cinema, Emily shared her plan to arrange a meeting with Nigel Hatfield.

"Are you sure? I won't try to dissuade you, but playing devil's advocate for a moment, what more do you want to know that you don't already?"

"Fair question. I want to understand what was driving Julie in those last weeks and days. Once she'd decided on a course of action, she was ferociously committed to pursuing it to a successful conclusion. She was the one who kept the three of us going on the Backlash investigation when Deepak and I were getting disheartened, but she always balanced the potential prize against the level of risk. Yet in this case, she was willing to take enormous risks with her safety – and our relationship – for what? To find out whether it was Trafford who killed Marion? It made no sense. There was little chance that he'd tell her, or guarantee that he'd tell her the truth. And she knew what he was capable of. The only explanation that makes any sense is that she felt she owed it to Marion to do everything possible to uncover her killer, to somehow make up for playing a role in her death. She knew it was unlikely she'd succeed, but she couldn't live with herself if she didn't explore every lead."

Louise was silent for a minute, then said, "I get that, and I agree, you should see him. Have you contacted him yet?"

"We've spoken on the phone. He's a journalist, so his number was easy to find, but he's insisting on meeting at his flat in Dolphin Square in London because he's being hassled by the press whenever he leaves home. Must be some family money around if he can afford to live there; the *Guardian* doesn't pay that well. The advantage is that entry to the block is controlled by a concierge, so visitors are screened. I've arranged to meet him this Saturday afternoon."

"Do you want an escort?"

"That's a lovely offer. It did cross my mind to ask you, but he said that I have to come alone, which is fair enough, so thank you, but no."

"I could take you there and wait outside; be on call if you need me."

"It's in London; it's ridiculous to go all that way just to wait outside."

"Where's your spirit of adventure? We could drive down in the morning, stay somewhere romantic overnight, then meander back here the next day. You used to live in London; you must know a few places to take a girl for a good time."

Emily looked at her, smiling. *Why didn't I think of that? Don't get boring, Emily.* "I'll check with Lily that she's happy to stay with a friend, make sure the friend's mum is OK with it, and we're on. It's a brilliant idea; I'll sort out the hotel."

Getting into Dolphin Square was as simple as Nigel had assured her it would be. The concierge in the lobby had all of Emily's details, checked her in efficiently and gave her concise directions to Nigel's flat on the eighth floor. He was standing in his doorway as she came out of the lift, looking grey and wan.

"Emily, do come in."

"Thank you so much for seeing me, Nigel."

"I thought it was the least I could do, given your relationship with Julie. What would you like to drink?"

"A gin and tonic, please, if you've got it."

"Coming up."

She was standing in the centre of the large, bright lounge overlooking the River Thames. Light flooded in, reflected from the white walls hung with original art. "Your flat is stunning."

"You're welcome to have a look around."

The rest of the two-bedroomed flat was almost a disappointment, except for when she walked into the oriental-style, marble-lined bathroom-cum-steam-room. "Wow. Forgive me, but how do you afford this on a journalist's salary?"

"You'll find I'm not the only left-wing journalist who has the good fortune and the misfortune to come from a wealthy family. Cheers."

"Cheers."

"I understand that you'd like to know more about the last week of Julie's life. What was happening; what she was like in those last days..."

"That's one part of it, yes. But she'd always balanced the risks she took against an astute calculation of the consequences. That was my experience, anyway. But from what I understand, she completely disregarded the danger involved in cornering Trafford. And for what? On the slimmest of chances that he'd give her a truthful account of how Marion died? It doesn't make sense."

"You're right. I was indebted to her for getting us as far as we got, but increasingly she behaved as if a reasonable assessment of the risks we were taking shouldn't apply. For example, we'd been on Benbecula for four days without any real lead as to where Trafford was living, so she proposed that we flush him out by circulating copies of his picture around the island. That way, he'd come and find us. Which he did. He burst into our cottage around dawn with a gun, instructed us to sit down, then bound our wrists together with those plastic ties the police use. Unbelievably, Julie started arguing with him, until he threatened to put a bullet in her thigh."

Emily finally understood. Yes, part of Julie's quest had been driven by guilt for her role in exposing Marion to danger. But she'd also needed risk and excitement to feel properly alive, and to quell her dread of leading an ordinary, humdrum life. That recklessness had defined her. She'd needed more than a loving, straightforward relationship with Emily, so once the thrill of seducing her and uncovering Backlash had worn off, she'd resumed her relationship with Marion and embarked on a succession of one-night stands. The hunt to confront Trafford had been the next, more extreme manifestation of her need for a constant adrenaline fix. She became aware Nigel had started speaking again.

"After our first two meetings, while I was convinced of her integrity and determination, I never thought that we'd ever become friends. I carried on with our partnership because I sensed that she could help me get what I wanted – an interview with Trafford. It was purely transactional. But as we got to know each other during the journey to Benbecula and then during our time in the cottage before Trafford found us, I got to like her more and more. We forged a strong trust between us and looked out for each other – she had my back and I hers. There's one thing I can tell you. Everything happened very fast after the two assassins burst in, spraying bullets around the room. Julie was sitting next to me when she was shot and I'm sure she didn't suffer; it was clear from her wound that she'd died instantly. Do you want to know about the firefight? It was horrific."

"I can imagine; actually, I can't even begin to. I've been given the version of events that the police have put together. It's good to know that Julie didn't suffer or have time to feel afraid.

How did you get out of there?"

"When the shooting stopped, I waited until there were no further signs of activity, then cut my ties with the knife that Trafford had thrown to us. When I finally screwed up the courage to go outside, Trafford had gone and the assassin he'd wounded lay dead in the field behind the cottage. I got off the island as fast as possible, caught the sleeper to London that evening and only reported the incident when I woke the following afternoon, for which I may be facing a prison sentence."

Emily stood looking out at the Thames, the colour of milky coffee in the late afternoon light, and downed the rest of her gin and tonic. She was imagining the scene: Julie confronting Trafford, her shock as the assassins burst in and then dying before she'd had time to feel any fear. Her eyes began to water. "It sounds horrific. Thank you for taking me through it. Do you have any idea who the assassins were?"

"I initially thought they were after me, but on reflection that doesn't make sense. My source in MI5 has indicated that they were almost certainly hired by senior figures connected to Backlash, to carry out a revenge hit on Trafford for his role in foiling their conspiracy. They also told me that Trafford has gone AWOL from his place of safety."

Emily's phone pinged as a message arrived.

Louise had dropped Emily outside Dolphin Square, then parked on a yellow line. After ten minutes she'd put the 'Police Officer On Call' sign on her dashboard to prevent an overzealous traffic warden ticketing her, and taken a walk towards the river. There was a gentle breeze blowing up the Thames Estuary, but even a southerner wouldn't call it cold, so the thickset, bearded man with a coat round his shoulders, hurrying towards Dolphin Square on the opposite side of the road, caught her attention for a second. Then she realised that his left arm was in a sling, which explained the coat.

As she was about to turn away, the man stopped to look at a street sign and then down at a map, and Louise knew she'd seen him before. He hadn't had a beard then, but it was him, the man in the Mondeo she'd stopped at the roadblock. It was Ben Trafford, who'd now turned into Dolphin Square West Side, heading towards the block's main entrance. *You don't need to be a detective to work out that this isn't a coincidence*, she thought. *Either he's followed us all the way from Manchester – highly unlikely – or he's come to sort things out with Nigel Hatfield. Given the security at the front of the block, he'll have to do some serious bluffing to get in that way.*

She held back for five seconds, then followed him, keeping around fifty metres behind. He stopped, looked through a set of iron gates at the side of the building and turned both ways to check the road, looking straight at Louise in the process. He paused for a moment, trying to remember, then walked into the building. She ran up to the gates, cautiously looked through and saw a narrow road leading to a loading bay used for deliveries. *Shit, he's got in.*

She texted Emily:

Have just seen Trafford enter Dolphin Square by a rear entrance, presumably heading for Hatfield's flat. You're not his favourite person, so please leave now. I will be waiting in the car at the main entrance.

She carried on walking, glancing at a parked BMW M3 saloon with two male occupants: late twenties or early thirties, one white and one black. What particularly caught her attention was the object the black guy was holding to his ear: not a mobile phone, but a two-way radio, and not the type used by the police, but by another service entirely. As she walked on, she heard two car doors slam and the sound of running footsteps. She turned just in time to see the spooks entering the delivery entrance. As she got back to her car, she noticed another BMW parked at the front of the building, to one side of the main entrance. *They're not taking any chances with this guy*, she thought. *Come on, Emily, get the fuck out of there.*

"Nigel, that information from your source has just got serious. The friend who drove me here has messaged me that she's just seen Ben Trafford enter this building by a service entrance. Don't ask me how she knows him. He's obviously here to see you, but I certainly have no desire to meet this guy again, and I'm leaving now. Are you coming? I can't imagine he's making a social call."

"Christ! But no, I'm going to stay and take that risk, Emily. This is my opportunity to put the story to rest, but you should go now. Good luck."

"I understand. Thank you for seeing me. Be careful; I hope everything works out for you, Nigel."

"It was good to meet you, Emily."

As she ran towards the lift she heard it coming up. If it was Trafford, he'd almost certainly recognise her. She pushed open the door to the stairwell just as the bell pinged to signal the lift's arrival. As she hastened down the first flight, she heard voices coming towards her. *Carry on down or go back up? Chances are, Trafford will be on his own if he's gone AWOL.* Her mind was made up when she glanced behind her and, through the glass panel in the stairwell door, saw a man in an overcoat walk past. As she reached the fifth-floor landing, two fit-looking young men ran past her, one revealing a shoulder holster as his jacket flapped open. They carried on without giving her a second glance.

She raced down to the ground floor, strode through the lobby, smiling broadly at the concierge and calling out, "Have a good evening," in her cheeriest voice, then slipped out of the doors that had already opened for her. She saw the headlights of Louise's car flash twice, ran across the road and got in.

Louise kissed her. "Tell me all about it later. All you have to do now is put on some good music and tell me where to go."

"How good are you at following directions?"

"You're about to find out."

"OK. Straight on, turn right, down to the Embankment, turn left and after a third of a mile turn right at the lights and go over Vauxhall Bridge. I'll pick up the route again on the bridge."

As they drove through Stockwell towards the A23, Emily gave an audible intake of breath. "The next road on the left is where Robert and I lived for six years. I haven't been here since we left nearly eight years ago. We had some happy times there. It always feels weird when I think about what he became. Of course, I have to face up to the fact that those sides to him were probably always there, only dormant. Sorry, I didn't mean to start reminiscing."

"Don't apologise. I want to hear everything about your life before we met; especially the part where you were sleeping with the enemy. Put some music on."

"Have you got any Joan Armatrading?"

"*Walk Under Ladders* should be in there somewhere. Where to now?"

"Bear left into the one-way system ahead, then right at the lights onto the A23. Then keep on that road for fifty miles or so—"

"Fifty miles?! The A23 – are you taking me on a dirty weekend to Brighton?! Wow! Emily Fowler, I love you! I haven't been there since I was a kid. A road trip, just like Thelma and Louise."

"Sort of. But let's stay clear of Beachy Head."

ACKNOWLEDGEMENTS

I would like to thank my wife, Francesca, for the love, support and wisdom she brings into my life. Huge thanks to Farquhar, Philip and Linda for their invaluable and perceptive feedback on the early drafts, and to my daughter Tania, a historian of feminism, for sharing her thoughts and research about the men's rights movement. To Neil for his ongoing encouragement and suggestions and to all my other friends whose 'how's it going?' questions helped to keep me motivated.